Watchman

JANE MORELL

ROBERT HALE · LONDON

Typeset in 10½/14pt New Baskerville
by Derek Doyle & Associates, Shaw Heath.
Printed in Great Britain by St Edmundsbury Press,
Bury St Edmunds, Suffolk.
Bound by Woolnough Bookbinding Ltd

Damascus 6 October 2003 04.00 hours

Side by side the two men walked quickly and quietly along the narrow cobbled side street, two-storeyed houses rising either side of them. They have a mission to carry out, and their orders stipulate that it be completed before sunrise. Both are wearing khaki combat jackets, jeans, and trainers; each carries a loaded handgun in a shoulder holster.

The younger of the two, glancing about him as they drew near to their action site, found his eye caught for a moment by the sky-rise beauty of the minaret of a nearby mosque silhouetted ghost-pale against the moonless night sky. The other, known among his comrades simply as 'Edara', was oblivious to the world around him: his mind, his senses, his very soul, dead to everything other than his twin purposes this night – one of which has, so far, been kept secret from the man at his side who, for the first time in his life, will shortly implement the most dreaded of Sarsen's unwritten, merciless law.

Reconnaissance of the target dwelling had been thorough, and they halted facing the green front door which opened directly off the street. The place was a medium-range rooming-house, a well-maintained but insignificant building. Each of its four rooms is let to a man in Sarsen's employ, and whatever happens there this night, none of the three men left alive in it will make any attempt to interfere or, later, report events to the authorities. One of them is the informer who has been instrumental in bringing about the imminent disciplinary action and, besides, they all value their lives too highly to put them at risk.

'Open it.' Edara gestured at the closed door.

Producing a key, the other obeyed, then followed his superior into the house, shut the door behind him and stood in the small square hall with his eyes fixed on Edara who is his inspecting officer this night.

'Justice must be done. Proceed.' Edara's words were bitter with loathing and contempt: over the years he had stored a great deal of hatred in his heart.

The Hamas activist to whom they are about to deliver Sarsen's justice lived in the first room on their right. Drawing his handgun the younger man tried the door, found it locked so knocked quietly on the white-painted wood. After a moment he heard footsteps within approach . . . then come to a halt.

'Who is it?' Even a whisper can communicate intense fear: knowing himself guilty, the man inside the locked room sensed his doom in the pre-dawn knock on his door, and dread has him by the throat.

'Sarsen sent me. I have a message from him for you.'

'But. . . . Who are you? Give me your name.'

'You have no need of that. Open the door.' But the young man knows exactly what he has been sent here to do, also that he is under examination and must show initiative and determination. So without more words, he shot out the lock, slammed the door wide open, darted inside and took up firing stance, gun out in front of him sweeping from side to side of the room in search of Jabal.

'Freeze, or I fire!' he ordered, centring his weapon on the back of the man reaching a desperate hand towards a drawer in the desk against the wall to his right.

Swinging round, Jabal stood rigid, both arms raised, eyes glaring at the gun and his fleshy face a mask of terror because he *knows* now and knowledge has killed all hope. 'I can explain!' he gabbled, voice high-pitched, breathless. 'Listen – listen to me! I didn't tell him anything of value; I was just trying to trap him into saying—'

'Silence.' The order was quiet but loaded with authority. 'Your accomplice Abdali has co-operated, his testimony proves you a traitor—'

'For the love of Allah the All-seeing the Merciful, *listen to me!*' Falling to his knees, Jabal beseeched mercy, arms outstretched towards the man holding the gun on him, tears streaming down his face.

'Stay on your knees and turn round.' Closing in on Jabal, the man charged by Sarsen with his execution advanced the muzzle of the gun to within inches of his eyes. 'For traitors, the bullet to the back of the head,' he said to him, quite softly.

On hearing him say this, Edara moved from behind him to stand to one side of the two figures locked into their duality of life and death, his hand snaking up to the breast pocket of his combat jacket, which had been tailored to contain the small hi-tech camera he has secreted inside it, its lens married to the round spy-hole in the camouflage-patterned drill material. He wanted a photograph that left no doubt as to the identity of the executioner – and slanted the interpretation of the picture towards the act shown being premeditated, deliberate murder. Switching on the camera, he smoothed his fingers around it and then, as the killing proceeded, directed the lens at will so that his pictures achieved that end.

Faithfully, mercilessly, it recorded Jabal's abject terror, his pathetic clumsiness as he shuffled round on his knees until his back was to the gun; then sliding up to the executioner it captured on film, first his hand wrapped round the butt of the gun, then in turn the gun, his hand ... and finally his face, hand and weapon as he advanced the muzzle to within two inches of Jabal's skull and squeezed the trigger. ...

The images of the killing, the killer, and his victim are fixed on film, clear and unequivocally damning: Edara has procured what Sarsen ordered him to procure this night. Switching off the camera, he stepped closer to the man he has played false.

'At the beginning, you talked too much,' he commented coldly. 'That is doubtless the Brit in you coming out. You would do well to correct this fault if you wish to retain Sarsen's favour.'

But a few minutes later, as the two of them went out into the hazed pre-dawn coolness of his birth city, Edara recalled the reason for Sarsen's ... not favour, he admitted in the privacy of his mind, rather Sarsen's *love*, his father-to-son love for this half-Brit. And then in his heart, Edara cursed the young man walking at his side for stealing from him Sarsen's high regard: not Sarsen's love, that had never been his, and he knew it. Knew only this half-Brit had that – and had it not because he had earned it the hard way, but simply because of a woman who was long since dead.

Chapter 1

He was a quiet man. Nevertheless he was what he has been through-out his life: a power-seeker. A loner by nature, he cultivated so-called friendships only with those he believed would at some time, in some way, be of use to him. And for years now his power had been increas-ing. He had worked for his present high position: schemed for it and played men false for it – killed for it also, lesser or less ruthless men and one woman. (However that last was a death he was still trying to expunge from all the records.) Among the internationally active terrorist élite this quiet man, this power-lover, was known simply as 'Sarsen'.

Standing at the window of his study on the fourth floor of an ostensibly run-of-the-mill apartment block, Sarsen was looking out over this beautiful city he'd been born in fifty-four years ago. But his mind was not engaged with its ancient splendours: behind his guarded brown eyes, narrowed now, he was seeing a very different city . . . *London.* As he conned over the terrorist hit that in mid-August would cause death and destruction deep beneath the city's prosperous, arrogant streets, Sarsen was envisioning the wild-eyed panic, the screaming, tearing pain and the dying of the people who would be trapped down there because there's no safe passage up to ground level where the air is sweet and fresh, is truly the breath of life.

Operation Zephyr. A mission intended to have major impact on the morale of the enemy in two disparate ways. Firstly and obviously, by virtue of the resulting casualties, devastation and general havoc; secondly, and even more importantly, by exposing to the British public the frightening inability of their anti-terrorist organizations to detect and prevent such an attack. And in order to facilitate the achievement of that second but paramount objective, Sarsen had planned Zephyr so that, while the ancillary and auxillary components of the mission consisted of a complex network of sleepers, IT experts and logistical back-up, its 'sharp end' personnel was restricted to as few as possible. That way, Sarsen thought now, our preparations for the hit will continue to remain undetected by Brit Intelligence: our minimalist strike force hidden within its support systems. And only myself and three others are cognisant of certain important details in the master plan – and one of those three is totally ignorant of one particular, key element in the security precautions in place at Red Pillars, the house at which my suicide agents will rendezvous and from which Edara will direct the final phase of the operation.

It had taken Zephyr two years to get this far, he reflected. Driven forward from its inception by Edara, its currently London-based commander, it would climax in that city on 14 August.

But. But, he now had to despatch to London the final agent required for Zephyr's success: the one man in his terrorist organization who could – and within a few days' time would – slip smoothly into the role there required of him, *able* to do so because of his own particular personal background, and *willing* to do so because of Sarsen's unremitting, insidious but beguiling use and misuse of his trust in him, his father-figure in childhood and, in manhood, his mentor in all things.

Swinging round, Sarsen strode across to his desk and, sitting down, unlocked its bottom drawer and lifted out one of the files inside, the one with the scarlet cover, the dossier of Jake Messanger. He had no need to read it. He knew – or, nowadays, perhaps only *thought* he knew? – all there was to know about the man who had come into his life as a very young child. To Sarsen, Jake was the son he had never had, and over the last twenty-seven years or so he had devoted a great deal of time to ensuring that the child he had marked for his own grew up to be a man he – to his mind – as such 'owned'.

Opening the file, he browsed through it: entered the self and life, to date, of Jake Messanger; as he did so once more assessing his suitability for the imminent mission that had the potential to make – or break, should it at any point go wrong – Operation Zephyr. It gave these facts about the man, with which Sarsen was already familiar.

Messanger, Jason (Jake): Born Manama, Bahrain, 1973.
Mother: La'ali Messanger, maiden name La'ali Mehrab. Third daughter of prominent Bahraini family of considerable wealth. Married John Messanger, British national and medical practitioner. Deceased 1976.
Personal Details
Height: 6' 1"
Eyes: Brown.
Hair: strong-growing, straight, black.
No permanent scars on face or body.
For face and head bone-structure see att. scans.
Strong, rangy physique. Fit, athletic.
Sports: rugby, cricket, tennis, riding.

NOTES

1.   Practises no religion. Steers clear of involvement in that of both mother (Islam) and father (Christianity).

2.   Mother died three years after his birth. Following her death her Bahraini family insisted on the child spending at least six months of each year with them in Bahrain; this period of time increased following the second marriage of his father, John Messanger.

3.   For CV in the organization devoted to the service of Islam see attached appendices.

Sarsen closed the red file. He had no need to read the mass of appendices: he had known Jake Messanger since the day he was born, and he had been his controller in every one of the terrorist

missions there detailed. Getting to his feet again he crossed to the
big window, stood looking down over Damascus . . . and was caught
up in memories. Personal memories. Behind his eyes he was seeing
La'ali Mehrab as he had seen her on a certain afternoon over thirty
years ago, when he was twenty-five years of age and had recently
received her parents' permission to pay formal, purposive court to
her. That day, he had caught a glimpse of her which had changed his
life for ever and which he had never forgotten; had never tried to
forget, treasuring it rather, and consciously using it to nurture not
only his continuing love for her but also the vicious, directed hatred
born of it which – as he watched her that day – had rooted itself deep
in his heart. La'ali had been walking along Dar Izz Street in Manama,
Bahrain's capital city: young and lissom in her body-loving silk
cheongsam, lustrous black hair swirled up around her head, La'ali
was beautiful to look upon. A family friend, Sarsen had lusted after
her since she was fourteen; and the lust was still in him now as, in his
memory, he saw her turn and smile up at the man walking so close at
her side, she leaning towards him lover-like, giving him the slum-
brous invitation of her lovely face, those full, enticing lips, those dark
eyes lit with promise.

Then suddenly La'ali vanished from inside Sarsen's mind and in
her place he saw the man she'd smiled up at in that seductively intimate way. Saw the Brit doctor, John Messanger. *Messanger*: the man
La'ali had married, breaking free of the understanding he, Sarsen,
had reached with her parents barely two months earlier, choosing
the Brit above him. Leaving him so easily: 'Sorry,' she had said to
him, 'but whatever my parents say I'm going to marry John
Messanger. I love him.'

It hadn't been La'ali's fault. All the fault and all the blame lay with
the Brit, John Messanger. . . . On that bitter thought Sarsen came
back to present realities. He saw below him the dramatic panoramic
view of his native city, nevertheless his soul was still engaged with the
man he blamed for his loss of La'ali Mehrab. A great hatred had
come to life inside him on that afternoon he had seen her, to his way
of thinking, give herself to the Brit doctor through the smouldering
passion in her smile as she looked up into his eyes. That hatred had

stayed with Sarsen, feeding on the loneliness of his life after she walked out of it to marry her chosen man. And then when only three years after her marriage she died in a car crash – *with John Messanger driving the car they were in*, La'ali sitting at his side, to die there while he came out of it alive – then, Sarsen's hatred had metamorphosed into a pathological determination to *destroy* the Brit. Because, in spite of a courtroom verdict exonerating him from all blame for the accident, Sarsen would have none of it: in his mind John Messanger stood for ever as La'ali's murderer and, as such, must die.

But his death should not be a swift and easy one, Sarsen had decided during those desert-days he had lived through after La'ali's body had been put into the earth. Messanger had to suffer, and suffer over years as he, Sarsen, would do from then on. There would be no satisfaction in killing him outright – which fate already lay in Sarsen's power to deliver. His rise through the hierarchy of the anti-West terrorist organization he had been recruited to at the age of thirteen was continuing apace, he could arrange for a fatal accident to befall a Brit. But Messanger would not suffer enough that way; the desolation of loss must last his lifetime, as would Sarsen's. The way to avenge La'ali's death, he had decided, would be to run in-depth surveillance on John Messanger's lifestyle – and then take it apart piece by piece, destroy in one way or another as many of the people the Brit loved as came within the compass of his, Sarsen's, power.

And that *I have done* – and indeed John Messanger suffered because of it. On the thought Sarsen's dark eyes were lit by an intense, malicious pleasure: for years now – even after John Messanger's death some years back – he had been enjoying his revenge and now the exaltation of it came again in his heart, hot and sweet. . . . During those years I have, in effect, stolen from him his first-born son, *La'ali's* son. Working on the child throughout his boyhood and on into manhood, I have instilled in him a deep love of his mother's people and way of life – while at the same time making him mine in his heart and in the ethos he lives by. And now, *through him*, I shall pursue John Messanger beyond the grave: I shall bring about the deaths of his other two children, born to him by his second wife. Only then – and provided of course that Jake succeeds in and survives the mission I am about to appoint him to – will my revenge be complete.

However, the current mission is my present priority: Operation Zephyr. Edara has signalled from London that the groundwork for it is completed, so it will move into its active phase – which means it is time to send Jake to him.

Resuming his seat at his desk, Sarsen used the intercom, instructing his secretary to send in Agent Messanger.

As Jake Messanger came in and walked across to the desk, Sarsen eyed him with approval. Jake moved with assurance and the easy grace natural to a fit, young and agile body. His thick black hair was cut short; his olive skin lay smoothly over the cut planes of his face and his eyes were La'ali's in colour and the directness of their regard, but, whereas hers had been vivacious and a touch reckless, his were sombre, and had a certain guarded wariness about them. The two greeted each other in Arabic, then as they went on talking they used mostly English but slipped into Arabic from time to time, each being fluent in both languages.

'Edara reports Zephyr on course and ready for action.' Sarsen's voice was hard, but his eyes and manner made it clear that he was speaking as to a beloved son, for what he was about to say to Jake Messanger had to be put to him firmly but diplomatically if he were not to be alienated. 'I want you to take part in it, work with him.'

A frown creased the skin between the younger man's strongly marked eyebrows. 'I was not aware of this,' he said slowly.

'I only made the decision yesterday.' This statement was a straight lie, the plan of which he was about to apprise Jake had been part of Operation Zephyr from the outset. But nothing in Sarsen's eyes or body language betrayed the fact; he was an accomplished and experienced liar. 'A major alteration to the plan was agreed on then, an idea of Edara's.'

'You approved it, so late in the day?'

'Without reservation. Edara has already prepared the ground for it. It is a brilliant scheme, it will add . . . it will make things run more smoothly in one very sensitive area where, otherwise, suspicions might easily have been aroused.'

Jake Messanger's eyes slid past Sarsen to the window. 'What would be my . . . contribution?' he asked, looking out over Damascus dreaming, brilliant under a burning sun.

It was time for plain truth now – part of it at least – Sarsen perceived. 'Your half-brother and half-sister are both living in London at the present time,' he began. 'He lives and works there, and for the moment she is on vacation from university and staying in his house. Those two figure importantly, albeit peripherally, in Edara's plan: it calls for you to reestablish contact with them and work your way into their confidence—'

'I can't do that! It's not – I've lost touch with both of them, sir.' Dismay, disbelief and sheer astonishment in every line of Messanger's face. 'I haven't seen either of them for ten years and more.'

'Do you not correspond?'

'No. Gemma still sends me cards at Christmas and on my birthday, but I haven't reciprocated for years.' His darkly handsome face was angry and mutinous.

'Very well, you have lost contact with them.' Sarsen's voice was clipped, decisive: nothing of the father-to-son in him now, he was the commander giving orders to a junior officer. 'So, you will immediately build bridges with them – to your half-sister Gemma in particular. When the three of you were children you were always closest to her. Edara has identified a friend of hers whom he will use to put pressure on a certain man whose role is pivotal to Zephyr's success—'

'What man? I thought—'

'You have not been privy to all aspects of the mission. That, I shall now correct. Sit down and listen.' Sarsen indicated the chair facing him across the desk.

'Thank you, but I prefer to stand.'

'As you will. . . . The man selected as our Brit cat's paw in Zephyr will at one vital point in the action have to be subjected to near-intolerable coercion. Your job will be to insinuate yourself into the social circle of Gemma and this friend of hers whom Edara plans to use to provide it. You will *inform on* them and their affairs, to Edara. I will brief you now, and you will travel to London in two or three days' time—'

'No! Sir, I cannot—' But Messanger broke off, seeing an unaccustomed balefulness sudden in Sarsen's eyes. I've just refused a direct order – from *Sarsen*, he thought, and was appalled. Sarsen: the man who – perceiving and understanding the agony of loneliness laying waste the boy Jake as his father took a second wife, had two children by her and then ruthlessly sidelined him from the closed-against-him circle of his new family – had befriended that sad child and introduced him into a new and wonderful world in which he was given love, the Arab world of his dead but dimly remembered mother. Sarsen, whom I have come to love as the only 'father' I've ever had.

Jake Messanger took a step back, stood stiff and straight. 'Sir, I apologize most humbly for the way I spoke to you,' he said in formal, excessively polite Arabic. 'But, please, understand. Gemma and Jared, they are my close relatives. It would be a monstrous thing for me to use them in furtherance of a terrorist strike against their native land. You know I am at one with with you in the fight against the Western capitalist countries: on your orders I have carried out intimidation, courier work – and one execution. But to use my half-sister. . . .'

'Your refusal to accept the mission would have severe consequences for you.' Sarsen's voice and manner were hostile.

'In what way, may I ask? Surely, sir, you would not—'

'Not me. Edara. He is intensely jealous of you; to bring you down would give him a great deal of satisfaction.'

'Bring me down? How could he do that? You are the only man who has the power to do that.'

'Power comes in many forms. In this particular situation, I would be unable to stop him. It would be a matter for the criminal courts of this country.'

'I don't understand, sir.' Nevertheless, a coldness stirred in Jake Messanger's heart.

Slowly, Sarsen got to his feet: as tall as this half-Brit whom he had – skilfully, secretly, and over many years – suborned to his service, he looked him in the eye. 'Do you recall the execution you carried out last year?' he asked.

'Of course. Edara was my inspecting officer.'

'And you shot a man dead in cold blood.'

'On your orders, sir.' He was tense and apprehensive: there was something here which, quite plainly, was building up to—

'Edara had a spy-camera on him that night,' Sarsen said. 'He has in his possession the negatives of film taken of that execution. The victim's face is not shown, only the back of his head. But the killer is shown almost full face, and the death is recorded on film, killer and victim are locked together in the same frames.'

'It's still not clear to me how—'

'Then think harder! Edara is pathologically jealous of you, his dearest wish is to see you removed from my inner circle. He wants you on Zephyr because he is in command of that mission and he believes your participation in it will facilitate this new and incisive plan he has for it, rooting you firmly into an innocent, family background as it does. So take this on board: if you refuse to co-operate, he will pass his negatives to certain friends of his who will then pursue the matter in the criminal courts. They will ensure that you are charged with murder in the first degree.'

'But that's impossible. . . .'

'Edara has the ear of men in positions to *make* it possible. Men who are seriously beholden to him for past favours rendered.' Then, seeing Jake Messanger prey to doubt and fear, Sarsen administered the *coup de grâce*. 'Best to roll with this one, Jake,' he said in English. 'It gets even worse.'

'It couldn't.'

'It could – and *will* if you don't accept the mission.'

'Tell me how.'

Turning away Sarsen said harshly, 'Gemma and Jared will both be killed if you refuse to work with Edara in this.'

'*Killed?*' Horror coursed though Jake Messanger. What Sarsen had just said was surely madness, there was neither sense nor justice in it. But he knew from experience that, in the world Sarsen, Edara and he inhabited, the absence of those two qualities was seldom allowed to frustrate the aims and desires of certain men in positions of power. 'But Gemma and Jared . . . neither of them is involved in the operation.'

'They will be – peripherally. They will not be aware that they are, of course.'

'But sir, I cannot—'

'Get with it, Jake! I can only brief you on your mission after you've accepted it, and we're wasting time.'

Messanger's world had gone chill and grey about him. Staring bleakly at Sarsen's back, choosing his words carefully, he asked a question he had never before had reason to put to this man he had come to love and trust above all others, his 'father' in all but blood. 'But . . . you, sir? If I refuse this mission, you will *permit* Edara to carry out his threat against me? The murder charge?'

'Zephyr is a Class A operation, as you well know!' Sarsen swung round, and Messanger saw nothing in him that spoke of the special relationship that existed between them, saw only the overriding passion of a man obsessed by an envisioned aim. 'As such, automatically, it claims my unqualified support,' he went on, in Arabic now, and holding Messanger's eyes, seeking to impose his will on him. 'Therefore I would remind you of a certain maxim with which I unreservedly concur: those who are not positively *for* us are perceived as our enemies; as such they become expendable, together with all those individuals close to them if that should serve our purpose.'

Messanger found himself unable to stand firm against such a statement of belief from this man who had dominated his life so far; for whom he had cut himself off from his blood-father, cleaving instead to the Arab side of his heritage, committing himself to Sarsen as he came to manhood, to his Islamist terrorist agenda.

'To me, to be counted your enemy would be a kind of death,' he said in Arabic, and from the heart.

'I think of you as my son.' Sarsen's voice and face smiled, for he had won and victory was sweet.

'And as your son I accept the mission to London,' Jake Messanger said.

'So we will sit down together and I will brief you on the revised plan for Zephyr; Edara will brief you further on your arrival in London. As you will quickly appreciate, the new plan is a great improvement on the original: from the cover of your position as Gemma's half-brother, you will undoubtedly be able to provide Edara with information that will open the way to the abduction which will kick-start the final phase of Zephyr. . . .'

Sarsen and Jake Messanger slipped back easily into the intimacy customary between them, the rift rapidly spanned by their mutual interest in Operation Zephyr, masterminded by Sarsen and with Edara in command in London.

Spanned, yes, but not forgotten by either man. An hour later, with Jake's mini-briefing concluded, each of them went his own way. And in the sudden silence of his own mind, each found his thoughts returning to what had been said between them immediately prior to Messanger agreeing to work with Edara in furtherance of that operation. And each discovered, then, that what had passed between them had sown seeds of doubt in his perception and understanding of the other. Seeds, only. So far.

Thus, and for the first time, Jake Messanger – casting his mind back to the execution he had carried out *on Sarsen's order* – questioned what might have been behind that order. Now, walking to his apartment near the pharmaceutical company he worked for, he recalled the night he had eliminated the traitor, with Edara present throughout – his examiner and, if necessary, his back-up – since it was the first time he had been entrusted with carrying out a death sentence. Edara, Sarsen had just told him, had been carrying a concealed camera and had photographed the killing in such a way that it could be construed as a murder *and with the murderer's face shown clearly*. And he had done so, apparently, with the express purpose of using those pictures to blackmail Jake Messanger as and when it suited his purpose.

But, thought Jake, oblivious to the suffocating heat of the streets he was passing through, he had only Sarsen's word for that interpretation of what Edara had done. So what if the photographs had been taken on *Sarsen's* orders? To give *him* a hold over his half-Brit agent?

It seemed on the face of it a possibility but – surely? – a remote one. A possibility, because Sarsen was, above all things, devoted to the cause the members of his terrorist network fought and died for; but remote because Sarsen was his mentor and his professed and acknowledged father in all but blood . . . *or was he?* Sarsen must have realized he'd balk at using his English half-sister in furtherance of a terror strike against her own country, which meant he'd have known he would need some sort of leverage if he was to get his way. And another point: why hadn't Sarsen himself briefed him fully on his part in Zephyr? Why had he given him only the preliminary information now, leaving the details to be given him later by Edara?

By the time Messanger let himself into his apartment, he had pushed his doubts aside. For them to retain credibility he'd have to accept that his 'father' had lied to him: had lied to him with malice aforethought and concerning vital, close-to-the-heart matters. And such a suggestion had to be – it *was!* – no less than absurd, impossible, *insane,* in the real world inhabited by Jake Messanger and Sarsen; it had no place there. It was so way out crazy that Jake laughed it to scorn, poured himself a gin sling and set about planning his approach to his half-sister in London – she was staying in Jared's house there, Sarsen had told him. It was the summer vacation and her brother had invited her to stay with him for as long as she liked.

Nevertheless, the seed of doubt regarding Sarsen which had been sown in him that day did not die: it simply curled up deep within his mind and, living on its own certainties, bided its time.

As the door closed behind Messanger, Sarsen leaned back in his chair and ran a hand through his thick grey hair, a faint – and faintly derisive – smile on his lips. Things were working out well, he thought. Jake had accepted the London mission, with its commitment to work with Edara, so that side of Zephyr could go forward immediately. Under cover of a business trip (pharmaceutical contracts for his company) Jake would get started on his infiltration of the Brit side of the Messanger family within a few days now, be in position to inform on them to his mission commander.

Suddenly, Sarsen's mind was caught and held by thoughts of that family: the two children born to John Messanger's second wife, the American woman the bastard had married within sixteen months of La'ali's death. Jared, four years younger than Jake; Gemma, now twenty-three. And for a moment he wondered what those two were like *in themselves*. He knew a multitude of facts about them. From photographs, he knew what each looked like. He knew the addresses each lived at, the names and addresses of the closest of their friends; knew that Jared worked – on the IT and Records side only – for MI5, and that Gemma was about to begin her third year of study at medical school in Edinburgh, specializing in epidemic diseases – knew the 'bones' of their lives, as it were. He had had sleepers in Britain reporting to him on them for years: John Messanger's blood ran in their veins, so he kept track of them in order to fulfil, when the time was right, the vow he had made to himself when La'ali died – was murdered, to his mind. So much he knew; but of their person-alities he knew nothing and, until that moment, had had no desire to know more.

Now, however, since Jake was about to reestablish contact with them, and consequently they would figure in Zephyr, the situation was different, and Sarsen's curiosity was aroused. Were they serious-minded, like Jake was? Were they clever? Gifted in any particular way? Politically minded, politically active? Given to partying and such diversions of the young? And, far more important than any of that, what were their feelings towards Jake – and what might *his* feelings be towards them as he got to know them?

Abruptly, Sarsen cut short his wonderings. Got to his feet and crossed over to a small but exquisite glass-and-rosewood display cabi-net on the far side of the room. Within it stood his four most treasured 'objects of great beauty', but he had eyes now for only one of them: the rose-quartz flower bowl he had given to La'ali on her fifteenth birthday, and which her mother had gifted to him after her death. He did not take it out of the cabinet; he simply looked at it – and considered Jake Messanger, her son by the Brit doctor.

What Gemma and Jared Messanger will feel towards Jake when he visits them in England is of crucial importance to the success of Zephyr, he thought, because it is essential that they accept him and invite him into their lives, thus enabling him to work for me from within that cover. But even more important, possibly, is what Jake feels, or might *come to feel*, towards them. The blood of John Messanger runs in all three of them, so what if he is drawn – strongly, *irresistably* – to them? What if he is claimed by the blood-tie? Now all three are adult, that might happen. And if it should, all my work on him will come to nought: I would lose him, and then Zephyr would perhaps fail. Consequently, *I myself* would fail in my private, long-term purpose, the destruction of John Messanger's bloodline. Therefore I must watch Jake closely when he is in London – have him watched, rather.

Thus, and for the first time in his life, a tiny crack developed in the hard, shiny carapace enclosing Sarsen's certainty of Jake Messanger's absolute and unquestioning loyalty to him: a seed of doubt slipped into that crack, bedded itself down in there and – waited.

Chapter 2

Ealing London, 8 July 2004

'God! I'll just have to get to work on those two shrubs; they look dreadful, and right in front of the house, too! How Jared can pass by them every day and not *do* something about them – it beats me.' As Gemma closed the street gate of her brother's home in Ealing behind her and, sports bag in hand, walked on along the path to the front door, her eyes were on the twin bushes growing one either side of it: bursting with life, each stood over eight feet high and riotously overgrown, its mass of foliage brilliant with yellow flowers.

Ahead of her Delyth Stanton reached out and drew a spray of them towards her, smelt the trailing blooms. 'Given any luck his new lodger will turn out to be a keen gardener,' she said, as, key in hand, Gemma joined her.

'Little chance of that. Jared says he's a forensic scientist, rather ancient and immensely brainy. Luckily for me, he's in Germany until mid-September, finishing a book he's doing, so Jared and I have the place to ourselves.'

In the hall now, and Delyth at her shoulder, Gemma dropped her bag – they'd been playing tennis at the local club Delyth belonged to – then shrugged out of her jacket and tossed it over a chair.

'I'm dying for some tea,' she went on, and started for the kitchen, but stopped alongside the hall table, picked up the mail and began sorting through it, taking out her own letters, most of which had been forwarded from the digs in Edinburgh she and Delyth shared.

Meeting at medical school the two young women had become fast friends, and when Jared – the upstairs flat he rented out presently unoccupied awaiting his new tenant – had invited Gemma to holiday at his London home in Ealing for as long as she liked during the summer vacation, she had accepted gleefully, aware that Delyth and her father lived near Walpole Park, just a few miles away.

'I'll get tea going.' Seeing her friend preoccupied, Delyth went on through to the kitchen at the back of the house. Light and airy, this was a big, friendly room, and used for most meals. From it the back door opened on to a terrace, beyond which lay a fair-sized lawn bordered on all three sides by a broad shrubbery, tall trees rising above it. Inside, brightly curtained windows took up most of the space to left and right of the back door, a large oak table close to the one on the left, a deeply cushioned window-seat running the full length of the one on the right.

Unlike Gemma, Delyth was a very self-contained person. Her face spoke of a quiet, perhaps introspective nature, the bone-structure sculpted, classic, the brows above the sea-green eyes bird's-wing graceful in line. But it spoke also of a determined spirit, for her mouth was firm and well defined, her regard uncompromising, direct – and suggesting a wariness which habitually preserved distance between herself and 'outside people'.

As she was warming the teapot, Gemma came in. 'Guess what?' she said, sitting down at the table and placing an opened letter in front of her on the polished wood, her fresh-complexioned face flushed with excitement. 'My brother Jake has actually written to me!'

'Only half-brother, isn't he?'

'Sure. But back when we were both kids growing up together he and I . . . well, I loved him a lot.'

'More than Jared?' Delyth flipped her long auburn hair back from her face then brought the tea things to the table, poured out for both of them and looked down at her friend.

'Yes – but differently, I suppose. Jake and I . . . it was really good between us whereas with Jared. . . . Oh, I dunno. Whatever, Jake and I were – there was a bond between us.' Hooking one arm over the back of her chair Gemma sat lost in memories, her short blonde hair tousled, a smile in the blue eyes as halcyon days from childhood lived again inside her head.

Delyth sat down facing her. 'You must have been sad, when Jake left to make his home with his mother's people.'

'I was.' Gemma's eyes strayed out to the garden. 'Jared, he was quite relieved when our half-brother finally broke with us, I think. By then the two of them didn't get on at all. Even our father was glad, too, because my mother loathed having her stepson around – loathed *him*, actually, and made that fact blindingly obvious to everyone, including him.'

'Poor Jake.'

Gemma laughed. '*Poor?* That's not an adjective I or anyone else I know would associate with Jake!' she said, but then frowned and corrected herself. 'No, that's not altogether true. For a while, sure, he was one really really unhappy, lost, sort of, little boy. But then a bloke out in Bahrain, a long-time friend of his mother's family, became his . . . I don't know how to put it . . . he *succoured* him. Anyway, Jake came to put this man in place of the real father who supported him financially, full stop! As for the rest – all those glorious things like *love*, etcetera etcetera, Dad gave him nothing, absolutely nix.'

For a few minutes then they sat quiet, drinking tea and eating biscuits from the tin open between them on the table. Then Delyth asked curiously, 'So, why this sudden reopening of communication on his part? You said you haven't heard from him for years.'

'I hadn't, till today. Even the Christmas cards I sent him went unanswered – but now this!' She flicked the letter with one hand, a quirky and slightly cynical grin tilting the corners of her mouth. 'He's coming to London on a month or so business trip, and wants to visit us. Says he'd like to "forgive and forget", and hopes we're ready to do the same.' Picking up her mug of tea she sat hunched over it in thought, her hands clasped around it.

Delyth watched her, giving her time to mull over the implications of this completely unexpected letter from the half-brother who had cut himself off from the English side of his family – how long ago was it? Twelve years at least, Gemma had once said – and 'gone Arab' as she'd heard Jared phrase it.

'So, *are* you going to forgive and forget?' she asked eventually, breaking the silence.

Gemma drank the last of her tea, then pushed aside her mug and folded her arms on the table. '*I* will,' she said, a frown clouding her face. 'There's nothing I'd like better. But whether Jared will – that's another matter. And since this is his house ... well, whether he'll want Jake visiting here is for him to decide, isn't it? Not me, even if I have been cooking him some fab meals recently – *and* started in on this jungle he calls his garden. ... When Jake was last with us – he came over just briefly, stayed with us for a few days when Mother walked out on us – well, things were pretty fraught altogether then, but between him and Jared the situation was plain frightful, they were barely speaking to each other.'

'Will you try to win him over? Persuade him to allow Jake to visit here?'

'You bet I will!' Getting to her feet, Gemma started to clear the table. 'I'd give anything to see him again – to welcome him back, have him with us for a bit. Then hopefully, if this time it's a success he'll ... we'll all three be friends. I'm dying to know all about Jake's life in Damascus, and about Bahrain, his mother's family. He'd never talk much about them, and none of them have ever visited us or invited us there.'

'Strange, really. In your case, anyway. I wonder why?'

'Haven't the faintest. God knows they're wealthy enough to spare a bed and a crust for the odd in-law.'

Pushing back her chair, Delyth got up and wandered across to the window, stood looking out over the paved terrace to the sun-bright lawn beyond it (the grass seriously in need of cutting) and the bordering shrubbery (running riot, crying out for pruning).

'What's Jake like?' she asked. 'To look at, I mean. Does he take after his Bahraini mother, or after your father?'

'Both, I suppose.' Closing the cupboard door on the biscuit tin, Gemma went across to stand beside her, the quiet attractive 'stranger' she had, over the last couple of years, come to care for very much. 'In height and build he's pretty much the same as Jared,' she said. 'But his hair's black, not blond like Jay's and mine, and his skin's a bit darker than ours, but then we're very fair. Eyes, though . . . that's where there's a big difference. Jake's are brown – like his mother's, I guess.' She paused for a moment, caught up in remembering her half-brother. 'Then of course the bone structure of his face is different from Jay's,' she went on. 'Jake's face, it's wide at the forehead then angles down to a strong, narrow chin – though his mouth's full-lipped and strong too. It's a very compelling sort of face, somehow. He's not so good-looking as Jay, I suppose, but he's the kind of bloke people tend to look at twice, if you know what I mean. He looks *interesting*—' She broke off, laughing at herself. 'Crikey, I'm remembering him from years ago, God knows what he looks like now.'

Delyth saw a deep longing in her; hoped for her sake that this man by the name of Jake would prove worth the love Gemma felt for him.

'What sort of business brings him over here?' she asked. 'Does he say?'

'Sure. He trained as a doctor – like we're doing – and now works for some big pharmaceutical company.'

'Yes, I remember. You said.'

'He says he's coming over to negotiate a couple of drugs contracts with two companies based in London and will be here for at least a month. The deals are a bit hush-hush, apparently – some of the stuff involved is still being tested.' Turning back into the room she made for the door. 'I do so much hope Jared will agree to him spending some time with us – and won't mess things up if he does.'

'Surely he won't do that—'

'There's no sureness about it!' Gemma swung round, her face angry, unhappy, but then at once she composed herself. 'I want him back, Del,' she said quietly, reasonably, 'but I'm pretty certain Jared doesn't. Certain, too, that he'll neither forget nor forgive. You see, Jay was very close to Dad, and what Jake did hurt him enormously.'

'I still find it hard to believe your brother would behave like you're suggesting. He must know how much Jake matters to you.'

Gemma smiled, but was only half persuaded, Delyth saw. 'I hope you're right,' she said. 'Forget it now, Del. Let's you and I get stuck into some gardening. That should put Jay in a good mood, then I'll tell him about Jake's letter.'

At 11 a.m. three days later, Jake Messanger arrived at Heathrow, having travelled via Qatar, Lebanon, and Egypt. Signing in at his pre-booked hotel in West London he ordered his luggage taken up to his room, then left for his meeting with Edara at the Knightsbridge safe house. Arriving there – he had been to the place once before, three years earlier – he produced his ID to the hard man who opened the door to him, answered the questions, was body-searched and then conducted to the same room as on his previous visit, a small one with the look of a slightly seedy office. Here the hard man opened the door, stood aside for him to enter, then closed the door behind him.

'Salaam Aleikum.'

'Wa-aleikum salaam.' From his chair at the central table Edara returned his formal greeting but there was no real welcome in the words or in the man, he used both his tone and his manner to put Messanger firmly in his place as no more than one of his two senior lieutenants for the duration of the present mission.

You're clever, devious, and vicious, thought Jake, meeting the hard black eyes. So it's as well for me that I am aware – as I now am, having discovered how you betrayed an unspoken trust and photographed the execution we were sent out on together – that you are unreservedly my enemy. My enemy to the death, since you have come to see that as the only way you can supplant me in Sarsen's favour.

'You observed all security precautions on your way here?' Edara demanded sharply.

'Naturally.'

Gesturing him to the chair facing him across the table, 'You may sit,' he said. 'You are, of course, aware of the aims of Operation Zephyr?'

'Sarsen briefed me before I left Damascus.'

'Outline them for me.'

'But—'

'I have to be sure of exactly how much you know. Proceed; but you may present a resumé, there is no need for detail.'

Messanger complied. 'One: the Watchman conference has been convened here in London to co-ordinate information from countries taking part regarding methods of, a) preventing, or, b) dealing with the effects of chemical warfare attacks by so-called terrorist organizations on major conurbations. Two: one of the methods of delivering such an attack is via the underground transportation systems of the target city. Three: in order to facilitate discussion of this subject, the delegate from each of the six participating countries has brought to conference blueprints of the ventilation systems in operation throughout the underground travel network in his country's capital city. In the interests of security all such blueprints are kept in—' Messanger broke off, frowning, annoyed at being required to give this recitation of facts which Edara surely knew by heart. 'What's the point of all this?'

'Obey the order I gave you. Continue.'

Messanger did so. 'Operation Zephyr will mount simultaneous toxic gas attacks at three stations on London's underground network, using sarin, or other toxic substances.'

Edara nodded. 'The toxic agent has been decided on. Stocks are ready.'

'What agent will we be using?'

'Knowledge of that is restricted to those who need to know. . . . So, Messanger, we come to your own part in the operation.'

'Sarsen told me you would brief me on that.'

'I shall now apprise you of the action I shall require you to take, and of its purpose,' Edara said. 'Zephyr targets three stations. In order to ensure that at those stations the lethal gas is released at locations which will maximize its effect, we need to have detailed knowledge of their ventilation systems in regard to their entrances, exits, platforms, connecting subways and escalators. The best source of such knowledge has been identified by our agents, and we shall access it thus. Blueprints of the layout of the ventilation systems at the three target stations are currently held and used by the British delegate to Watchman, which is in progress at Devon House in London. We shall gain access to them, and photocopy them. Having them will enable us to pinpoint on each target station the most advantageous position from which our suicide personnel will release the lethal gas.'

'Sound reasoning.' Messanger was deeply attentive now: stimulated by the prospect of action, he had put aside his personal feelings towards his commander. 'Presumably though, it won't be easy to access those blueprints? They'd be kept under tight security—'

'Watchman is not classified as high risk; the security measures in place can be . . . circumvented.'

'You have *insider* information to that effect?'

Edara smiled faintly, a smile which, if anything, merely served to increase the studied menace implicit in his face, Messanger thought. 'Indeed we have,' he said. 'One of the delegates is ours. . . . In addition to that, all our preparations so far, including acquisition of the gas and its safe storage, have been carried out without being detected by the British Intelligence services. Provided we continue to operate at this exemplary level of secrecy, Zephyr's success is assured.'

'You are to be congratulated,' Messanger said smoothly. 'Am I correct in assuming that my job will be to photocopy the blueprints?'

'You do yourself too much honour.' The smile was gone. 'You will be . . . an accessory, an *enabler*, shall I say, facilitating decisive action during that particular phase of the mission. You will assist – crucially, I grant you that – in the creation of the planned situation which will make it possible for us to carry out the photocopying required *and* ensure that what we have done is kept secret for a minimum of twenty-four hours.'

'During which time our hit will come to climax.' Getting to his feet Messanger padded across heavy-duty carpeting to the picture facing him on the wall to Edara's left and stood studying it. It was a reproduction of Van Gogh's *Marigolds* and the thought flashed across his mind, how odd to find all that brilliance of life and colour in this room where two terrorists are plotting death and destruction.

'What are you thinking?' Edara's voice sharp, suspicious.

'Our spy at the conference – what's his name?' His answer followed hard on Edara's question, but he warned himself – watch yourself, Messanger, and never lose sight of the fact that this man is your enemy. Yes, you're working with him and yes, he'll assist and protect you as may be called for to safeguard the successful prosecution of your part in Zephyr. Nevertheless, in his heart *he is your enemy* and, at some later stage, will surely seek to destroy you – providing always that he can see a way to hide from Sarsen his own guilt in any such destruction.

Debating whether or not to trust him, Edara hesitated. Eventually, said stiffly, 'His name is Alain Oufkar. A specialist in biological warfare, he is of Franco-Algerian parentage, a second generation citizen of France educated in that country and then, as a postgraduate student, in the United States. A long-time agent of Sarsen's, he is now reporting to me personally on certain aspects of the Watchman conference which are relevant to Zephyr.'

'Do I know him?'

'You do not.'

'Does he know me?'

'He knows *of* you.'

'In what way? And why?' Because something in Edara's voice as he gave that last answer had rung warning bells in Messanger's mind, it had seemed almost as if Edara were somehow *mocking* him.

'Leave it, we have more important matters to discuss. Sit down again, I have reports you should see.'

Edara was – probably – right, so Messanger resumed his seat. 'First things first, though,' he said, folding his arms on the table – and a certain challenge in him now for although Edara was leader of the mission he, Messanger, was vital to its success, he had Sarsen's word for that. 'This "planned situation" you just spoke of which will allow the photocopying to be done and then kept secret for the necessary period of time: I will *help to create it*, you said. Therefore, I'd like to know exactly what that situation is.'

'Very well. The Watchman conference is being held at a venue here in London called Devon House. The blueprints vital to us are stored in the conference-room there, in one of six specially designed cabinets. Each delegate has his own cabinet, the lock to which is operated by his handprint. We shall require the Brit delegate to open his cabinet for us. Naturally, he will not do so voluntarily. In order to force him to comply we shall abduct a relative of his, a woman close to his heart, then hold her captive – and under threat of immediate death should he refuse us his co-operation.'

'Suppose he does refuse. What then?'

'First we carry out our threat on the abductee. Then we inform him of her execution, and work on him personally.'

'Extreme measures?'

'What else? If he has already allowed the killing of the abductee, such will surely be necessary. . . . I've never yet known those particular measures to fail,' Edara added, soft-voiced.

'Who will – who will take charge, if it comes to that?'

'I shall deal with it in person. I have the neccessary means in my possession.'

'And how – where – do I fit in?'

Sitting back, Edara looked down, resting his bony, long-fingered hands on the edge of the table, considering exactly how much to tell Messanger. Given the way things were between himself and this half-Brit, this rival of his for Sarsen's favour, he had to watch out for his own interests as well as those of Zephyr, that was something he had determined on long since. Therefore he must withhold from him certain highly important facts regarding his part in the mission until closer to the hit itself. And in the course of Zephyr and its aftermath there might well be a chance to, at the very least, discredit him in Sarsen's eyes, possibly even—

'Where do I come in?' Messanger asked again, not liking the silence.

'When you need to know, I shall tell you.' Snapping out of his introspection, Edara stood up, indicating the end of the meeting, pressing the intercom button on the desk. 'Meanwhile you are to concentrate on mending fences with your two siblings, particularly with the woman, Gemma. Give her what I believe is termed a good time; take her out, spend money on her, so that in return she invites you into her social life.'

'But I'm not *close* to them! I haven't seen either of them for years—'

'I already have considerable *information* regarding both she and her brother; I do not require you to investigate them. I require you to insinuate yourself into their present lifestyle, to win their liking and trust so that you are invited into their social circle and meet their friends, particularly Gemma's. You will report to me, in person, immediately after your first meeting with your siblings. I want, and expect, results fast.' Sitting down again, Edara reached for a file, opened it and bent his head over it.

'This way, sir.' The summoned guard's invitation to leave was respectful, but clearly not to be gainsaid. And thus the first meeting in London between Jake Messanger and Edara ended with the formal, barely cordial farewells of two men forcibly united for the prosecution of a terrorist attack but bitterly – and on one side murderously – opposed to each other in their rivalry for the favour of Sarsen, their overall commander.

Chapter 3

Ealing, London 17 July

'Oh *hell!*' Glancing at her watch as she pushed Jared's front door shut behind her and rushed on into the kitchen, Gemma saw it was already five o'clock. She had a hundred and one jobs to do before Jake presented himself at the house. He had been invited for drinks and a meal when, two days earlier and just arrived in London, he had called her from his hotel in Victoria. Jared had been out when she took the call, (a good thing too, she'd thought at the time) but, on his return, he had taken her invitation to their half-brother in his stride. Without enthusiasm, yes, she recalled now, as she set about preparing a bowl of salad, but at least he hadn't been cross or dreamt up some excuse and cried off. And then as she set the table in the dining-room, checked supplies in the drinks cabinet in the sitting-room and, finally, cleared up in the bathroom, her mind was taken over first by memories of their childhood days together and then by wonderings about Jake's long-dead mother and her family in Bahrain. How strange, she thought, the way Jake, right from when he was a child, only seven or eight years old, was drawn so strongly to the Arab side of his parentage. His mother La'ali Mehrab – La'ali means 'pearls', Jake told me once – met our father when he was at medical school and she was a student, on an English course in Leeds. Her parents were very wealthy and hugely influential in Bahraini affairs, Jake said, and I remember him telling me that before they would approve their daughter's marriage to him he had to promise, on oath, to live and work in Bahrain for at least five years following the wedding.

Didn't work out like that, though, did it? she thought. La'ali died in that car accident, and soon afterwards father came back to London to live and work, leaving the infant in the care of his mother's family for a while. So, maybe during those baby years an awareness of – or love of, perhaps? – all things Arab bedded itself deep down inside Jake's psyche, within his spirit, his *self*? Because once something like that has lived in your blood and brain, perhaps it's there for ever?

And then of course there was the fact that our father married again so soon after La'ali died. . . . *Stepmother!* And *shit*, when Jake came over and lived with the family for a bit, did Sandy – sorry, Alexandra – did she live up to the wicked stepmother image! Deliberately, she shut Jake out of the life she was building. The family had to be the close-knit unit of Sandy, John and their two kids Jared and me. Of course, Dad always did the right thing by Jake in material and financial matters; saw him through school and college, funding him liberally all the way. But from the day he married Sandy he showed – *showed*, who knows what he actually *felt*? – no affection towards Jake. Sandy made sure of that; she made Dad's life hell if he did. I remember one day—

No, stop it! It doesn't do any good, it's too late now, Gemma thought, the damage was done long ago. But maybe it isn't too late? Now Dad's dead and Sandy's gone back to the States for good and married again, I'd like to . . . draw Jake back to us, to Jared and me – to *me*, anyway. Maybe I can make that happen. I'll have a damn good try, whether Jared wants it or not—

The phone in the hall interrupted the flow of her thought, and she hurried to answer it, thinking, I just hope it isn't Jake saying he can't make it. I'll blow my top if I've done all this shitty housework for nothing—

'Hi, Sis. Jared,' said the voice in her ear. 'Look, I'm sorry, but we're into an emergency here and I'll be a bit late back.'

'But you *promised* me!'

'I know I did. One of our own's in trouble, though, and I'm needed.'

'Sure. Understood, then. Get here as soon as you can.'

'Will do.'

'And Jay, please be nice to him. *Please!*'

'He's our guest, Gem. Have you ever known me to be other than my usual charming, witty, considerate, intelligent self to a guest in my house?'

'Idiot. But—'

'Well, then. I have to go now. With luck, see you around seven-thirty. OK?'

'Has to be, doesn't it? See you.' As she replaced the phone, Gemma thought, perhaps it's a good thing, anyway; now, I'll have Jake to myself for a while. Could be things'll go better this way: it'll be Gemma and Jake like it was when we were kids, the rapport between us will bridge the divide between him and me that Sandy created and was always seeking ways to make deeper. And *crueller.*

'Hello.' Gemma got out the one word of greeting but then for a moment stood silent, smiling up at the tall stranger to whom she had just opened the door. *Jake* was standing there: like Jared in physique since in that both took after their father, fitness and strength evident in their lean athletic bodies. But there the likeness ended, for Jake had his mother's dark eyes and raven-black hair and was gifted with the high cheekbones and narrow, determined chin which had bestowed on her the dramatic beauty evident in the framed photographs which – until Alexandra Rostov came into his life – John Messanger had displayed around his house.

'You haven't changed much,' Gemma went on, a joy coming alive within her as she saw his eyes lose their guarded look and speak to her just as they often used to during their shared childhood years. 'It's wonderful to see you, Jake. Come in, you're very welcome here. I only wish you'd never gone away.'

Stepping into the hall he took her hand, raised and kissed it. 'You look lovely,' he said. 'Grown up now but still . . . Gemma.'

She laughed and closed the door behind him, shutting the outside world away to go about its own affairs so that she and her half-brother would, hopefully, have privacy in which they might revive the love which had existed between them in times past, which she remembered so vividly and yearned to enjoy once more.

'I hope I look happier than I did when we last saw each other,' she said, turning to him. 'It was the day your taxi carried you off to college, out of my life, and I cried my eyes out when you'd gone.'

Reaching out he ran his hand over her bright hair, then laid it against the curve of her cheek in a brief intimate caress. For, as he drove to Jared's house, he had recalled the gesture as one which used to give her great pleasure, and he had decided to use it again now in the hope that it would rekindle in her the empathy – the love, even? – there had been between the two of them, so that she would seek to have him close to her once more and would draw him into her social circle as was apparently called for by Edara's plan for the Zephyr strike.

'Only now do I realize how much I've missed you,' he said.

'Me, too.' Impulsively she stepped forward, reached up and kissed him on the cheek, sister-to-brother kiss, light, tender.

That one kiss seemed to Jake Messanger strangely sweet; but it felt to him as if it came from another world, and for a moment he was suddenly invaded by an unnerving sense of loss of will and direction, a kind of emotional disorientation. Then the feeling passed and he was Edara's tool in a mission masterminded by Sarsen, who had stood proxy for his blood-father and whom he revered above all men. 'Now I'm here with you it's as if I've never been away,' he said, carefully.

'So let's make up for the lost years,' she said. 'Now you *are* here, I want to see you as often as possible – when you've got the time, of course, this being a business trip I guess you'll be pretty busy.' As she spoke Gemma smiled up into his eyes, and in that moment he realised that for her the years had already been bridged between them. Already, she wanted him with her; so provided he played his cards right that evening, their first together, she would indeed invite him into her life. And he would be able to manipulate her then: would surely have the opportunity to do whatever Edara's abduction plan required.

*

They were halfway through their second drink before Jared's name was mentioned. It was a sunny evening, and they were in the living-room at the side of the house, Gemma sitting at one end of the sofa facing out over a flagged courtyard, Jake ensconced in an armchair nearby. He was pleased with the way the evening was proceeding: talk was easy and absorbing between them, flowing effortlessly as they asked and answered each other's questions regarding work and lifestyle. Already he had arranged to take her out to dinner the following evening, while she had invited him to a birthday party for her closest friend – Delyth – which was to take place at Jared's house on 13 August.

'I'm sorry Jared's so late,' Gemma said into a silence that had fallen, glancing at her watch, frowning.

'Personally, I'm glad of it.'

'Oh Jake! Surely now you're both grown men—'

He put his whisky down on the side-table by his chair and looked across at her. 'Glad of it because it gives me more time to . . . to *find you* again, Gemma. I think that's easier without Jared present to come between us.'

'D'you believe he'll try to?'

'It's certainly what he used to try to do when we were kids together.' He got to his feet and went to her, met her eyes as she looked up at him. 'He didn't succeed then, did he? And it's my sincere hope – my *belief* – that he won't now, if he does try.' He smiled. 'If he's the man I hope and expect he is, he won't even try; he'll have grown out of such stupid, childish jealousies.'

Sometimes, though, Gemma thought, turning away and staring out at the flowers she had planted days ago in the big glazed pots which, when she arrived, had been standing empty out in the court-yard; sometimes when we were teenagers and you were away with your mother's people, those long visits to Bahrain, Jared used to cause me to . . . to be *unsure* about you. He made me see you as an outsider among us and in some way *hostile* towards us – to him and me, and to our parents. But then, as soon as you were with us again all my doubts would vanish. . . . I loved you then, Jake. And now you're here I believe I still do. Big word, though, love.

'I've always thought of you as my full sister, you know. Whereas to me Jared was always and quite definitely my *half*-brother.' He spoke softly and with intent. 'I loved you. And what was more important, to me I mean, was that I felt sure you loved me. To the boy-me, knowing you loved me in return was my lifeline when I was at home in England with Dad and his second wife. You were always there for me when life in Alexandra's house became almost unbearable.' Jake had prepared this approach to her carefully, in the hope that opportunity might arise for him to employ such a line of 'infiltration'. Yet now, as he made his pitch to win her to him, a faint sense of — regret? Guilt, even? – stirred briefly within him, and he was glad that when she answered she did not turn her head and look at him again.

'D'you know,' she said, 'just before you said that about Jared I was remembering how, back when we were in our early teens, although *he* was my full brother, it was always you—' She broke off, for the living-room door was opened and Jared came in. He halted at once, his eyes going directly to Jake.

'Hi,' he said to him coolly, pushing the door to behind him. 'It's been a long time, hasn't it? Sorry I wasn't here when you arrived.' Then he went across to his half-brother and shook him by the hand, but there was no real warmth in either his voice or his handclasp.

'It's very good of you to invite me here.' Jake had got to his feet. 'I apologize unreservedly for failing to keep in touch with you for so long and, as I wrote in my letter, only hope you will forgive me for that and forget any bad times in our shared past, as I have done.' There was a smile on his face, warmth in his grip, the offer of friendship in his voice as well as in his words. But none of it was sincere: from an early age he had been well schooled by Sarsen in duplicity and emotional control; by now these assets had become second nature to him. As he looked at his half-brother, Jared's thick blond hair, fair skin and blue eyes all spoke to him of Alexandra, the woman who, to his way of thinking, had stolen his father John Messanger from him. All the bitterness and enmity he had felt towards him during their childhood and youth came to life again inside him, but he betrayed none of it.

Surprisingly, an easy grin spread across Jared's face as Jake fell silent. 'Nice speech,' he said, with friendly mockery. 'You're right, though. That stuff you're speaking of, it's all long in the past as far as I'm concerned; it's gone and forgotten. . . . Hi there, Sis, you're looking gorgeous as usual,' he went on, turning to her. 'I'll pour me a drink – it looks like I've got some catching up to do.'

They had so much to talk about, those three. And for the greater part of the evening Gemma found it easy to steer the conversation away from any topic likely – even guaranteed – to spark an argument between Jake and Jared, or to bring out into the open the hostility towards the other which she intuited still ran deep and strong inside each of them. Both disguised it well. Nevertheless it quickly became clear to her that it was Jake who was making the greater effort to avoid overt discord, always managing to deflect the flash-point questions his half-brother threw at him now and again. If only we can get through this first time together without real conflict, she thought, I think everything will be all right; I'll be able to build up from there, talk Jared round. I do so much want to keep Jake with us from now on.

As the evening progressed each of them learned quite a lot concerning the others: heard about their jobs, their friends, the things they liked and those they hated or despised, their hopes and plans for the future. However, naturally each divulged only as much about themselves as they wished known – which was not in each case the whole truth, or even a part of it. But when supper was over and they were sitting out on the terrace at the back of the house, coffee and drinks to hand, Jared put to his half-brother a question he was not prepared for. He chose his moment: Gemma had just gone back into the house to freshen up.

'What's become of that bloke your mother ditched so she could marry our father?' he asked, seemingly casually. 'Syrian, I think he was. Dad certainly made an enemy there. He told me quite a bit about him once. Said the man was absolutely gutted at being thrown over like that. Said, too, though, that the Syrian was pretty influential in those parts and would see you right as time went on. Did he?'

Sarsen. Jolted out of the sense of well-being which had grown in him during the evening, Jake picked up his brandy and cradled the glass between his cupped hands, looked down into it. Would it be safe to answer with a certain amount of openness, he wondered. And decided that it would be: the true identity of Sarsen was ring-fenced, surely impenetrable – besides, why should either of these two try?

'He did indeed,' he said. 'He was very good to me.'

'Does he still figure in your life out there?'

'Of course. Both working in the medical field, we see a great deal of one another, professionally *and* socially – mostly the latter now I'm no longer practising as a doctor.'

'So he's still a close friend of yours? With you being the son of the woman he was engaged to before our father came on the scene, I guess he'd like to be.'

'He's far above me in medical circles. I consider myself honoured to know him.' Desperate to change the subject, but fearing that to do so might appear suspicious, Jake spoke stiffly, hoping Jared would move on to some new topic.

Jared, however, had no intention of doing so. He leaned back in his cushioned garden chair, very relaxed, surveying his half-brother lazily. 'Did he ever marry, then?' he asked.

'A year after my mother died, he married a Kuwaiti girl. It didn't last, though. He divorced her and she. . . . She'd been educated in the States. She went back there, took a degree in law and made herself a new life.'

'Did they have kids?'

Now, Jake looked up, frowned at his half-brother. 'Why are you asking so many questions about this man? Yes, he had one child with his Kuwaiti wife, a daughter. But I can't see why you should be interested.'

'I'm interested because it's a fascinating story: "unrequited love", "the loved one lost forever", "love of my life" and all that. So may I ask one more question?'

'On condition it's your last on the subject.'

'I don't recall this bloke's name: what is it?'

'Khaled Adjani,' Jake answered automatically – then realized he had given Sarsen's real name and covered up the error at once, going on smoothly, 'but for family reasons he uses his mother's patriarchal name, Ansari, has done ever since he came of age.'

As he finished speaking Gemma rejoined them, and the conversation became general. And from then on until Jake left, Jared was careful not to make any further reference to the Syrian who had loved and lost the girl John Messanger married: decided he had learned enough about him – for the moment.

It was a few minutes after eleven o'clock that night when Jake Messanger left Jared's house and returned to his hotel. The evening had been spent profitably, he thought. He had, quite definitely, won Gemma to him; she had made it plain she would be only too happy to spend time with him whenever he was free. As for Jared. . . . Not much success there, he decided, as he drove through the lit London streets. However it didn't matter that he hadn't found out much about him and his job: he was surely no danger to Operation Zephyr. Edara's agents in the Brit capital had vetted Jared and reported him no conceivable threat since although he worked at MI5 he handled nothing of a sensitive nature.

But all was not quite as Jake supposed. For the last four months Jared had been operating as a low-level spook for MI5, and Edara's agents had not penetrated his cover. After questioning Jake that night about himself and 'the Syrian', he had decided it would be worth his while to find out more about both, if that were possible.

Thus it came about that, three days later, in the evening, Jared Messanger made his first active move to discover more regarding his half-brother's probity of purpose in coming to London and re-establishing himself within the English side of his family. During those three days, using such IT facilities at MI5 as he had clearance for, he had satisfied himself that Jake's bona fides in respect of the stated reason for his visit – discussions with two pharmaceutical companies re the purchase of certain analgesic drugs – were indeed all in order. That done, he turned his attention to the Syrian: called Simon Croft, an oppo of his from boarding-school days who lived nearby. Croft was a neighbour to Delyth Stanton, and since she and Gemma had become fast friends at medical school, the four of them socialized together whenever Gemma was staying with him during vacations. Croft was now a lecturer at Whitehaven College, an establishment offering two-year advanced English Language courses relevant to special subjects – such as medicine, English literature, IT – to mature students from the Middle East.

Croft answered promptly, but seemed impatient. 'Look, I'm with a colleague,' he said, 'I don't have time to chat.'

'I didn't call you to chat.'

'Then ten to one it's to ask me a favour—'

'You're dead right there. I've got a name I want you to check via that database at Whitehaven you told me about; they rack up a fair amount of personal info concerning their students, you said.'

'They do. Mostly, but by no means all, academic. So?'

'Anything political?'

'Some, I guess. Nowadays. I've never really thought about it.'

'Then I'm asking you to think about it now – more, actually, I want you to find out something for me if you can. This bloke, I want to know if he's got connections with any *political* activists or organizations in the Middle East, most particularly in Syria and the Gulf States.'

There was a pause, then Simon Croft asked, 'Political, as in terrorism? Is that what we're talking about?'

'Yes, it is.'

'Ah. Now look, Jared, I don't—'

'As you've said yourself, we're talking terrorism here, and I have to tell you this concerns the possibility of it hitting Britain, so surely you—'

'OK, OK. I'll give it a try. That's as much as I can promise. And – presumably? – there might not be anything to discover. Give me the name you want me to look into.'

'Khaled Adjani. Syrian by birth, in his mid-fifties—'

'Hold it there, the name and nationality is enough for now. If I find out anything dramatic I'll call you, otherwise it can wait until I see you at Levensholme – Tom's barbecue; you said you're going?'

'Sure, I'll be there. And Simon—'

'Yeah?'

'Get on to this as quick as you can, and give it your best shot. It could be important.'

'All right, will do. Cheers.'

But, as he switched off his mobile, Jared wondered whether he had done what he had simply because he wanted to *get* Jake: wanted to see him damned before the world, to bring ruin on him. Suddenly disturbed, unsure – Jake was *his half-brother*, for God's sake! – he flung himself down on his bed, linked his hands behind his head and stared up at the ceiling, frowning. He had no actual proof that Jake was in any way involved in terrorism. All he had was this gut feeling that the bastard wasn't levelling with him and Gemma, was somehow *using* them. *Why* Jake's sudden desire to mend fences with us? he debated. For ten years and more now he's apparently never given me and Gemma a thought, and now suddenly he rushes over to see us the minute he arrives in London. Asks Gem out to dinner pronto – even gets himself invited to the party she and I are giving for Del on her birthday. It all seems a bit weird. Doesn't *add up*, somehow. Because if he *is* on some sort of clandestine political mission, why this urgent desire to get cosy with *us*? What's the point of it? What possible use can we be to him? None, that I can see. Absolutely zilch—

But! Jake is obviously fully identified with the Arab world, he's lived and worked there for many years. . . . Yes, on balance I'm glad I got Simon in on this. And I'm not going to give up on it unless and until I'm convinced Jake's on the level. It's conceivable there's even bigger things at stake here than I imagine. The more I think about our relationship, the more clearly I see that to put him in London as an intelligence-gathering agent working on a mission against Britain – shit, he'd be God's gift to a hostile Arab organization. Gemma and me his cover while he beavers away on his own agenda. However, none of all this gives me any justification – yet – for putting the whole thing up to Rawlings for investigation— Rawlings, Christ! He'd have me for breakfast, slice me up every which way and fry me, spread me on his toast. . . .

Nevertheless Jared Messanger slept well that night, satisfied that he had taken one small step which might, at the very least, lead to some clarification of his half-brother's background in the Middle East.

Chapter 4

Central London 17 July

MEMORANDUM
To be circulated to all delegates
attending the WATCHMAN *conference*

1. The WATCHMAN conference will take place in London
    from Monday 26 July to Thursday 19 August inclusive.
    Venue: DEVON HOUSE London.

2. All delegates have been security vetted by both their own
    national intelligence services and by those of the UK. All
    have been given clearance.

3. Competence of conference delegates:
    The delegates are scientists with high-level relevant expe-
    rience in cybernetics; medical research specialists;
    weapons engineers; experts in germ and chemical warfare
    and the methods by which such weapons can be delivered
    to target locations.

4. Purpose and remit of conference:
    To consider and discuss means and ways of delivery of
    toxic agents – lethal gases, bacteria etc – to selected and
    vulnerable targets. In the light of international knowledge

and experience to date to revise, pass on and suggest improved strategies for combating hostile action of this kind, with particular reference to:

a.   Contamination of water suppplies.

b.   Contamination of air supply in confined spaces (e.g. Sarin in underground network as successfully carried out in Japan in 1995).

c.   Interruption/contamination of food supplies to resident populations.

5.   Final report of conference:
Not only should this include proposals for improving protection against terrorist activity as outlined in Clause 4 but also given worst-case scenarios and such attacks being successfully pressed home, how best for the relevant authorities to deal with the resultant difficulties, public anxiety etc.

6.   All government departments in Britain are under orders to afford full and rapid co-operation to all conference delegates.

In his office at MI5 HQ in Central London, Mike Edwards replaced the month-old memo in its file and locked the file away in the bottom drawer of his desk. Then he leaned back in his chair, linked his hands behind his head and conned over the present state of play concerning Watchman. On the day he had received the memo, an informant of his had reported third-level intelligence – that is, intelligence unsubstantiated by any other source – suggesting that one of the delegates was either working directly with Al Qaeda, or had secured his appointment to the conference with the intention of leaking information on its proceedings to someone who had links with that organization. Edwards had had the lead followed up, but nothing concrete had been discovered: no delegate had come anywhere near being marked as a suspect, so Edwards had pulled his agent off the investigation.

But that just isn't good enough, Edwards thought now. Here we are with – perhaps – a chance to nail *an Al Qaeda activist!* It would be little short of criminal simply to leave the matter lie – hell, as soon as Watchman's over all the delegates'll go their separate ways, so any undercover agent among them will pass out of our jurisdiction. I'll take it higher, have to. . . . I'll take it to Rawlings, see what he thinks. There's Professor R. Stanton, the British delegate to Watchman: maybe Rawlings'll authorize an approach to him?

Chapter 5

Uxbridge Outer London 18 July

A hardline fanatic in his fifties, Edara had risen to his present position in Sarsen's organization the hard way, seeing action in both
Chechnya and Afghanistan. It was now his hope – no, more, it had
become his expectation – that success in the Zephyr operation would
see him rise to his ultimate goal, Sarsen's acknowledgement of him
as his rightful successor. The only threat to his realization of that
ambition that he was aware of was his fellow agent Jake Messanger.
Sarsen's attitude towards *him* seemed to Edara to be ambivalent, and
now he was looking for possible allies against the half-Brit.

Agent Nine, the second of his lieutenants in the Zephyr mission
was, he judged, such a one. In the safe house now, Edara handed the
summarized action schedule for the operation across the table to
Nine. 'Check through it,' he said. 'It outlines the bones of the hit. I
have made one slight alteration to the arrangements we agreed on
two days ago.'

Rising to his feet, reading the two-page schedule as he went, Agent
Nine crossed to the one window in the small back room of this subur-
ban house selected for their meeting. He was well aware of the facts
detailed in it. Every facet of the hit had been discussed time and time
again over the last six months in the course of the innumerable
sessions Edara and he had had – sometimes working together, sometimes separately, but always in close collaboration – with the various
weapons experts, cadre leaders, sleepers and so on involved in the

mission. Nevertheless he studied this final schedule intently, a kind of greediness in him. For he and Edara were the originators, the creators, of Zephyr: the dream of a spectacular strike from which it had come into being had been theirs, and theirs alone – and both men loved it with an abiding and jealous love.

The schedule detailed these facts:

OPERATION ZEPHYR: ON-SITE ACTION AT UNDERGROUND STATIONS

TARGET LOCATIONS: Green Park
                            Holborn
                            Knightsbridge

TIMING:

Saturday 14 August
12.00 midday: simultaneous release of toxic gas from pressurized containers secreted in prepared holdalls carried by suicide agents.

ACTION:

One suicide agent assigned to each station. Agents report to Red Pillars safe house by 04.30 hours.
Final briefing there by Edara.
Each agent to be armed with his container of toxic gas immediately prior to his departure.
Each suicide agent to travel to his target alone, following given instructions.

NOTES
1.   Optimum success requires precise positioning of the suicide agents. To this end a blueprint of the ventilation system at each target station will have been obtained. With reference to these, each agent at Red Pillars will be shown where he is to position himself at his target station, and will memorize that position (each being already familiar

with the layout of his station, learned during his period of intensive training for his mission).

2.　Commencing at 07.15 hours suicide agents will depart from Red Pillars at half-hour intervals, and travel to their destinations.

3.　On their departure, Edara will shred and burn all documents used by himself and the three suicide agents during the final briefing.

Coming to the end of the schedule Agent Nine returned to the table, handed it back to Edara and sat down again.

'Good, is it not?' Looking into Nine's seemingly guileless eyes Edara marvelled – by no means for the first time – at the contradiction between his urbane physical appearance and his ruthless, devious persona and, mentally, congratulated him on the way he so skilfully used those contradictions in his work for Sarsen. Many of the enemy had been destroyed by Agent Nine's machinations: deceived into trusting him by his apparent warm-hearted good faith, had been conned into making mistakes and thus caught in a trap of his devising. 'All our agents are established here, all logistics are in hand,' he went on, 'Zephyr continues on course and – most important of all, naturally – we remain undetected by Brit Intelligence.'

'Provided we get what we want from the abduction, all should go well.'

Catching a note of scepticism in the – when Nine so chose – mellifluous voice, Edara asked quietly, 'To which of the two abductions do you refer?'

'That of the woman. The other is straightforward.'

'And you have . . . what? Doubts? Doubts regarding the plan for seizing the woman?' Edara's voice was still quiet, but his eyes had hardened: the kidnapping of the woman and the use of her captivity as their main enforcer had been his own idea and he resented criticism of it.

'It relies too heavily on one particular agent.'

'Messanger. Yes, Sarsen's personal choice.' Edara clasped his hands on the table. 'As you are aware, my friend, I detest the presence of Messanger within Sarsen's close circle as much as you do. But surely it is beyond dispute that, in this particular situation, he is the agent best placed to ensure the success of the plan for the woman's abduction and, following it, to oversee her continuing detention at safe house Alpha.'

'All of which places a tremendous amount of trust in him.'

'And you don't consider him worthy of it? You suspect – you *have reason* to suspect the sincerity of his commitment to Zephyr? *To us?*'

Nine hesitated. Finally said, 'It is my opinion that Sarsen should deny Messanger further promotion until and unless he converts to Islam. As you know, today will be the first time I have met him in person. However I have made it my business to investigate his past, and I have discovered matters which cause me to mistrust the way he has come to be the recipient of Sarsen's trust . . . his affection and trust, I understand.'

'Perhaps you *understand* the situation between them in the way the outside world is intended to perceive it.'

Agent Nine's eyes – cold now, and a dawning malice in them, his only feature that is beyond his *total* control of expression – searched his commander's face as he discerned one possible interpretation of what Edara had just said. After a moment he asked carefully, 'Are you suggesting that Sarsen is not sincere in the trust and affection he shows towards Messanger?'

'That is something which will become apparent in the course of time.' Edara's remark had been a deliberate lure: from Agent Nine's reaction to it he had hoped to be able to judge whether he could count on him as an ally against Messanger, should the need for one arise, or should he, Edara, decide to precipitate such a need. And now, intuiting from that sly malice towards the Brit which Nine had been unable to hide, and recognizing within it a jealous desire as strong as his own to destroy their common rival for Sarsen's favour and patronage, he spoke freely – relatively freely only, having an axe of his own to grind when the time was right.

'All is not as it seems between Sarsen and the Brit—' He broke off, said in a grim aside, 'To me, he is *Brit* and always will be, the blood of the father is dominant.' Then he took up the thread of his reasoning. 'Sarsen has *brain-washed* Jake Messanger. He began the exercise during the boy's childhood, then pursued it through his teenage years and on into his manhood. . . . It is an undertaking that has been completely successful, so rest assured, my friend: in the Brit, Sarsen has made a tool to his hand,' he added softly.

Slowly, an expression of malign satisfaction spread across Nine's face. 'An extremely useful tool in the prosecution of Zephyr,' he observed.

'Indeed. However, all tools wear out in time – or, as in this case I suspect, come to the end of their usefulness to their owner.' Leaning forward, Edara pressed a bell on the table, 'I shall have our Brit in now,' he said. 'While he is with us you will leave the talking mostly to me.'

The bell rang in the narrow front hall of the house. It startled Messanger, and he glanced across at the guard who had admitted him, subjected him to a severe body-search, then pointed to an upright wooden chair just inside the door, barked a peremptory 'Wait there!' and stationed himself at the foot of the stairs on the far side of the hall, the handgun in his right hand held alongside his thigh. Half an hour had gone by since then. During it no word had passed between them: Messanger sat deep in thought, going over such knowledge as he had regarding Zephyr, and the guard standing at attention, his eyes never leaving his 'prisoner'.

Now, sharp on the summons of the bell, he marched across to Messanger. 'Upstairs!' he ordered, gesturing with the gun. 'You first, and keep your hands where I can see them.' As they reached the first floor he moved ahead and opened the second door on his right. Messanger walked in, hearing it close behind him as he advanced to the table in the middle of the room.

'*Ah-leen.*' Edara's voice was as hostile as his eyes.

'*Elf' salamaat.*' Messanger's response was measured, and without waiting for invitation he sat down in a chair facing Edara. He was aware of one other man sitting to one side of the table, and guessed it must be Agent Nine, his fellow lieutenant on Zephyr, but for the moment he kept his eyes on Edara, this personal enemy of his.

It seemed that Edara also wanted it that way since for the time being he neither introduced Nine nor made any reference to his presence.

'You report good progress with your two siblings,' he observed sharply, 'but I must remind you that our time is limited.'

'I'm aware of that. This evening my half-sister, Delyth Stanton and I are going to a barbecue at Levensholme, the home of one of their friends; it's in the country, south of London.'

Both Edara and Agent Nine were extremely pleased by this news since it suited their plans, but neither betrayed the fact.

'Interesting, and potentially useful,' Edara commented drily. 'Your half-sister will soon be giving a party for the Stanton woman. Have you been invited to it?'

'I have.'

Sitting well back in his chair, Agent Nine had been watcbing Messanger closely. He knew a great deal about Delyth Stanton and her father Professor Robert Stanton. Much earlier in the mission he had headed the tangential exercise which had first isolated and then decided on Gemma Messanger as Zephyr's best chance of penetrating the social circle surrounding one delegate to the Watchman conference. Directly out of that decision had come Edara's idea of using Gemma's friend Delyth as 'forced enabler' in their prosecution of the main hit through the co-operation of her father.

'This will be the first time you have met Delyth Stanton,' Nine put in now, with deceptive mildness.

Messanger turned to him. 'May I know your name?'

Nine sat forward so that the light from the window fell on his face. 'We have not met before, but Edara will have told you of me, I am known simply as Agent Nine. It is a pleasure to meet you, Jake Messanger, and I have no doubt it will be a pleasure to be in action with you during the course of Zephyr. You stand high in Sarsen's esteem, and since I know him to be a discerning judge of men I count it an honour that he has sent you to work with us in the final stages of the mission.'

Surprised by Nine's affable appearance and slightly over-the-top welcome, Messanger responded with due politeness, then turned back to Edara. 'You gave me to understand that you called me in today to apprise me of the final schedule for the hit and to give me more detail regarding my part in Zephyr,' he said. 'May we move on to that now?'

Edara picked up the schedule and handed it to him. 'Finalized and summarized,' he said curtly. 'Study it.'

'Shall I be given a copy?' Messanger asked as he took the papers – then cursed himself for asking the question. Grow up, you fool! That's a stupid thing to suggest, bloody infantile – and in front of these two, of all men!

'Copies of the final plan for an operation are never passed to agents,' Nine cut in hard before Edara could speak. 'The original remains in Edara's keeping. You are required to commit its salient points to memory.'

Messanger nodded, then, head down, memorized the definitive plan for Zephyr. No one spoke while he did so. And in the given secrecy of the silence, Edara took stock of the body language of this Brit who stood four-square in his way, blocking the realization of his savage, driving ambition to become Sarsen's chosen and anointed heir apparent and who, doubtless, would remain so while he walked the earth. Meanwhile Agent Nine watched both of them, perceiving the blood-deep hostility coursing between them, controlled at the moment but – on one side at least – surely bent on destruction? And he decided then that, should it come to a showdown between them during the present mission, he would be well advised to be on the winning side: the big question was, which side would that be?

The key facts of the plan for Zephyr's climax taken on board, Messanger looked across at Edara. 'How do we obtain the photo-copies of the blueprints?' he asked him, eye to eye.

'Through the enforced co-operation of a delegate to the Watchman conference who has access to the cabinet in which the ones we are interested in are kept for the duration of the talks.'

'*Forced?*'

'We shall subject him to intense pressure.'

'What kind of pressure?'

'Personal, emotional pressure, which, as you well know, can be the most difficult of all to resist. We shall break the will of the man concerned, destroy his psychological ability to stand firm against us. Rest assured, Messanger: he will open his cabinet, and we shall photocopy the relevant blueprints.'

'But surely it will quickly be discovered that this has been done?'

'Not so. No one bar our own agents – and, naturally, the reluctantly renegade conference member – will be aware of what has occurred until at least twenty-four hours after Zephyr's climax.'

'The plan states that the photocopies will be delivered to you at or before 02.30 hours. Zephyr blows at midday, so this means that our collaborator will have to be kept quiet all through one morning: won't people – his friends, his colleagues – be concerned about him? Think something's wrong, and probably inform the police?'

'Zephyr climaxes on a Saturday, Watchman will not be in session. The traitor will be held prisoner in his own house, and we have reliable information that on the day concerned he will be known to be working at home, as he often does. No one will disturb him—'

'But what the hell!' Suddenly, Messanger, was really angry. 'No man on earth could behave that way! Not when he must surely guess that—'

'He will not know our reasons, so how can he guess our intentions? Also, we shall still be holding, under severe duress, the person who was the source of the intolerable pressure which enabled us to dominate and suborn him in the first place.'

'In God's name, who is this *source* you speak of? Who matters to him so much that he'll—'

'Did Sarsen not tell you?' Edara's hooded eyes mocked him. 'Shortly before we seize our collaborator we shall abduct a woman who is close to his heart. Then we make clear to him that should he *at any time* or *in any way* fail us, she will die, and that her death will not be an easy one. . . . We keep her under duress for as long as it is necessary to enforce his compliance with our orders.'

'You seem completely sure of him: that he'll both turn traitor to his own country *and* keep quiet for as long as you so order.' But the anger had gone out of Messanger, he had driven it out because Edara was commander of the mission and as such not to be called to account.

'You use the word *traitor.*' Suddenly, Nine intervened, putting his elbows on the table and leaning towards Messanger, searching his face. 'It seems to me unequivocally . . . judgemental on your part. Yet what would *you* do, yourself, if you were thrust into a situation like that? A situation in which the very life of a person you deeply loved was the other half of the equation you were faced with?'

Surprised – for from what he'd heard of Agent Nine he was not the sort of man to be either interested in or troubled by moral scruples or niceties – Messanger stared at him, frowning; thinking that while it was indeed a very perplexing question, it was not one he was prepared to answer off the cuff, and certainly not in the presence of Nine or, even more definitely, Edara. 'It would depend on—'

'We have not met here for a discussion of ethics,' Edara interrupted. 'Messanger, I will now brief you in detail on the logistics of the hit. Nine, you will leave us; you know it all.'

'There's something I'd like to know, Edara,' Messanger put in quickly, 'and I think maybe it's better asked about while all three of us are present. What are the names of these two people? The conference delegate, and the woman you're so sure he will turn traitor to keep safe from harm?'

Nine was already on his feet ready to leave but he stiffened where he stood, his eyes going from Edara to Messanger. He was already privy to the names of the two people involved, but he was intrigued to discover how Edara would deal with the question.

'You have no need of those names yet.' Edara's eyes and voice were ice cold. 'In this operation you have no independence of action whatsoever: your part in it, your duty, is simply to follow whatever orders I give you.'

'That is true. Nevertheless I would regard it as an indication of your trust in me were you to tell me.'

Edara turned aside, gesturing to Nine to be on his way. 'Trust has to be earned,' he remarked to no one in particular, then handed one of the files on the table to Messanger. 'In there you will find reports from our agents obtaining and collating information on security arrangements at Devon House. Study them now, before I start on your briefing.'

Chapter 6

Ealing 20 July

After lunch the next day – a warm and sunny one, the occasional fleecy cloud sailing dreamily across blue sky – Jake drove to Jared's house. Gemma had invited him for tea – 'Well, I'll promise to give you a nice tea,' she'd said to him over the phone, when he told her he would be free the following afternoon, 'but really, I'm asking you over so you can help in the garden, too. So please get here around two o'clock, then we can have a good go at it. Bring your stuff so you can shower and change afterwards.'

So now, clad in navy-blue sweatshirt and jeans, a change of clothes in the holdall he was carrying, he walked up the front path and went round to the back of the house as Gemma had suggested, telling him she'd already be at work there, probably in the shrubbery that bordered the property. But as he went round the corner and into the back garden he could see no bright blonde head amidst the unkempt greenness massed on the far side of the raggedy, dande-lion-infested lawn.

However, there was an auburn one: a mass of gleaming auburn hair tied at the back of the head with green ribbon. A young woman was at work among the trees and bushes across the lawn, and, putting down his bag, he stood watching her, realizing she must be Gemma's friend Delyth Stanton. Her back was to him, and she was wearing pale-brown shorts and a dark, sleeveless T-shirt. She was cutting back a bay tree twice her height, he saw, and now as she reached up for a high branch – revealing a slender, athletic figure – her hair swung free and cascaded down over her shoulders, brilliant against the greenery, glinting in the sunshine.

Then, as he watched her, a small branch of the bay, falling as it was cut off, landed on a rose bush in full bloom. She twisted round to lift it clear of the flowers and, as she tossed it out on to the grass, she caught sight of the tall man standing at the corner of the terrace. He began to walk towards her. For a moment she stared at him, but then as he drew close, quite suddenly she turned away and began dead-heading the roses.

'Hi,' he said. 'Sorry, I didn't mean to interrupt you.' Halting a few yards from her, he saw her face in profile to him as she snipped off blown roses. She has a beautiful profile, he thought: high cheek-bones, the features clear-cut, the jawline smooth, elegant.

'You must be Gemma's half-brother, I think.' Her voice was very cool, very self-possessed, but she did not turn her head and look at him and her secateurs were still busy, withered blooms still falling to lie sadly on the dark soil. 'She'll be back in a minute. She's just gone down to the shops, we ran out of butter.'

'I'm a bit early.'

'Why don't you put your bag inside and come and get started? There's an awful lot to be done here.' Snip, snip went the secateurs.

'In a minute.' He wanted her to look at him, wanted her to talk to him: unreasoned and seemingly arrowing in out of the blue, these two desires suddenly possessed him. 'You're Delyth, aren't you?' he went on, 'Delyth Stanton. Gemma told me you'd got hair to die for, so it's fairly obvious;. . . . You like gardening?'

'I hate to see a garden left uncared for as this is. All the good things smothered with predators—'

'Predators – that's a strange word to use about plants.'

'You think?' But there were no more withered roses left to cut off, and she straightened up. 'Wouldn't it be a good idea if you stopped standing there doing nothing and started work?' she said, looking straight at him.

And he saw then: there was quite a bad scar on the right side of her face. Low down on her cheek a sickle-shaped macula showed russet-red and faintly wrinkled, its semi-circular edge ridged pale against undamaged skin.

'How did you get the scar?' he asked quietly. But he was no longer looking at it; he was looking into her eyes – and she was allowing him to do so, which surprised and delighted him. 'It looks as though it happened a long time ago.'

'It did. I was ten. I got kicked, in the face by a horse – a pony, rather.'

'Do you still ride?'

'Of course.'

'Surely it hurt a lot.'

'I don't really remember.' But suddenly, she smiled at him. 'Lying can waste an awful lot of time, can't it?' she said. 'I remember perfectly well. It hurt like hell, but for a while then everyone made a tremendous fuss of me. I could get away with anything. So it wasn't all bad.'

'You and Gemma, you first met at college, she told me.'

Delyth nodded. 'We did,' she said, and stepped forward on to the lawn. Then in the sudden ease each found in the other's company they strolled across the grass and sat down on the wooden seat built around the trunk of a chestnut tree in the far corner of the garden. 'Very soon we discovered that Jared lived close to where Dad and I do and – well, it's great, we get to spend time together during vacations,' she went on, stretching her slim, tanned legs out in front of her. 'And what makes it even better is that Simon and Jared have known each other since they were at school together – Simon Croft, that is, he's a family friend of ours; he's been our neighbour for ages.'

But mention of Jared's name had jolted Jake out of the sun-gold little world this girl and he seemed somehow to have spun into existence around themselves. Abruptly, he returned to his real one. Sarsen; Edara; Agent Nine: they, surely, were his real world? The world he lived in, had *chosen* to live in: under the guidance of Sarsen, and because of his love for him, had *chosen* to live in? Sunshine was simply sunshine. This person sitting beside him was simply a very attractive woman; was, moreover, one from whom he had been instructed to glean as much information as possible regarding Gemma, Jared, and their circle of friends. So, he should tailor his conversation with her to that end.

'This bloke Simon, is he in the same line of work as Jared?' he asked.

'Simon Croft? Lord, no. He's a lecturer at a college for post-grad students to whom English is a second, but foreign, language. You'll meet him at the barbecue at Levensholme, Tom Smithyman's place. He and Tom have been mates for a long time. Levensholme's beautiful. I've known it since I was a child, and I love it. It's old, with a character all its own.' She sat silent for a few moments, then said, 'I don't mind about the scar.'

Oddly moved that she should want him to know it, he turned to her at once, saying, 'It made a difference to you, though, didn't it? Inside you, I mean?'

A wariness came in her eyes. 'I can cover it up quite easily. Cosmetics do that.'

'That's not what I asked you, is it?'

'No.' The clear, sea-green eyes studied his face; then her hand strayed up to her cheek and, smoothing her fingers over the scarred skin, she smiled at him – a little. 'It taught me certain things,' she said. The words came slowly and – it seemed to Jake Messanger – with a wry regret.

'Such as?'

But now she shied away from the intimacy between them, broke it into pieces with a light, dismissive laugh. 'I learned that it's not a good idea to get too close to horses, or to people either,' she said.

'What the hell do you two think you're doing?' Gemma, coming round the side of the house pushing a wheelbarrow loaded with garden tools, stopped dead at the edge of the terrace, staring at them in amazement. Then she burst out lauging and went on towards them as they got to their feet. 'OK, break over! Hi, Jake, sorry I wasn't here when you arrived – not that it seems to have bothered you,' she added, as he came across to her, her eyes following Delyth who was on her way back to the bay tree. 'Take care, though,' she said quietly, turning to look up at him, all flippancy gone. 'She's a self-sufficient lady, that one, and she's very, very bright. She's going places, is Delyth. She's a high-flier, they say at college and by "they" I don't mean only her peers, I mean the Establishment as well. So please, unless you're serious about it, don't set out to . . . to get really close to her. You might get hurt.'

'Does it show that much?' He quirked an eyebrow at her.

'Not really, I guess. It's just that I. . . . Well, it's like when we were kids together: you and I, we had this understanding, this rapport, so that quite often we knew what the other was thinking and feeling.'

'True.' Jake put his hand over hers where it lay lightly on the handle of the wheelbarrow, and felt hers turn under his own and clasp it. 'I'm glad to be here with you,' he said.

'It won't stop at this one visit to England will it? You'll come over again – to see *us*, I mean, not just on business? And maybe I can come out and see you.'

'I'd like that.' But he knew it for a lie, and for a moment hated himself for it. Then the dream broke and, again, he was back in Sarsen's world: he was on a mission for him, and the girl he was talking to was no more to him than a tool to his hand in the execution of that mission. However, he did not lose sight of the fact that it was his duty to keep her happy and on his side for a while yet. 'We'll set a date for you to come to Damascus,' he went on, and raised her hand, kissed it, released it.

'That'd be lovely.' Then throwing him that gamine grin of hers he remembered from childhood, Gemma took a Strimmer from the wheelbarrow and held it out to him. 'But right now it's time for grass-cutting for you and weeding for me, else come party night the guests will have to be told to bring their wellies.'

Chapter 7

Levensholme and London 22 July

Ten o'clock, and afterglow still flaring the western sky. At Levensholme the barbecue had been going for three hours, and on the softly lit veranda running the length of the back of the house, the dozen or so guests – friends, neighbours and business colleagues of Tom Smithyman, Simon Croft's crony – were enjoying themselves, their talk and laughter drifting light and convivial on the warm summer air.

Jake Messanger, however, was standing alone at the edge of the veranda. Delyth spoke no more than the truth when she told me Levensholme was beautiful, he thought, gazing out over the stretch of immaculate lawn that, bordered by flowerbeds with mature woodland trees rising behind them, ran down to the brook bordering Smithyman's property. I had forgotten the breathtaking colours, the greenness of England in summertime—

'Cooler than Damascus?' A hand on his arm and, turning, he found Gemma beside him, drink in hand and dressed easy in prettied-up jeans and a darkly pink top.

'I'd certainly rather be here than there tonight,' he said.

'What's the best time of year to visit?'

'October, or maybe April, early May.'

'Not good months for me—'

Which was why he had suggested them. 'We'll fix something,' he interrupted. He had no intention of inviting her – yet, at the back of his mind he was conscious of regret that it should be so. Stifling the feeling, he went on at once, saying the first thing that came into his head. 'Simon seems a good bloke. Lives near Delyth, I think?'

'He does. He grew up there, then stayed on with his parents while he was at college. In fact, he still lives in the same house – it's a bungalow, actually, but some bungalow! It was architect designed with Simon's dad in mind – he had bad arthritis – and it's absolutely super, got this gorgeous garden all round it, too. Anyway, his parents moved to Western Australia a couple of years ago and the place came to him. He's a terribly nice bloke. I like him a lot, but he's got absolutely no sense of humour. None whatsoever, and for an extrovert like me that makes him hard going sometimes. Actually, it's Delyth he wants, not me – nor any other woman in this wide, wide world.'

'You mean—?'

'He's been proposing to her regularly for years, and rejected with equal regularity. He is resigned to it now, I think. And as you see here tonight, they stay close friends.'

But Jake, unaware that he would regret it later, had lost interest in Simon Croft. 'Would you like to eat?' he asked.

'I already have. Ages ago, I was starving. You?'

'Long since.'

'So let's sit down over there at the far end of the terrace and just talk. I'd like another drink first, though, please.'

Collecting a glass of white wine for her and a lager for himself at the bar alongside the barbecue, Jake carried them across to Gemma, who had seated herself in a garden chair beside one of the white-painted tables.

'I haven't seen Jared here,' he said, sitting down facing her. 'You did say he was coming?'

'He said he was, so I guess he'll turn up eventually.' Gemma was annoyed at her brother's lateness, and her voice showed it. 'A while ago I asked Tom and he said Jay had called him – the usual thing, crisis at the office.'

Jake sipped his lager, considering how to respond. Jared's hostility towards him, thinly disguised since that first time he had visited them, seemed only to have increased, and he did not like it: having an enemy inside the close family circle within which he was operating was deeply worrying. He knew from Edara that Agent Nine himself had vetted Jared and declared him clean, his job with MI5 purely administrative. So, thought Jake, things must be all right, Nine's vetting will have been both exhaustive and aggressive.

'Delyth seems to enjoy your company, says she finds you so easy to talk to.' Seeing him apparently not interested in discussing Jared, Gemma had changed the subject. 'You will come to the party Jay and I are giving for her on her birthday, won't you?' She laughed. 'She's not a great one for parties, so please do come – if *you're* there she might for once stay late, not do her usual Cinderella thing and take off before midnight!'

Looking up, Jake found her regarding him quizzically, bright blonde head tilted sideways, the half smile on her face teasing him. You're very attractive, Gemma, he thought, and I'm drawn to you strongly, things are so damned good between us, like they used to be when we were children. Nevertheless, I have to keep you at arm's length and do it without you realizing I'm doing so. Which is a mean, devious, despicable way to behave, especially when you're so trusting. Sure, it's all of those; but my mission here calls for it to be done, so I will do it. I'll go to that party because I want to go, but also because Edara has ordered me to. I wonder why he has? No particular reason, probably; just him playing his cards close to his chest like he always does, bastard that he is.

'I'm looking forward to being there,' he said. 'I had a business dinner invitation but I've called it off, fixed it for another evening. And . . . I'm glad Delyth likes being with me. To me, she seems . . . different from most.'

'Most what?'

Jake smiled. 'Most women I've met, I suppose. Sorry, it was a stupid thing to say.'

'Not really: Delyth *is* one in a million. . . . But like I said to you before, Jake, take care with her. Two years ago she was . . . well, I have to call it jilted, but that's such a crummy little word, isn't it? The bloke was someone she'd known from her teens, and it hit her really hard. Since then she's been pretty much on the defensive with men.'

'Tell me about it.'

Gemma looked across at him, and the intensity in his lean, strong-featured face disturbed her. 'No, I'm not going to do that,' she said slowly, her eyes meeting his, warning him he must let the matter go. '*She's* the only one with the right to tell you – or refuse to.'

He looked away. 'That's true,' he said. 'I agree. I shouldn't have asked.'

Deliberately, she broke the sudden tension between them. 'So, what's Damascus like?' Picking up her drink, she favoured him with her gamine grin. 'Somehow we never seem to find time to get round to that, but we've plenty now.'

Already regretting having betrayed his serious interest in Delyth Stanton to his half-sister – to do so had been unforgivably unprofessional – Jake followed her lead readily. 'What do you want to know?' he asked, switching his mind to the city's many glories, the sites of interest most visitors usually wished to see.

But that was not what Gemma wanted from him. 'Tell me about you living there. The area you live in, your friends, the people you work with, what the shops are like, what you eat – also, please, places where we can eat together when I come to see you . . .'

Although based solely on his own intuition, Jared Messanger's suspicions regarding his half-brother had increased as the days went by. Consequently, a little after ten o'clock, immediately after he arrived at the Levensholme barbecue, he sought out Simon Croft and, finding him on the edge of a lively group of guests on the terrace, laid a hand on his arm, asking as he turned to him, 'So you didn't get anything on that name I gave you, Khaled Adjani?'

'I drew a complete blank.'

'Then come inside and we'll talk, I've got another idea,' Jared said, and led the way indoors, into a study at the side of the house.

'The name doesn't figure at all in the records at Whitehaven,' Simon said, sitting down in an armchair. 'Not in the data banks I've got access to, anyway, which include stuff on the students' referees on application.'

'Shit. Not surprising, though, really. . . . But realizing it was a long shot, and knowing how good you are at your job, the way you strike up some pretty good friendships with one or two of the blokes studying at advanced level on your Medical Practice course – I don't reckon politics would figure much on the English Literature one – I've thought of a different approach.'

'What've you got in mind?'

'This: I don't know if you'll go along with it, but here it is. I remember you telling me a while ago that one of your present students you've become friendly with is from Lebanon, and that the two of you often go out together for the odd beer after class, and so on.'

'Sure, I know who you mean: John Nestorian. He's a good guy; in his fifties now, and fairly high-powered. He's hoping to land an advertised post in the States, so he's studying like crazy to get his professional English up to speed. He was working in Damascus before.'

'I remember you said; it's what gave me the idea. What I thought was, do you know him well enough to ask him about Adjani? Since he was based in Damascus, could be he might come up with something?'

Simon sat forward, his interest caught. 'You never know. John and I, we're . . . well, he *trusts* me, I'm pretty sure of that. If he does know anything about Adjani, I think he'd pass it on to me. I've been giving him private tuition for the last six months, and he's been to my place a few times. I brought him down here to Levensholme once.'

'How long did he stay in Syria? Any idea?'

'Actually, yes.' Simon drank off the last of the vodka sling he had brought in with him and put the glass down on the floor beside his chair. 'Nearly five years. Mostly in Damascus, doing research for the last year.'

'Does he get on well with the other students?'

'Indeed he does. He's very popular.'

'Politics?'

'He never expresses any views publicly – none of them do. He talks quite a bit about that stuff to me, though. He was very guarded at first, naturally, but by now he's pretty open with me, we have some fairly frank discussions. He's a Christian—'

'Maybe, just maybe, we're on to something here,' Jared interrupted, his eyes alight. 'Jake's building himself a career on the medical scene – which is the sort of career that could make great cover for a hush-hush political activist, couldn't it?' And then, in his mind, he carried the premise further: it would make good cover for *Jake*, wouldn't it, if he really is committed to some Islamist group hostile to the West, and has come over here to prosecute a mission on its behalf.

'I don't see where you're going.' Simon was eyeing him warily.

Jerking to him an upright chair Jared turned its back to Simon then sat astride it and put him in the picture. 'I have serious doubts as to the real reasons for my half-brother's business trip to London,' he said. 'Doubts, too, as to just *why* he's suddenly become so interested in Gemma and me, so eager to socialize with us, to get to know our friends, and so on. To me, all this he's doing doesn't ring true. His wanting Gemma and me to "forgive and forget" and all that – it doesn't ring true.'

'Doubts about *Jake*?' Simon stared at him in amazed disbelief. 'You're out of your head!'

'You don't know him; I do. Think on it, Simon. Jake's completely bilingual, English and Arabic. His mother was Arab, so he's half-blood Arab. Add to that the fact he's spent the greater part of his thirty-one years living in the lands of his Arab relatives and under their influence. Now put all of those facts together and, surely, it follows that he'd be an absolute gift to any Islamist terrorist organization looking to recruit an undercover agent to carry out a mission in the UK? And even more so, a gift to any Arab master-terrorist who had been in a position to win his trust, and then influence him right from when he was young. To mould him into what *he* wants him to be?'

Jared had spoken with such passion, such total belief in what he was saying, that Simon found himself convinced – at least sufficiently to be ready to give him any assistance he could in finding out the truth behind the whole situation. There remained, however, one point he wanted to be clear about. 'When you refer to a master-terrorist,' he asked, 'it seems to me likely you have in mind this bloke Adjani?'

'Yep, I do. So, are you up for it? You'll tackle your friend Nestorian?'

'You've made a case all right, but I'm not going to commit myself until I know exactly what you want me to do'

'Fair enough. Listen, then. I want you to get me any information you can about Jake and his life in Damascus. Specifically – and hope-fully – anything which might point to him having, or ever having had, some connection with covert political, even *terrorist* activists or organizations based in and operating from Syria. I want information on the people Jake works with, socializes with, or appears to have any sort of unexplained contact with. Now, about Nestorian. Where does he stand, politically?'

'With the students, discussion on any subject even remotely connected with politics is almost always . . . well, academic, theoreti-cal. But thinking back to conversations I've had with Nestorian, I believe he might have been politically active in Lebanon, covertly of course. He's certainly pro-West, no question.'

Jared pushed himself up from his chair, stared down at Simon Croft. 'So, here's what I'm asking you to do. I want you to use this bloke to try to get info on my half-brother so that if there's the slight-est suspicion he's involved in anything anti-Brit, it can be killed off. I'll take it higher and it'll be dealt with. So you give Nestorian the name Jake Messanger, saying you're interested in him – say you've got business with him and need to be sure you can trust him, so would be grateful for any help he can give you in the matter. You'd better make it plain that it's political stuff about him you're after – even, if you think your Lebanese friend won't shy off at the mention of it, possible connection to terrorist cadres.'

Simon stood up, frowning. 'You really do have grounds for suspecting Jake?' he asked earnestly. 'I respect Nestorian enor-mously, we get on well. I don't want to jeopardize that.'

'Sure. Yeah. I understand. I can't say I'm dead certain about Jake having some secret anti-Brit agenda he's working to, but I *am* sure –

bloody near certain – that if he is, then it's vitally important he's stopped in his tracks. And I can't see how anyone else but me is going to try and do it.'

'Suppose Nestorian does come up with something that fingers Jake as being linked to terrorist activity, what will you do?'

Jared searched Simon Croft's eyes, and finding a particular fear in them, he laughed it to scorn. 'No, mate, I wouldn't do that,' he said. 'If it comes to the crunch I swear to God I won't smite Jake dead one dark and stormy night. I shall simply report, in full, to people I can reach if I have to.'

'Withholding the name of your informant? Permanently?'

'Christ, yes; I promise you that, on oath. . . . So what do you say? Will you do it – give it a try, at least?'

'Considering all you've said it seems to me it'd be practically criminal not to. I'll get on to it tomorrow; John'll be at college all day.'

The tension drained out of Jared's face. But all he said was, 'Thanks. Let's go get ourselves another drink.'

As they went out on to the veranda, Simon asked, 'What about Khaled Adjani?'

'Don't give up on him.' Jared grimaced wryly. 'Could be you might unearth something that ties him in with Jake, stranger things have happened. You never know your luck until – not often, but maybe once in a lifetime if you're one of the chosen few – it serves you up a dream come true.'

The moon had risen by the time Jake succeeded in getting Delyth to himself that evening. Searching for her then, he spotted her on the edge of a group at the far end of the terrace that had gathered around a girl with long black hair and a beguiling voice who was playing guitar and singing sad Spanish love songs.

'I've been looking for a chance to talk with you, Delyth,' he whispered, touching her arm as he came up beside her. 'Just you and I, I mean. Will you come with me now? We could go into the garden.'

'I'd like that.' She turned to him at once and began moving towards the lawn. Jake followed her. She was wearing a darkly gold-coloured tunic of some soft, silky material that fell smoothly over matching trousers. As she walked ahead of him across the grass she seemed to him to shimmer moth-like in the moonlight.

I don't want to lose her: suddenly the words stood clear inside his head, but then he looked at them in amazement and, angrily, blacked them out. This woman has no place in my life, nor ever will have! he told himself passionately. I do not belong in her world, the sort of world I'm living in here – and she certainly doesn't belong in mine, nor ever can! Besides, what I thought just then is nonsense, for how can one lose something one doesn't actually have, something that's. . . only a chimera. Won't go away, though, will it?

'If we go right on down to the brook there's a path off to the right that runs alongside it,' Delyth said, when they were halfway across the lawn. 'I like it along there.'

'So let's go that way. . . . You told me you know this place well.'

'I've known it since childhood. Tom's Simon's friend, and I'm Simon's. He and I used to come here together when we were little. Used to play adventure games in the woods, swim in the brook, things like that.'

'I'm surprised it's deep enough to swim in,' he said; thinking, how strange to be here with this woman I hardly know yet somehow do know, and the moon shining on us.

'There's just the one place where it is. If we go on downstream we'll come to it.'

Reaching the brook they turned off on to the springy-turfed path and walked on, a tall hawthorn hedge on their right, woodland trees behind it, and the stream running close on their left. Then, suddenly, the path opened out into a broad grassed clearing, and Jake saw on the far side of it a big sawn-timber summerhouse, moonlight casting its shadow black upon the greensward.

'Tom's parents built that for him as a birthday present,' Delyth said, as they went on towards it. 'His mother wrote children's stories and in the summer she liked to work at that trestle table over by the brook. Simon loves this place. Four years ago he planted yellow irises below the bank here, there's huge swathes of them now. Beautiful, in late spring.'

The table had a long bench running either side of it, and they sat down facing each other. 'It must be fun, having brothers and sisters.' Delyth said, smiling. 'You were so lucky, having Gemma and Jared to grow up with.'

But Jake had no intention of talking about himself. 'You're an only child, aren't you?' he observed, voice carefully neutral.

She looked full at him then. The moonlight fell on her face, and he realized she had perceived that he was deliberately evading her. But she simply smiled again, then turned to look out over the water. 'I am,' she said and, as she went on, he heard a great tenderness come in her voice and knew she was speaking straight from the heart. 'But I have to tell you – and in my case this is truly so – that there can be one huge advantage to not having any siblings. It's this: my father was widowed when I was six and, since all he had left of his marriage was me, from then on he's been giving me all the love he has in him to give. It's a lot of love, and it's mine for life, as is mine for him. . . . So I'm sad for you, Jake, that you never had anything like that for yourself. It's a lovely thing.'

He sat silent, deeply moved, but not knowing what to say – or, indeed, whether he should say anything at all; whether what she had said should be left to stand by itself, something of herself she had allowed him to share.

Then, she laughed across the moonlight – as deliberate an act as had been his change of subject a few minutes earlier – and broke the spell she had woven around him. 'So, what else do you want to know about me?' she asked, the long silky hair swinging loose as she ran a hand through it. 'No, wait – I'll tell you. My father lectures at Cambridge and is deep into research, molecular biology, but it's vacation time now for him, as it is for me. Which, of course, is marvellous, we have time to do things together. He still lives in the house I grew up in, and to which I return as often as I can. It's too big for him really but he likes it there. He plays the piano rather well, and sometimes I sing for him – never for anyone else, though, as I don't have much of a voice—'

'I'm sorry, I didn't mean to be inquisitive.' Seeing he was in danger of losing her, he interrupted, only to discover he had no idea how to go on. So reaching out, he ran his fingers lightly, smoothly, over the scar on her cheek. 'It doesn't show at all under your make-up,' he said. 'When you go out you choose to hide that bit of your life away from other people. I'm glad you didn't mind me seeing it the other day, in the garden at Jared's place.'

Delyth had not moved under his touch because it seemed to her almost like a caress and, as such, should not be rebuffed unless one really wanted to hurt. 'Reconstructive surgery.' She spoke lightly but her eyes, he saw, were anguished. 'Sadly, it wasn't as good a job as it should have been. But then we all make mistakes sometimes, don't we? Some of them matter a great deal to other people, some don't. Those my surgeon made did, to me. . . . He was a good surgeon, my father made sure of that, but very few people go through life without getting *anything* wrong. That surgeon became a very good friend of mine.'

'Is he still?'

'Only in my memory. He died last year.' She stood up. 'Time to go back,' she said.

'I'm glad you brought me here.' Jake, too, got to his feet.

She smiled, but moved away towards the path. And then as he fell into step beside her and they strolled on together, asked, 'Why should you be glad? It's . . . just a special place. A fun place for Tom and his mates before we all grew up and went our separate ways. So I don't see why me bringing you here should make you feel glad – or miserable either, come to that. You weren't part of it.'

'I think you know why.' Moonlight was falling on them but a side-ways glance at her gave him nothing; she was looking down and her hair had fallen forward, hiding her face from him.

'Perhaps.' Then she quickened her pace and looked up, smoothing back her hair. 'Jared's arrived, did you know?' she said coolly. 'I want to talk to him when we get back, there's something I want to ask him.'

It was eight o'clock in the evening three days later when Edara got the phone call from Paul Marsh, one of Sarsen's long established sleepers in London. Marsh was a trusted employee with a big travel company – at senior management level now, Middle East department

– which specialized in arranging flights and accommodation for foreign students either taking educational courses in Britain or visiting the country for personal reasons. Over the years Marsh had put in place a useful network of informers and conmen and women who, each using their own tested methods, selected from among the company's clients people likely to prove sources of useful information, gained their trust – also, sadly, quite often their real friendship – and then cozened from them various types of saleable intelligence regarding their respective homelands or particular individuals there.

Edara switched his phone to 'scramble' as soon as Marsh gave his name, then simply said, 'Speak.'

'Reference agent Jake Messanger, as of now active here in London and currently on my "all ears" list.'

'Understood. Proceed.'

'Action linked to Messanger has occurred at Whitehaven College, London—'

'Which enrols post-graduate students from the Middle East. Offers English for special purposes courses at advanced level, aimed at highfliers in medical practice and English literature. I recall you pulled off a very useful coup for us there last year.'

Marsh was pleased at the compliment, for Edara was known to dole them out sparingly and they invariably led to monetary rewards. 'My suspect is one Simon Croft, a lecturer at the college. Croft has been asking a certain student there about Messanger's life and contacts in Damascus—'

'Names?'

'One. Khaled Adjani.'

'A certain student, you say?' Edara cut in sharply, his decision already made in principle. Khaled Adjani was Sarsen's true name and, as such, had to be safeguarded at all costs. 'Tell me about him.'

'Name, John Nestorian. Nationality, Lebanese. He's been working in Damascus recently so he may know, or have informed knowledge concerning agent Messanger, since it is quite possible the two moved in the same work-related circles.' Marsh paused, having heard Edara hiss out a vicious expletive. However, no other curses followed it.

'How long is it since Croft began this questioning?' Edara asked.

'Yesterday only. He met Nestorian for lunch and again later, at five o'clock, for a drink at a pub near the college. My informant reports Croft the instigator of both meetings, and says his social contacts with the Lebanese are usually more widely spaced. These happenings seemed suspicious to me, so I called you.'

'You were right to do so. This informant of yours – is he a friend of the Lebanese in question?'

'He cultivates a friendship with him, among others. He reports that, at those last two meetings, Nestorian gave Croft considerable information on Messanger.'

'How can he know that?'

'He was there, at the second meeting, sitting not far away. He eavesdropped.'

'Were you able to find out exactly what information Nestorian passed on?'

'My informant drew the line at that. Refused to give details.'

'And you *accepted* his refusal?' Suddenly, there was ice in Edara's voice.

'Any rough stuff from me and he'd simply pull out and sell his information elsewhere from now on. There's plenty of takers for such merchandise in my world, and he's too valuable to lose. Besides, what he gave me seemed to me enough for action to be taken. Was I wrong?' he asked, curiously.

'That is not your affair. As of now, you will drop all enquiries relating to both Croft and Messanger. I will be in touch with you later; there may be follow-up work to be done on Nestorian. Edara out.'

Pushing the phone aside, Edara sat quiet at his desk, leaning back in his chair, hands clasped beneath his chin as he ran his mind over the situation Marsh had just outlined to him. He already knew quite a lot about Simon Croft. As a family friend of the Stantons since childhood, and still a close friend to Gemma and Jared Messanger, Croft figured in the Zephyr database compiled during the exploratory investigations by Sarsen's agents into the Stanton family's background. Nevertheless, as was now obvious in the light of Marsh's telephone call, either those investigations had not been sufficiently thorough, or they were outdated, the work-related side of

Croft's life had not been dug into deeply enough.

Too late to remedy that now, Edara thought. Two meetings in suspiciously close succession Croft had just had with the Lebanese, who was quite clearly a possible source of suspicion-arousing and damaging information regarding Messanger and his presence in London. Croft might *already possess* such information about Messanger's contacts in Damascus, and were he to report it to the British Intelligence services, Messanger's cover story would at once be rendered suspect. If that should come to pass Operation Zephyr would have be aborted. Of course, it was possible that Croft might hold his fire in expectation of acquiring further information, but only a fool would count on that.

So, Croft had to be stopped – and stopped before he had any more time to get in touch with the British authorities.

Edara reached for his emergency phone. In a matter of seconds he was through to the controller of the Immediate Extreme Action section of the London branch of Sarsen's network of agents.

Chapter 8

London 25 July

A few minutes after one o'clock that night, and the sky overcast. Four hours had passed since Edara's call to the controller of the Immediate Action section and two of his special agents, a man and a woman, were approaching Simon Croft's bungalow in Shelley's Grove. Both in their late twenties, both dressed in casual but stylish, good-quality clothes suited to this up-market area in which their target lived. The woman carried an overnight bag, and was clad in designer jeans and a severe, dark-red overblouse; the man wore black chinos and a grey jacket of heavyweight denim open over his black T-shirt. He was around six feet tall, the woman a good four inches shorter; but whereas he was broad shouldered and moved with virile, controlled power showing in every line of his body, she was lightly built, her strengths in action lay in her speed, agility, and a certain vicious cunning. She did not like the man – she's Polish, he was born in Germany, but she had a great respect for his leadership, his expertise and his utter ruthlessness in termination jobs such as the one they were committed to that night.

'Number fourteen. We're nearly there.' The woman's voice had a hard quality to it even when, as now, she spoke quietly.

'The chestnut tree marks it for us, just by the gate.' The man was, for the moment, equally soft-spoken.

'I hope he's asleep in bed.'

'Easier for us if he is, means you and I will get home earlier. The scout control had here within thirty minutes of Edara's call reported him back at midnight so he's had time enough.'

'That's it ahead now. The tree.'

They turned in through the gate into number fourteen, closed it behind them. In front of them there was a paved path leading across the lawn to the long, many-windowed bungalow, but they did not take it. Separating, they circled the lawn, one to the right, one to the left, and then, keeping in the cover of the tall conifer hedge enclosing the property, each worked his way round the bungalow then closed in on it from behind so that they came together at its back door. Leaning down, the man gave its lock a knowledgeable once-over with hand, pencil-torch and eye, murmured, 'Not a great one for security, this bloke,' then slipped his lock-picking kit out of his jacket pocket and went to work. The woman watched him, saying nothing.

'We're in.' He gave the door an experimental push, found it free of inside bolts so eased it half open and stepped forward from the half dark of the outside world into near total blackness. But he had always liked the dark. When he was a boy it terrified yet fascinated him; it drew him to itself and, in time, allowed him to learn its special, arcane ways. Since coming to manhood he connived with it, working best within its collaborative secrecy. As it embraced him now, he heard the three whispery, telltale sounds made by the woman. first she closed the door behind her, then she unzipped her bag and, a couple of seconds later, zipped it shut again. So, knowing now that she had her gun ready – it's a special job, silencer built in – he took his torch out of his pocket again, switched it on and directed its strong, narrow beam along the corridor opening off to their left, as reported by Edara's scout.

With the man in the lead they passed swiftly along the corridor, then halted at the second door on their right. It was closed. Putting away his torch, he wrapped his hand around its glass knob, turned it smoothly to its full extent, eased it slightly open, stepped inside – then swung it wide with one hand, reached up and switched on the light, moving aside as light flooded the room and the woman darted in past him.

The man asleep in the bed facing her jerked half upright staring at her – then brought both hands up in front of his eyes to shield them from the shocking glare of the light overhead.

'Don't move!' She spat it out standing at the foot of the bed, the gun in her right hand aimed straight at his head.

'Who the hell are you?' he said, but it was pure reflex, he was barely awake.

'Do exactly as I say and you won't get hurt. OK?'

He nodded, squinting out at her from behind the fragile shelter of his hands. 'OK. I'm not one to argue with a gun, so OK.'

'Put both hands down flat on the sheet.'

As he did so he saw she was not alone; behind her there was a man just inside the door and now he was moving further into the room.

'Get out of bed and stand beside it, facing me,' the woman ordered. 'Keep both hands where I can see them.'

He was wide awake now, and fear ran wild inside him – but the gun was aimed straight at him, so, thrusting aside the covers, he swung his feet to the floor. As he did so he glimpsed the man padding past him, tall, dark hair—

'Keep your fucking eyes to yourself!' snapped the woman.

To get out of bed under the threat of a gun took only a few seconds. He slept in boxer shorts and that night his are pale blue. Feet planted squarely on his bedroom carpet, toes curled tight into its deep blue pile, he stood up and faced her – then mortal terror surged through him because she was smiling at him and he sensed the man close at his back, a little to one side of him – he reached out his hand to the woman because *he knew now—*

Her two bullets hit him fair and square in the chest. Already dying, he was slammed backwards, arms outflung, and the dark-haired man received his body with practised ease. He bent to lift it, then slung it over his shoulder and walked across to the door – stopped there, turned to watch the woman as she put the finishing touches to this part of the job.

Having slipped the gun back into her travel bag, she threw one of the two suitcases she'd spotted on top of the wardrobe on to the bed and began packing into it the specified items of their target's belongings. This turned out to be easier than she'd expected: clearly a tidy and well-organized bloke, he had hung up shirt and trousers ready for the next morning and placed his black shoes, polished, beside the chest of drawers – on the top of which he had laid out his wallet, card-case, house and car keys, together with his loose change in a slim, gold-initialled leather purse. She crammed all of these into the case, then – opening drawers as needed – took out a clean pair of pyjamas, two clean shirts and a complete change of underwear and threw them in too. Lastly, she went into the adjoining bathroom, stowed his washing and shaving gear into his waterproof washbag and took that back into the bedroom.

'Hurry. Time we left.' The man clipped it out as she came in.

She considered it a rebuke, and her lips tightened. But she said nothing, simply chucked the washbag into the case, clicked it shut and slid it down on to the floor. Swiftly, deftly, she made up the bed, turned down the covers, placed his slippers neatly in front of the side-table – then picked up the case and headed for the door. As she drew level with him, the man turned off the light. She halted for a moment, slightly disorientated in the sudden darkness – then he switched on his torch and set off back down the corridor. Closing the bedroom door, she followed him, seeing ahead of her his figure bulked misshapen against torchlight, black, grotesque, with the body of their victim humping up from his shoulder like some monstrous leech clamped into his life-blood, engorged.

They left the bungalow the way they came into it: out of the back door together, separating to skirt the front lawn – only starlight to help them, the moon hidden behind cloud – then met again at the gate.

The woman got there first. 'Timing OK?' she whispered, as the man stopped beside her.

'Good. Four minutes to rendezvous.'

'Is he dead?'

'I didn't check. The more you move him, the more chance of leaving blood around at the scene – so *don't*. If he's still alive Edara's special duties types'll finish the job later.'

'And disposal the same as with the Australian last May?'

'Yeah. Night trip out to sea, then over the side into deep, deep water. . . . Right, let's move.'

The evergreen hedge girding number 14 Shelley's Grove afforded good cover. Going out through the gate, the man and the the woman waited side by side in its dark shadow, both silent now.

The black collection van arrived dead on time.

Chapter 9

With the agenda for that morning completed, the room in which the Watchman conference was being held was emptying fast. As the Italian delegate hurried out through its double doors, Professor Stanton and Alain Oufkar were the only ones left sitting at the long, highly polished table. This had often been the case since the conference began. Placed next to each other – not by chance, though the professor was unaware of that – both invariably took their time over the transition from concentrated discussion – heated argument, occasionally – to the pursuit of one's normal life: Stanton because he was by nature a man who preferred to take things with due deliberation; the Frenchman – of Algerian extraction – solely because he had quickly observed it to be Stanton's habit, and his mission demanded that he rapidly develop a friendly relationship with the professor who was London's delegate to the conference.

'One of our colleagues here fails to take the proper security precautions,' Oufkar observed, frowning at the eighteen-inch square blueprint the Italian, who had been sitting opposite him, had left lying on the table.

'His exposition of Rome's modernization programme was quite masterly.' Stanton was leaning back in his chair, his eyes on the ceiling, his mind still engaged with evaluation of the proposals he had just referred to.

Turning his head, Oufkar studied the British professor: grey-

81

haired and narrowly built, his sharp-boned face handsome in a mature and austere way, Stanton had an air of informed intelligence about him. A reserved, hard-to-know sort of man, Oufkar had found him; a man wrapped up in his work and with little time or inclination to socialize – something of a loner, in fact.

But he's easy enough to converse with, particularly when the subject has relevance to Watchman's agenda, Oufkar thought to himself now, and he's certainly been most usefully ready to talk shop with me, secure – he believes – in the knowledge that I, like himself, am the soul of probity.

Seeing Stanton still preoccupied, Oufkar got to his feet.

'I'll put his blueprint away for him,' he said, and reaching across the table rolled it up then took it over to the row of six grey steel filing cabinets along the opposite wall. Four feet high and two wide, these were designed specifically for the safe storage of sensitive maps and diagrams and their locks were electronically controlled, each responded solely to the handprint of its owner.

'You can't lock it for him, unfortunately.' Stanton had rejoined the world.

'At least it'll be better than leaving it lying around.' Oufkar slid the blueprint over one of the rollers inside the open cabinet, then closed it and turned to face Stanton. 'We did good work today,' he went on. 'The conference has gone well so far. I have to say that, speaking for myself, I have learned a great deal from it . . . much of it from you,' he added, 'and I'm grateful to you.'

Stanton invariably found compliments difficult to deal with, 'I also have learned many things, and some of them from your good self,' he said stiffly, but then produced a smile. 'As a matter of fact I was saying that very thing to Delyth last night. She came in as I was writing up my notes and asked me how my day had gone, so I told her about your excellent evaluation of Dr Schwartz's address to us.'

What a stroke of luck, he's brought his daughter into our conversation himself! Oufkar smiled, he had been wondering how he could do that without it looking forced. 'Your daughter's party is fairly soon now, isn't it?' he said. 'I remember you saying—'

'It is indeed.' There was a real warmth in Stanton's voice now, and the severe lines of his face softened, the stern regard of his grey eyes lit with a sudden inner tenderness. 'August the thirteenth.'

May Allah ensure that the party isn't cancelled when she and her friends realize Simon Croft won't ever be coming home again, Oufkar thought. But asked, 'Will you be attending it?'

Stanton gave a short laugh, then stood up and began to gather up his papers and put them in his briefcase. 'I shall not. I *don't do* parties given by the young, as Delyth would phrase it. She isn't much of a party lass herself, in fact. But this one is special to her, being given for her by one of her fellow students. Even so, I doubt she'll stay much beyond eleven o'clock. I've never known her not to be back by midnight. As for myself, I shall be at home working. When she comes in I expect we'll make some tea, and she'll tell me about her party. I'm taking her out for a celebration dinner the following evening. Just she and I, at a place we've often been to together since her mother died. It's a quiet country pub, but they serve very good food. I've made a special order, all her favourites.'

'I suspect she may appreciate that celebration even more than the party,' Oufkar offered, smiling into the professor's eyes and thinking, but neither you nor your daughter will be at that quiet country pub as planned, my friend. In fact it's quite possible – likely, even, should Edara decide he can pull it off without repercussions – that you will never see her again after she's left home for this party Gemma and Jared Messanger are giving for her.

'You're too kind,' murmured Stanton, closing his briefcase, then joining the other as he made for the door. 'That presumption of O'Driscoll's earlier on this morning, what did you think. . . .'

After Oufkar had parted from Stanton and was on his way back to the sleeper's house where he was lodged, his mind moved away from the Stantons: considered instead Jake Messanger, Sarsen's agent so recently arrived in London. The word was that Edara deeply resented the half-Brit's high standing with Sarsen, seeing him as a serious threat to his own hopes of being named as Sarsen's heir, his chosen successor. If that rumour's true, he thought, walking London's streets in the midday sunshine, and I heard it from an informed source, then were I Messanger I'd watch my back after

Zephyr's accomplished: Edara's never been a man to play clean.

Twelve-thirty. Gemma poured herself a glass of orange juice, carried it into the sitting-room and sat down at one end of the window seat. After a moment she noticed her mobile lying half hidden behind a cushion, remembered Jared had asked her to invite Delyth's cousin Lisa to the party, and picked it up, only to realize she hadn't got her number. 'Shit,' she murmured, and decided to call Simon. He'd have it for sure, as he and Lisa were family friends; he'd probably know it off by heart. It would be lunch-break at the college so he'd likely be in the staff room, she'd rung him there before.

She got through at once. 'Whitehaven College.' A woman's voice answered, slightly irritated.

'Sorry to bother you,' Gemma said, 'but is Simon Croft there, please? I need to speak to him.'

'Who's calling?'

'Gemma Messanger.'

'I can't see Croft in here but he might be next door in the dining-room. Hold on, I'll check.'

'Gosh, no, never mind—' But she heard the receiver put down . . . then picked up a minute or so later.

'Sorry, he's not in college today, someone said he doesn't come in on Thursdays. Sorry. 'Bye.'

Shit, what a waste of time, Gemma thought, as the line went dead. Never mind, I'll call him this evening, at the bungalow.

Taken to the private house in a chauffeur-driven Volvo, Jake Messanger arrived there at 2.30 and was at once ushered into a small study opening off the entrance hall.

'*Misa il-kheer.*' Edara, seated at a carved oak desk on the far side of the room, a slender vase of peach-coloured roses close on his right, greeted him with the bare minimum of welcome then gestured towards the chair set facing him across the desk. 'Sit down. I expect no one else.'

'Good afternoon.' Briefly, Messanger looked around him, feeling the atmosphere of the room cold about him; it seemed a hostile place. Then he sat down, looked Edara in the eye, and on the instant his world narrowed down to himself and Edara.

'In eight days' time – the day preceding Zephyr's climax on Saturday 14th August – you will be at this party at your half-brother's house,' Edara began, his dark eyes hooded beneath the heavy brows, 'so we come now to your final briefing. As you know, the photocopies of the required blueprints must be in my hands by or before 02.30 hours on the morning of the strike, to give me time to use them to pinpoint on the ground plan of each target station the most advantageous location for the release of the gas.'

Messanger contented himself with a nod and a quiet, 'Yes, I'm aware of that.'

'So now to the details of our procurement of those photocopies, three in number. Our enabler in that exercise will be the British delegate to Watchman, Professor Stanton—' Edara broke off, seeing Messanger tense suddenly. 'Is something wrong?'

'No. I was surprised, that's all.'

'Why should the name of Professor Stanton in relation to our operation surprise you? You have not met him, and in your reports to me, written and oral, you have referred only to his daughter.'

'I don't know him personally—'

'But you know his daughter, and that is the key factor here,' Edara interrupted, watching the half-Brit – avid for his reactions, but concealing that fact from him, face and voice bland.

Christ Almighty! Shocked to the core of his being, appalled but uncomprehending, Messanger dropped his eyes. I cannot believe this! he thought. It's not possible, it's inconceivable. *I can't believe it!* Delyth and her father, involved in Zephyr? In God's name how *could* they be? From all I know of the operation there's no imaginable way— No, hold it! Stop right there, Edara's only a few feet from you and he'll be alert to every nuance of your body language so *don't give yourself away to him.*

Master of himself once more, Jake Messanger drove Delyth out of his mind and looked up at his commander, met his eyes. 'How so, the key factor?' he asked evenly.

Edara laid the plan on the line. 'At Devon House, the delegates to the Watchman conference have personal filing cabinets in which to store the blueprints they use to illustrate arguments for and against the measures they discuss,' he said. 'Access to these is electronically controlled, each opens solely in response to its owner's handprint. Now, for Zephyr to achieve what we want – that is, the highest possible number of casualties – we need to refer to the blueprints showing the ventilation systems, the exits and entrances, the platforms, escalators etcetera in the three underground stations which are our targets. Professor Stanton, being London's delegate, is in possession of these. He stores them in his cabinet. Therefore, since he is the only person able to access them, we shall abduct him, use him to access his cabinet, and take photocopies of the blueprints specific to our purpose. These will be brought directly to me at Red Pillars, my command centre. The suicide agents who will release the toxic gas will report to me there and, using the photocopies, I shall ensure that each of them knows exactly where he must position himself to release the gas. Each agent then departs from Red Pillars: they will leave at half-hour intervals, commencing at 07.15 on Saturday morning.'

'And the photocopies?' It was something to say, to give himself more time to prepare his response.

'Will be shredded and burnt to ashes.'

Messanger nodded, then sat quiet, conning over Edara's plan, probing it for weaknesses: one glaringly obvious one had struck him while Edara was speaking, and there might be others.

Watching him, Edara felt the familiar hatred well up inside him. Hatred of this young, handsome half-Brit: a man cross-bred, the blood of each line diluted – but, surely, the heritage of one preferred over the other and the rejected one never surrendering, living on inside the man, all the time lying, scheming, betraying even, in the attempt to regain supremacy. A half-breed is never to be trusted. Such a one must not succeed Sarsen so *I will destroy you, Jake Messanger.* Here in England, away from Sarsen's eyes, I will see you dead.

'The plan seems good in theory,' Messanger said. 'But in practice there's surely one huge difficulty? How do you secure the professor's co-operation? Get him to open his cabinet? By killing him and then making use of his lifeless hand?'

'No, not good enough – as I suspect you know. The technology has moved on. Besides, that way could lead to many problems—'

'Then?'

'By employing the severest *emotional* pressure. That will suffice, I am sure.' A smile thinned Edara's lips: he had been expecting the question. 'Professor Stanton's love for his only child, his daughter, is profound,' he went on. 'He will do anything – *everything* – in his power to keep her from harm. Rest assured: Stanton will co-operate.'

With a supreme effort of will – and already half-warned – Messanger let it settle in his mind, holding Edara's eyes, banishing all expression from face and voice. 'That's an enormous assumption to make,' he said. 'Surely there is a danger – a great danger – that Stanton will not give in.'

'Faced with the threat that his non-co-operation will inevitably result in first the torture and, ultimately, the death of his beloved daughter, the professor will do what we want.'

Cramming down the horror rising inside him, 'But you . . . what do you know of him, to be so sure?' Messanger asked, 'How do you know he loves his daughter . . . loves her enough?'

'Investigative agents have been reporting to me on that point over the last six months; as has, more recently, a certain delegate to the Watchman conference who corresponded with the professor during the preparations for the conference, and developed a friendship with him from then on.'

'Who? Which member?'

'Your question is naïve in the extreme. I shall in kindness forget you asked it.'

Already regretting that he had, Messanger got himself back on track; forced himself to assimilate Edara's plan and, at the same time, keep his emotions under control, hide his devastation from those fierce, intrusive eyes.

'I assume, then, that Stanton's daughter also will be abducted, and that I am to figure in her abduction,' he said.

'You will figure in her abduction and in her detention thereafter.'

'Give it to me in detail.'

Edara leaned across the desk. 'Both Stanton and his daughter will be taken at gunpoint,' he said, exultation firing up his voice and face. 'The professor at his house at eleven o'clock, the woman as she leaves the party, which is expected to be sometime before midnight. Stanton will be driven to a pre-arranged parking space near Devon House, then held captive in the car until the time comes for us to use him. You are with me so far?' His eyes searched Messanger's face hungrily, seeking to see into his soul.

'I'm with you. What about the girl? How and where will she be taken?'

'When she leaves the party you will escort her to her car which will be parked in the two-car area to the side of your half-brother's house. You know it?'

'Of course.' Only too well, he thought, it's perfect for an abduction by ambush, just a poorly lit little square of tarmac private to Jared's house, trees and shrubs on three sides of it.

'When the two of you reach her car you put the gun on her and force her into the passenger seat, assisted by our agent who has been waiting in the surrounding cover. He drives the two of you to the safe house in which she will be held. One other guard awaits you there. He will be under your orders throughout her detention. And know this: you will be personally responsible for the woman at all times. Is this understood?'

'Perfectly.'

'Then I will proceed. Both Stanton and his daughter will have their mobile phones with them; she always carries hers when she goes out, and his abductors will make sure he takes his with him from the house—'

'For what specific purpose?'

'Do not interrupt me. . . . As soon as you have the woman in the safe house, you will assault her. You will beat her until you have her begging for mercy and ready to do or say whatever you order her to since you will have informed her that you will not stop until she convinces you she will co-operate fully.' Pausing, Edara held Messanger's eyes, waiting for him to ask—

'And what do I tell her to do, or say?' Coldly, the words steady out of a dry mouth, Messanger put the obvious question. It hurt him.

'You tell her that you are going to put her in touch with her father on her mobile. That certain friends of yours are holding him prisoner because he is refusing to do something they require him to do – and that if he continues to refuse, they will kill him. Then, Messanger, you tell her that given this situation she is the only person in the world who can save his life, because as soon as he believes that by co-operating with his captors he will save her from further pain and terror, he *will* co-operate and, by doing so, save her.'

Rising to his feet, Edara placed both hands palm-down on the desk and, his eyes never leaving Messanger's, leaned towards him and spoke with the fierce passion of the true fanatic. 'My mole at the Watchman conference informs me that Stanton loves his daughter with a deep and abiding love,' he said. 'Nevertheless everything else in him – duty, loyalty, patriotism perhaps, for he will have realized by then that his abduction is almost certainly in furtherance of some terrorist plot – will be commanding him to deny us access to the blueprints. Therefore, when his daughter, *his beloved daughter*, speaks to him on her mobile it is essential that her voice is so tortured by physical pain and the fear of more pain, that he cannot – *cannot* – endure her suffering, cannot allow it to continue.' He drew back a little; and then with chill venom added, 'So you understand, do you not, why it is essential that you make the woman's physical agony a real and living torture to her?'

'The long explanation was unnecessary. I was there long before you got to the end of it.'

'You will have to go in fast and very hard.'

'Obviously. No problem.'

'The physical violence?'

'I've done it before.'

'Not on a woman, according to the records.'

'No, not on a woman.' Messanger's brows drew together in a frown and he gestured impatience. 'Look, Edara, why the cross-examination? You're running this operation, so naturally I accept your orders. But get on with it. Stop digging into side issues.'

89

Edara withdrew from challenge. Sat down, stiffly upright, saying nothing but continuing to watch this half-Brit, half-Arab he loathed with visceral ferocity.

'What happens after the photocopies have been secured?' Messanger asked. 'To the two captives, I mean?'

'Stanton is returned to his house, tied to continuing silence regarding all that has occurred by the ongoing threat to his daughter's safety and well-being. *Relative* well-being, that is.'

'And – what of her?'

'She remains a prisoner in the safe house. Under your strict guard.'

'How long for?'

Until I decide she is no longer of use to us nor a danger to us in any way.'

Christ, this is *Delyth* we're talking about! *Delyth!* I cannot— You have to. *Have to,* because you're part of *Sarsen's* operation and you are . . . you are *his son*; he has been as a father to you. Yes that is so, but nevertheless I must try—

'Yet Edara, since neither she nor her father can possibly pose any threat to us once Zephyr has blown and there has been time for all its engaged personnel to go into deep cover or leave the country, presumably you will then order her to be let go.'

'There are matters you have no knowledge of to be considered. She remains under your guard until I order her release.'

'I understood from Sarsen that—'

'Are you questioning an order of mine directly connected to the conduct of the operation?'

'No, but—'

'And Messanger, why are you so concerned about this woman?' Suddenly, Edara's voice was quiet, but his eyes were searching Messanger's face as though he would like to rip the flesh from it and claw his way into the half-Brit's inner self.

Messanger stood up, holding the raking, hungry stare. 'My sole concern is the success of Operation Zephyr,' he said curtly. 'Prolonging the woman's detention without apparent cause might put at risk the lives of certain of our agents, particularly sleepers resident here in Britain,' He felt himself sweating as he spoke.

'It will not be prolonged without good cause.' But then Edara decided he had gone far enough. His plans to effect his personal agenda in relation to Messanger were proceeding well; he would be dealt with in the aftermath of Zephyr when attention was elsewhere. 'Your part in our operation is vital to its success,' he went on smoothly. 'Keep clear in your mind, however, that mine is also; and that, therefore, if either you or I fail in our duty at any point during the operation, then Zephyr itself will fail. Any fault on the part of either of us cannot be glossed over and put right as can less pivotal errors.' He turned away. 'You may go now. Report to Agent Nine in person in three hours' time, as scheduled.'

Chapter 10

London 9 August

When Gemma called him on his cellphone at eight o'clock that evening, Jared was having a drink with a colleague at a pub some five minutes' walk from his office. Slipping off his bar stool he turned aside to take the call. 'Hi, Sis,' he said. 'This had better be good, I was just getting stuck into a well-earned—'

'It *isn't* good, in fact it's really shitty and quite worrying, which is why I'm calling you. It's Simon. I can't contact him—'

'Hang on, too much noise in here; I'll find somewhere quieter.' Although annoyed at being interrupted, Jared was vaguely disturbed by what Gemma had said, as he had arranged to ring Simon Croft himself later that evening, to find out if the Lebanese bloke had come up with any interesting info re Jake's contacts in Syria. He pushed his way through groups of drinkers and out into the relative quiet of the corridor. 'Gemma? It's OK now, I don't have to yell my head off. So what's this about Simon? He's usually fairly well-organized, unlike me—'

'Jared! Shut up and listen. I wanted to ring Lisa and invite her to the party, like you said, but I couldn't remember her mobile number so I decided to ring Simon, get it from him. Well, I tried Whitehaven at lunch-time – no dice, seems he doesn't go in on Thursdays. I didn't think anything of that, just waited till evening and tried him at home. But Jay, I've rung him four times since six o'clock and there's no answer. His mobile's switched off, and there's no answer from the home number, not even the Ansaphone.'

'I shouldn't worry—'

'Stuff that! I *am* worried, it's scary somehow. Anyway, I wondered if you'd call in at his place on your way home? It's not much out of your way, and you could just see if everything's OK?'

'Sure. No problem, will do.' Jared kept his voice light and easy to reassure his sister, but inside his head apprehension had flared into life, and even as he spoke was hardening into real fear for the safety of Simon Croft whom he, Jared Messanger, had persuaded to venture into what was, quite possibly, the ruthless world of terrorism. 'Leave this with me, Gem,' he said. 'I'll finish my drink quick then get over there.'

'Ring me if—'

'I'll do that. And look, Sis, don't get too worked up. You know Simon: he gets on with his own thing, doesn't always think to let even his friends know his plans.'

'But he might have been in an accident, had a heart attack – shit, anything might have happened.'

'Hey, loosen up! I'll take off right now, get back to you from there. Cheers.'

Sheathing his mobile, Jared stood stock still in the corridor of The Dancing Bear, head down, mind racing, people passing by him unnoticed as he confronted one appalling possibility: that as a direct result of Simon making enquiries re Jake Messanger and a man named Khaled Adjani – at his, Jared's, personal request – some sort of violent physical action had been taken against him in order to block those enquiries. On the thought, Jared shuddered, then hurried back into the bar, made his excuses and left at once, got on with what he had to do. Like he'd said to Gemma, he'd drive over to Simon's place and check it out; luckily he still had a spare key to the front door, left with him a month earlier so he could keep an eye on Simon's mail and so on while his friend was off in charge of a students' trip to Stratford-on-Avon. Surely, *something* inside the bungalow would give him a clue? Show that Simon had simply taken off for the evening or a day or two.

Move, man, *move!*

'Give you the ex-directory number of Superintendent Rawlings, a senior counter-terrorist officer?' The voice over the phone – belonging to that night's duty sergeant at Jared's section at the offices of MI5 – poured scorn on the suggestion. 'You know damn well I can't do that on your say-so. Tell you something, though, seeing as I know you for an upright citizen of the realm. The bloke often works late, and I haven't seen him sign out, so if you're lucky he might still be at his desk. You want me to call through?'

'If you will. Tell him it's urgent, needs to be dealt with at once.'

'That'll be up to him, won't it? Hang on, then.'

Some five minutes later Jared was in the office of Superintendent Jack Rawlings. Seated at his desk studying a file, 'Be with you in a minute,' Rawlings had said, as he came in, then continued reading.

Standing facing him across the desk Jared waited, running over in his mind the facts he was about to put on the table, and praying inwardly that Rawlings wasn't too wrapped up in whatever it was he was working on at that moment to at least give him a fair hearing, not instant dismissal, ridicule even. He was in with a good chance, he hoped, for although Rawlings was known as a stickler for correct procedures and the possessor of a temper run on a very short fuse, he also had the reputation of being a mover and shaker when needed.

'Right, Messanger.' Pushing aside the file, Rawlings looked up at the young man before him. 'You've got information relating to terrorism, you say. So lay it on the line, short and sharp, bare facts only. I'll ask for background knowledge afterwards, *if* I decide your info warrants it.'

'Sir.' Instantly and instinctively Jared responded to the resolute drive in Rawlings' piercing blue eyes, presenting a clear, cut-to-the-bone summary of his suspicions regarding the legitimacy of his half-brother's visit to England, his own consequent approach to Simon Croft asking for his co-operation re Jake's contacts in Syria and finally, the so recent apparent disappearance of Croft which had followed fast on him seeking information from a Lebanese friend of his, *political* information on a man going by the name Khaled Adjani—

'Khaled Adjani?' Up to this point Rawlings, leaning back in his chair, had listened without interrupting; now he sat forward, elbows planted on his desk.

'My half-brother gave me the name – mentioned it, just. It's the name of a Syrian who—'

'Yes, you said: the man who made himself your half-brother's stand-in father whenever he was in Bahrain with his mother's people – and later, too, Adjani being a medical man himself.' Rawlings, Jared observed with relief and mounting excitement, was now undoubtedly interested by the situation he, Jared, had outlined. Rawlings sat silent for a minute, staring thoughtfully at a point somewhere above the younger man's head. 'Tell me,' he said then, 'are there any other names – of people, or organizations maybe – you remember your half-brother mentioning? Cast your mind back.' He was allowing Jared to take his time now; what he had told him so far certainly did arouse suspicions.

'I think I've given you all the names I've heard. . . . No, wait. He spoke of another professor who helped him a lot at one stage, an Egyptian, Hussain Harawi. And once, when he was talking to my sister, Gemma, not to me, I heard him refer to some sort of brotherhood called The Closed Circle—'

'*The Closed Circle?*' Rawlings tensed visibly. 'What did he say about it?'

'I don't know. Like I said, he wasn't talking to me; I wasn't paying attention, just the name struck me. It was the title of a book, I thought at the time.'

'It was indeed.' Rawlings' face was grim. 'But it's also something else. The name was taken by an Islamic fundamentalist group active in Britain throughout the '90s. They were closely linked to Al Qaeda – ceased operations here around '98. Interesting, that your half-brother mentioned them.'

'He might have been referring to the book.'

'Might have.' But Rawlings' voice was sceptical, and he pushed himself to his feet. 'Right, Messanger, that will be all for now,' he said, and stood with his head down, going on to himself, quietly, as he considered his next step. 'I'll try the Closed Circle angle . . . Brodie, ex-MI6, he's the man: worked on the probe into their activities in the late '90s. Retired now, but it's not something he'll have forgotten. When they withdrew from Britain he fought for permission to pursue investigations abroad, but funds were denied him—'

'Sir.' Jared had stood his ground in the face of apparent dismissal, and now Rawlings looked up at him again so he seized his chance. 'Sir, may I, er, stick with this?' he asked, face alight with enthusiasm and a sense of purpose. Both were powered in part by his longstanding antipathy towards his half-brother, but Rawlings had no way of knowing that and, therefore, saw only a young officer eager to get in on the investigation he himself had generated.

'Have to earn your keep,' he parried, already half persuaded.

'Sir, if you do decide to initiate further action in this I'll be very well placed to report to you on Jake.'

But Rawlings had perceived possible – even *likely?* – quicksands in such a situation and, going around his desk, he looked Jared Messanger squarely and searchingly in the eye. 'The man is your half-brother,' he said to him. 'In the event of us proving him involved in terrorist activity here in Britain, would you, at a crisis point, be prepared to put the boot in against him? You are closely related to him by blood, and that status gives you favoured personal access to him and the details of his private life, but are you prepared to exploit that *all the way*? Mightn't you be traumatized by divided loyalties? Tempted to hold back, possibly?'

'No, sir, I would not. There's no chance of it.' Jared had stiffened and his face was stone-hard. 'I would be prepared to put the boot in, no question of it. My half-brother chose his own way, his own life. I owe him nothing, certainly no loyalty. And I'm absolutely sure I speak the truth when I say to you that he feels the same way towards me. The word half-*brother* is to both of us no more than a legal statement . . . Neither he nor I give a fucking damn about the other,' he added, a suddenly vicious hatred in voice and eye.

Yes, I can use you, Rawlings thought, perceiving it. If Ben Brodie comes up with anything and we do mount an investigation, you will gladly get stuck into this half-brother of yours given the chance, I can see that. 'Fair enough then, Messanger,' he said, 'if we act, I'll bring you in. How much longer did you say he'll be in London?'

'Three more weeks – at least, that's what he tells us. He says he'll stay on for a bit after his job's done, would like to spend time here with my sister and I now we've got together again. And, sir,' – Rawlings had begun to turn away but now stopped, faced him – 'what about Croft? Might it be possible . . . shall I inform the local police?'

'Not yet – and I'll deal with that college he lectures at. We'll give it another twenty-four hours; meanwhile you can press ahead with your own enquiries, but remember, *no local police.* Understood?'

'Yes, sir. Understood.'

'Right, then. I'll be in touch with you.' Turning aside, Rawlings reached for one of the phones on his desk, punched out a number, listened, then spoke. Jared opened the door to go out, but then paused, stood listening. ' 'Evening, Ben. Jack Rawlings. How's the back? . . . Glad to hear it. Look, I want to pick your brains. Cast your mind back to the Closed Circle days' – at this point Rawlings, phone held to ear and mouth, turned to perch on the edge of his desk, caught sight of Jared as he did so and broke off, giving him a look he could neither misinterpret nor ignore.

Jared went out, closing the door quietly behind him.

'Closed Circle!' responded Ben Brodie. 'Hell, yes. We missed out on a good chance there, Jack, years ago. If only they'd have backed us.'

'Water under the bridge, Ben,' said Rawlings. 'But you gave it your best shot then – and maybe, just maybe, you can put me on the track of some of their personnel who're still active. A whisper's come to my ears that certain members of the original Circle may be still at work, though probably not operating under the same names.'

'What info have you got?'

'Hold on. Listen, I know that, in preparation for the book you published a while ago, you encoded a stack of relevant detail on some of your cases, including that of the Closed Circle, then built yourself a comprehensive database and stuck it on your computer. Now, I've got some names which, meshing in with those on your database, might, with luck, enable you to home in on any individual who was connected with The Circle and is still involved in terrorist activities. So I'm hoping you—'

'You always were a lucky bastard. Yes, I've kept my database up to date, old running mates still oblige. Hang on a minute. I'm on my mobile, and all my IT stuff's up in the study. You've checked on the net?'

'Not yet, but we've been monitoring regularly, scanning for the re-emergence of sometime friends; nothing's come up.'

'So what *have* you got?'

'A couple of names, and some background facts which, I hope, will give you leads to follow up via the data you already hold.'

'And, hopefully, unearth info that ties in with whatever op you're into right now?'

'As yet there is no op. Whether or not there will be depends largely on what you turn up, if anything.'

Brodie chuckled delightedly. 'Ah-hah! Great to be involved again. Just give me a couple of minutes, then. Bloody stairs. Can't get up 'em so fast these days.'

Ex-Superintendent B. Brodie picked up his stick, negotiated the stairs, went into his study and sat down in front of his computer equipment. Resuming contact with Rawlings he asked for and was given the background facts the serving MI5 man possessed.

'That surname *Messanger* might get us somewhere useful,' he commented, as Rawlings fell silent. 'That, and *La'ali Mehrab* – prominent Bahraini family, that is. I'll start there. . . . This may take time, Jack. Keep a line open to me, it's likely I'll need to ask you things every so often.'

It took over three hours. Brodie worked with concentrated diligence. He made use of the net, and called various MI6 officers he had kept in touch with after retiring, but the greater part of his digging centred on the MI5 and MI6 reports and dossiers he had stored on his computer while researching material for the book he had published two years earlier. Meanwhile, Rawlings ordered up coffee and sandwiches from the canteen, answered Brodie's questions swiftly and to the best of his ability, caught up with some paperwork, lowered the level in the bottle of Black Label in his middle drawer by half an inch . . . and, eventually, was rewarded.

'Reckon we might be on to something here, Jack,' Brodie said. 'Hear this. I found that one of the blokes active in the UK branch of Closed Circle used the code-name Sarsen, S-A-R-S-E-N. Then, as I followed up that name, I discovered that Sarsen – or whatever the bastard's name may be when he's at home – is currently operating as one of the top dogs in terrorist circles in Syria, his cover being his normal surface life as a well-established and highly successful medical man now into trading pharmaceuticals, advanced stuff mostly. Now – and this is surely the clincher – I've just come upon an MI5 investigative report suggesting that this Sarsen operating in Syria is none other than the man who, years ago, was unofficially engaged to the Bahraini girl La'ali Mehrab, but whom she unceremoniously dumped when this British doctor by the name of John Messanger came into her life.'

'That same Syrian who, according to Jared Messanger, so damned skilfully "adopted" La'ali's son Jake when she died. The bloke – then know as Khaled Adjani – who was always there for the sad little orphan boy victimized in the big bad world of his English stepmother.'

'And who, according to what you told me before, Jack, pulled the orphan away from the British side of his family when he was very young, and then, as the boy grew into a man, may have indoctrinated him with his own values and Islamic fundamentalist beliefs. But there's no factual proof of all that, is there. None that could ever stand up in a court of law.'

'Nothing, either, that in any way incriminates Jake Messanger. Nevertheless, Ben, it's a situation liable to get the sixth sense of MI5 blokes working overtime, is it not? This stuff you've just come up with suggests there could be the possibility of a terror strike here in Britain in the near future.'

'One other thing I chanced on, Jack. Twice, and both times with Sarsen named as mastermind of a terrorist organization, there was reference to an agent of his going under the code-name "Nine" active here in London during the early '90s.'

'Minor cog or big wheel?'

'Somewhere in the middle – *then*. Now, who knows? He could be top brass.'

'Or long since dead. If the former, though, that earlier spell over here would make him damned useful if there is an op now either envisaged or in progress.'

Rawlings brought the call to a close. Thanked Brodie, and asked him to widen his search for information he deemed relevant.

'. . . And give it all you've got, Ben,' he ended. 'Top priority, eh?'

'I don't need a lot of sleep these days, I find,' Brodie said.

Edara had several safe houses in and around London always ready for his use, one or two of them the residences of established sleepers, others staffed by men and women tied to the service of Sarsen's organization either by their deep conviction of the inviolable rightness of its proclaimed cause, or by a blood-debt incurred on account of some crime they or members of their family had committed. His present meeting with Agent Nine was taking place in the sitting-room of a terraced house in Soho. He had called in Nine to check through his plans for the abduction of Professor Stanton and his subsequent co-operation, and the photocopying of the blueprints required for Operation Zephyr.

His questioning of Nine, however, had been aggressive. Nine had kept his cool under its unrelenting pressure, but as his resentment of it grew he decided to hit back. True, Edara was commander of the present mission, but he, Nine, was his equal in past deeds of death and glory, and was entitled to treatment as such. So now, as Edara indicated that the interview was over and relaxed into the comfort of his deeply cushioned sofa, Nine sat forward, hands gripping the wooden arms of his straight-backed chair.

'In my opinion, the fallout likely to result from the killing of Simon Croft has been most unfortunate,' he said, his voice silky-soft but subtly hostile. 'It was surely an error on your part to order it. Also, I should have been consulted in advance.'

Edara decided it would be diplomatic to lie. 'Naturally, I considered consulting you,' he said. 'But please understand, there was no time for that. And the killing was skilfully carried out: "murder" is not yet a word on the lips of any of those against us; they talk only of Croft's *disappearance;* and Oufkar has learned from Stanton that Gemma Messanger has decided not to cancel the party for his daughter which is, of course, vital to the success of Zephyr.'

'All you say is true. Nevertheless, we have been fortunate: had the party been cancelled—'

'Enough. It was not. Allah is our shield as well as our sword.' Having delivered this pious platitude, Edara rose to his feet in plain indication that it was time for this lieutenant of his to leave.

Agent Nine stayed where he was. 'There is one other matter I am greatly concerned about,' he said, sure of his standing with Sarsen whatever Edara might say.

'If you have a question, ask it.' Edara was brusque, annoyed by the – as he saw it – presumption of his subordinate.

'Did you place surveillance on Jared Messanger, as I suggested a week ago?'

'There was, and is, no need for it. As you know, he was fully vetted during the preliminary stages of Zephyr. He is of little account; he has no access to anyone of importance in British Intelligence.' Edara gave a thin-lipped smile. 'And as we have said before, as such Jared Messanger gives extra credence to the presumed innocence of his half-brother's visit to London. For what terrorist in his right mind would choose to seek closeness with a relative who was even on the periphery of his enemy's intelligence service?'

At the wheel of his hired Mercedes, Jake Messanger wondered what Gemma, sitting beside him in beige trousers and emerald overblouse, was thinking as they drove along quiet country roads, bound for a pub called The Green Man. She had been silent for at least the last five minutes, and a sideways glance had shown him her eyes downcast, a sad droop to the line of her mouth. He had invited her out for lunch and a drive in the country, her choice as to where they ate and where they drove afterwards. 'Take us somewhere you know and like,' he had said to her. 'Show me England in summertime. . . .' The last thing she had said to him now was that there had been no news of or from Simon Croft.

'I suppose Jared's right,' she said suddenly. 'Simon's simply taken off for a few days without telling any of us. He's done it before.'

Jake reassured her, pointing out that Croft had packed a suitcase of personal belongings, and that there had been no sign of break-in or disturbance at the bungalow. 'I'm sure you're right to go ahead with Delyth's party,' he went on. 'Croft would have wanted that, and likely he'll be back for it.' But inside himself he was uneasy about the disappearance; for although he could see no reason for it to have anything to do with Operation Zephyr, he still had a feeling it probably *was* so connected. He had approached Edara on the matter the previous day; only to be met first with a convincingly mystified denial and then with a contemptuous suggestion that perhaps he, Messanger, was losing his nerve – was, with the feverish imagination of an adolescent novice to undercover work, fancying conspiracy all around him.

Dismissing the memory, Jake set about lifting Gemma's spirits; talked and joked with her about her proposed visit to Damascus the following spring, and about the minutiae – some times funny, often annoying, and occasionally, as she put it, 'really really shitty' – of her life at college during term time. Thus, an hour flew by as they drove through a countryside alive with patterns of shifting sunlight and shadow as a westerly breeze kept the clouds sailing across the blue sky above them. It was not until they were sitting at one of the hardwood tables on the big lawn behind The Green Man that their conversation turned to Jared.

'I despair of my brother ever being really friendly towards you,' Gemma said, her eyes on her glass of cider, her fingers idling with it. 'Properly friendly, I mean, not this act he puts on sometimes.'

'What act?' Jake drank the last of his lager, looked at the distant hills to the west. He knew well enough what she meant, but he wanted to hear any thoughts she might have about himself and his half-brother. He was quite sure by now, and was unworried by the fact, that Jared was highly unlikely ever to become his friend; what did cause him unease was the possibility that Jared might be actively hostile towards him, might – somehow? – even be working against him behind the scenes. Reason told him that such a scenario was near impossible since Jared had been vetted by Agent Nine; nevertheless that nagging disquiet continued to bedevil him.

'Oh, you know.' Gemma frowned. 'He does it often enough: the solicitude for your comfort at the hotel, his insistence on paying for all drinks and things when the three of us are out together because "you're *our guest* over here" as he puts it. Things like that – he goes over the top.'

Play this carefully, Jake warned himself: unwise to be too anti-Jared with her. 'Doesn't seem over the top to me,' he said. 'It's very generous of him, I think, and it shows he's trying to be friendly.'

'But he's sometimes so rotten inquisitive!' she burst out. 'You give him an answer about the family stuff, your mother's people, I mean, and he questions it as if he thinks you're *lying*! Thinks you've come over here with a secret agenda of some sort and—'

'Has he ever said anything to you that suggests he really believes that?' A sudden sharpness in his voice, and Gemma stopped fiddling with her glass, looked up at him – and for a split second caught a piercing hardness in his eyes that she'd never seen in them before. Then it was gone and he smiled at her.

'I'd like to get to *know* him, Gemma,' he went on quietly. 'You, Jared, and me – we all had the same father. Don't you think it would be a good thing if we pushed the wicked stepmother right out of our lives and were simply John Messanger's children, the three of us together? After all, she's paid no attention to you two for years now.'

She smiled at him for that, which was what he'd hoped for. 'You're just great, and it's super to have you here with us,' she said, her eyes sending him the love creaming through her. And from the strength of it, she told him a lie: answered his question with a direct lie for fear that the truth might lead him to confront Jared and thus bring about an almighty row between them which would annihilate all hope of the concept of 'the three Messangers' ever being a reality. 'And no, Jake,' she said. 'Jared has never suggested to me that he believes there's some ulterior motive behind your coming over here and getting to know us again, he really hasn't. I think it's just that he can't forget all the shitty stuff between the two of you right from when you were just kids. And then there was the way you cut yourself off from us so totally, later on. You know how close Jared was to Dad; well, what you did then hurt Dad terribly – and Jared can't forgive you for it.' She reached across the table and laid her hand over his. 'Please, leave all that now,' she said. 'You and I make up two-thirds of the Messanger equation; with luck we'll pull my brother in to complete it, given time.'

He raised her hand to his lips, kissed it, released it.

'I love you, d'you know that?' she said, taking back her hand.

'I know it.'

'You love Delyth. I can tell. Different kind of loving, of course.'

'Not the brother-to-sister kind, indeed.' (But she noticed he did not dispute the existence of his love for her friend.) 'I love you too, Gemma; please believe it.' I know it'll be hard for her to go on doing so when she discovers the truth behind me and this visit of mine to London, he thought. I can only hope she'll try. Understand, and *try*. . . . And as for Delyth, she's out of my reach and always will be. I have to cleave to Sarsen, to the way of life I've chosen. Come Friday night, the night of her party, when the chips are down between she and I, I will . . I will *reason* with her, I will make her understand the stark realities of her situation and, therefore, *agree* to do what she must do to save her father's life.

'I don't find it difficult to believe you when you tell me that, Jake.' From across the table Gemma gave him her sudden, gamine grin. 'But could be you're one hell of a good liar.'

'It's my greatest accomplishment and possibly my greatest asset,' he said, summoning a smile. And thought, sadly, that statement's probably true on both counts. . . . 'Would you like another drink out here, or shall we eat now?' he asked.

'Let's go in and eat; I'm starving.' Gemma was on her feet, pushing one hand through her blonde hair. 'I'm going to have steak and mixed salad, the way they do it here is out of this world.'

Chapter 11

Damascus   Sarsen's office 9 August

Two top-secret reports received earlier that morning lay in front of Sarsen, on the tooled leather surface of his desk. He read through both, but now picked up the one from Edara and went through it again page by page. It fell into two parts.

The first dealt exclusively with Operation Zephyr and, to his great satisfaction, reported the mission continuing secure on all fronts and developing exactly as planned; escape routes in place for all agents requiring them; financial arrangements proceeding smoothly; communications and IT programmes on schedule; support logistics in place and geared for action – and, most importantly, preparations for the two abductions finalized.

He turned his attention to the second part of Edara's report, which was short, its contents categorized, succinct. He read through it again and then, sitting back and clasping his hands beneath his chin, considered not only the comments – the *judgements?* – made in it, but also the character and the already well-known to him ambitions of the man who had advanced them, because the two agents he has reported on are certainly viewed by him as his rivals for position and power within the organization. On the first of those rivals, Jake Messanger, the report was – revealingly? – middle-of-the-road, being neither derogatory nor complimentary. It is like a school report saying 'Satisfactory, but could do better', Sarsen thought, the suggestion of a smile on his lips. But then quickly he corrected himself: it is not like that at all, Edara would damn Jake in this report to me if he had any proof whatsoever to support his opinion. So I'll take what he says about Jake as questionable in itself.

That decided, Sarsen's thoughts moved on to the other agent named in Edara's report. Of him Edara stated baldly: 'Agent Nine has on two recent occasions displayed a critical attitude towards myself that borders on insubordination. This has been dealt with.' As he considered those two statements, Sarsen, being in possession of certain facts detailed in the other secret report he had just received, thought to himself – perhaps you would have been wiser to deal with Nine more circumspectly, Edara. For that second report had been sent to him under conditions of extreme secrecy by Agent Nine himself, and in it he put forward two criticisms – *accusations* perhaps a more apposite word? – against Edara. First, that he was guilty of culpable, panic-driven over-reaction in order-ing the killing of Simon Croft. Nine stated in his report that Croft's 'disappearance', as it was so far officially classified, was presently being investigated by the British police and, consequently, might lead to trouble for Zephyr and, later, result in police enquiries which would put at risk the security of some of Sarsen's agents in London. Both those difficulties, Nine pointed out, could have been avoided simply by abducting Croft and holding him incommuni-cado until Zephyr was completed. And Agent Nine's second accusation had even more immediacy to it, Sarsen thought. He stated that it was his opinion that, in the interests of Zephyr's secu-rity, Jared Messanger ought to have been placed under surveillance from the moment his half-brother arrived in London, and that he had advised Edara to that effect, only to be – Sarsen smiled thinly as he recalled the vulgar Arabic phrase Nine used – summarily 'slapped down'.

So, the situation in London is shaping up in accordance with my wider plans as well as those for Zephyr, Sarsen concluded. Judging from these reports neither Edara nor Nine will confide in the other, nor are they likely to conspire together against me when – after Zephyr – I need them to work separately to achieve the two, possibly three, murders-disguised-as-accidents I shall require of them. Which brings me to the one remaining uncertainty in my wider undertaking.

Getting to his feet he turned and gazed out of the window at Damascus, seeing his city hazed with afternoon heat; but his aircon-ditioned office was cool around him as his mind centred on the third of his leading agents engaged in Operation Zephyr, namely Jake Messanger.

That tiny seed of doubt which had been sown in Sarsen's mind by Messanger just before he left for London had rooted itself there – feebly, but sufficiently strongly to sustain life. In an earlier report to him Edara had laid emphasis on the fact that Messanger was devel-oping a close relationship with his half-sister Gemma. Edara had perceived only the value of that to Zephyr; but in Sarsen, knowledge of it had fed those embryonic roots. That nascent doubt regarding Messanger's continued loyalty to him had grown bigger, not in rela-tion to the prosecution of Zephyr – had that been the case Sarsen would immediately have ordered Jake's instant return under guard to Damascus for severe interrogation – but as to Jake's future value to himself, Sarsen, as his right-hand man in terrorist activities. He had had great hopes of Jake, seeing him as potentially a valuable agent in English-speaking countries, America in particular. But now?

For Gemma Messanger and her brother Jared my plans are set in stone, he thought. Those two are of John Messanger's blood and as such are to be wiped off the face of the earth. But what, now, of Jake? I adopted La'ali's son by John Messanger with the intention of using him as a weapon against his father. But then as the boy grew older, and I got to know him well, I came to see him as more La'ali's son than John Messanger's and, moreover, perceived his potential as a tool to my hand for the advancement of the Islamic cause. However, if he is beginning to move away from his Arab heritage and cleave instead to that of his blood-father, it is only right that he should share the fate I plan for his siblings.

But I will wait, he thought. I will bide my time until the whole of the picture becomes clearer. Because in regard to Jake Messanger, Edara may be grinding his own axe: for were Jake to die he, Edara, would be well-placed to become my heir-apparent. So, let Zephyr continue its course. Time enough to decide later what action to take about Jake; and it will allow him the chance to prove himself loyal to me even against the Brits – and, by doing so, keep his life.

Chapter 12

Ealing   Evening, Friday 13 August

'Do you think we were right to go ahead with the party as we have, with Simon still . . . well, you know, missing?' Standing at the edge of the terrace at the back of Jared's house Gemma looked up at Tom Etherington, a neighbour, her blue eyes moody, the generous mouth puckered with concern and uncertainty.

'Fuck it, what else?' Tom had been first to arrive and now, a few minutes after 7.30, his fair-skinned, regular-featured face was easy with well-being and good-fellowship, in his opinion all was fine with the world. 'When he does turn up you'd better not let him know you ever considered cancelling, or hc'll think you've gone mad. Besides, the love-sick idiot would never forgive you for depriving his beloved Delyth of a party on his account while all the time he was – hell, what? – probably holed up in the hallowed precincts of some stupendous library—'

'It's a lovely party and I'm sure Tom's right,' Clare Rivers interrupted, annoyed with her boyfriend because she thought he had drunk too much too fast and was talking rubbish. Then she looked around her and changed the subject. 'The garden looks a lot better,' she said to Gemma, 'you and Delyth must have been working like dogs; Jared never does a thing. And, by the way, that tall dark bloke over by the bay tree – is he your half-brother? I didn't make it to the barbecue at Levensholme but Tom told me about him and I'd love to meet him. . . .'

Right from daybreak that Friday of the party a vicious little war had been going on inside Jake Messanger's head, and in his heart. In the course of the morning he had made a presentation to the board of one of the pharmaceutical companies involved in the deal which was his cover story to account for his visit to London. During that he had succeeded in confining his private inner war to the sidelines of his mind and had, he thought, made a satisfactory fist of the presentation. Nevertheless, he gave thanks that that was not of vital importance since the greater part of the work was being done behind the scenes by other representatives more widely experienced in such matters than he was – and in fact the British companies concerned kept their eyes mostly on the ball, not on the individual players or the captain of the team.

But by the afternoon, when he was at Jared's house helping Gemma with preparations for the party, full-scale inner warfare had resumed and he had found himself in danger of becoming not only bereft of hope but also, even more damagingly, of self-belief and self-respect. *What kind of man have you become?* he asked himself. You cannot, you must not, go through with Zephyr! *This* is your country, *these* are your people! Delyth, Gemma – you feel close to them, feel at one with them in a deeper way than you've ever experienced before. And as they belong here, so do you. Are you some kind of monster, that in a few hours' time you're going to light the fuse to a terrorist strike here in London; going to *hurt Delyth* so as to make that hit happen simply because you've been ordered to do so?

How did you get to this terrible place where you now stand? Are you really that kind of . . . savage? In desperate search for answers to these questions Jake's tortured mind traced back along the chain of command that had powered in turn the conception, the creation, and, now, the implementation of Operation Zephyr: it led, as he had known it would, to Sarsen.

Sarsen. In childhood, Jake's refuge in adversity and loneliness. Then his father-figure, honoured and loved above all men. Through the teenage years his friend, role model and mentor, always ready to discuss and advise on both the self-centred ideas and questions of adolescence and the frighteningly wider concerns of the looming adult world. Then eventually, in manhood, still his mentor but also his – also the man who took him into the service of an Islamist terrorist organisation as an agent in one of its crack cadres, which he commanded. Jake Messanger had realized years earlier that Sarsen had as such moulded him to fit in with an agenda of his own, a political one. But until a few months ago he had never doubted the sincerity of Sarsen's motives, or his love for him: never until that April morning in Damascus when, in his office high above the city, Sarsen had in effect blackmailed him into accepting the role he had planned for him in Operation Zephyr, using against him an execution he, Sarsen, had ordered.

Now, suddenly, and with only about thirty hours to go before Zephyr was scheduled to blow, doubts regarding Sarsen's true feelings towards him blossomed within Jake Messanger's mind: the seed of doubt which had rooted itself in his psyche that morning earlier in the year thrust up stalk, leaves, buds and flowers with horror-driven speed. What if Sarsen has devised some similar betrayal of me here in London? he asked himself. What if the plans for Delyth – even for myself, also – are not as he has given me to understand? What if he, Sarsen, is working to a darker purpose here? Has a secret, ulterior plot under way in which Edara is, or will be, the mainspring of some tangential action in which I will be the fall guy – *as I was before?*

However, by the time the guests had arrived and the party was in full swing, Jake had allayed his doubts – partially, at least. He *must* stick to Edara's plan for that night's action. He was Sarsen's trusted undercover agent, he had to remain loyal to him. Life would make no sense if he were to betray him. Yet still a restless uncertainty tormented his mind. Perhaps it was that he, the man Jake Messenger, would make no sense if he turned traitor now. Years of his life would be lost, would become meaningless . . . *or was it really the other way round?* Was it that if he took Delyth hostage and beat her up in order to secure the co-operation of her father – if he did *that*, his life would become meaningless? Besides, how could he bring himself to do that to *Delyth*? It wasn't possible. . . .

'Hi. I'm Brett Gaveston.'

'Jake Messanger.' Turning as the stranger came up behind him on the terrace and introduced himself, he saw Gaveston to be a chunky, dark-haired young man, brown eyes lively and friendly. 'I've heard Gemma speak of you,' he went on. 'You have a sister named Rachel who's something of a star at the local tennis club.'

'Gem's not so bad herself, y'know. Me and Dan – that's him over there across the lawn, talking to the tall blonde – we often make up a four with Gem and Del when they're down from college.' He grinned. 'Guess you'd better keep an eye on Dan, he's got a crush on your sister.'

'Reciprocated?'

'God, no, Gemma's got more sense.'

'Delyth Stanton . . . is she involved with anyone local?' Gemma had told him she wasn't, but then Gemma wasn't local, and this guy was.

'Nah.' Gaveston took a pull from his can of Foster's then turned away, running his eyes over the guests partying in Jared's summer-scented garden. He soon found the one he was looking for: Delyth, standing beneath the chestnut tree at the far end of the lawn, deep in conversation with Tom.

Jake had followed the younger man's eyes. Delyth was wearing a sleeveless dress of some soft, flowing material the colour of pale honey and, as he looked at her, she seemed to him a figure of mystery and fascination. Desire welled up in him and with it came an urgent longing to be close to her, to share her thoughts, her feelings, her life—

'You beat her,' Edara's voice said inside his head, and dream turned to nightmare. '*You beat her up until she's begging you for mercy*' – *Jesus!* I can't *do* that, he thought.

'Not Delyth,' Gaveston went on, turning back to Jake. 'She's one very gifted lady and she's going places, I reckon. Career-wise, I mean. . . . Y'know, I fell for her like a ton of bricks when I was seventeen, we were in the sixth together and doing Arthurian legends in

English Lit. Delyth was my Guinevere and I'd have died for her if she'd asked.'

'Obviously she didn't.'

'How could she, she never knew. Anyway, after a bit I met a gorgeous girl, a local farmer's daughter – dropped the torch pretty quick then. We're good friends now, Delyth and I, on a very ordinary level.'

'Thanks for the party, it's great.' Coming out of the house to look for Jake, Delyth stopped to speak to Jared. 'I only wish Simon were here.'

'That'll work out OK, you'll see. He's a head-in-the-clouds sort of bastard, far too wrapped up in Shelley and Co to remember to keep us mortals informed of his comings and goings.' Jared grinned. 'Don't get uptight about it. When he comes back from wherever he's at, he'll be full of apologies – might even throw you another party to placate us all. By the way, where's Jake? I haven't seen him around.'

'I'm not his keeper.' But it was said with a smile, as she smoothed back her hair. 'Actually I think he's out on the lawn, I saw a big group there. And I'm not uptight about Simon. Only . . . sad, I suppose. I so much wanted him to be here. ... Nice, isn't it, getting together with people you like.'

'Amongst whom you now number Jake.'

'You sound as if you don't approve of that. Why shouldn't I consider him a friend?'

'No reason. None that I can tell you, that is. Forget it.' Jared looked at his watch and changed the subject, saying the first thing that came into his head. 'I've got to leave by quarter to eleven, damn it.'

'Don't tell me: another crisis at the office!' Laughing, she presented his usual excuse. 'You'll have to think up a new one soon, that's getting a bit threadbare.'

As she fell silent, his mobile buzzed and, turning aside, he answered it. To his surprise his caller was Superintendent Rawlings.

'Sir,' he said, and moved further away from Delyth, whereupon she murmured 'See you', and went down on to the lawn in search of Jake.

'There's been a promising development here,' Rawlings told him. 'That mature student at Whitehaven College whose name you gave me, John Nestorian, he's come up with a couple of things that look worth chasing up. We're doing that now – you want to come in, see how it goes?'

'I'm on my way. I'm at home. Be with you in—'

'Do you by any chance know where your half-brother is at this moment?'

'He's right here. There's a party on.'

'So presumably we can count on him staying there for a while yet? It's virtually certain he won't be called away on business like you are now?'

'Can't see that happening, sir. He's spent quite a few evenings with us recently – with my sister, mostly – and never been called away. I'd say you can count on him being here until at least midnight.'

'Right. You get over here at once, then; I'd like you around to refer to if necessary.'

Like me around because I've sketched my half-brother into a terrorist scenario, and you've sussed that I want him to be caught red-handed, Jared was thinking as he made his excuses to Gemma and went out to his car. Weird it is, this hunch of mine that Jake's come over here on some undercover terrorist mission – no, it's more than a hunch, it's a conviction. The way he's cosied up to Gemma, building on her memories of the closeness between them when we were all kids together – it doesn't ring true to me, never has. Jake's *using* us somehow, using us for some secret purpose of his own, I'm sure of it, dead sure.

And then as he drove across the city Jared's mind turned to Rawlings and what might come to light – if anything did – through his investigations based on the names John Nestorian had provided. So it was only much later that night that he realized how lazy-minded he had been to assume that his half-brother would stay on at the party after Delyth had left when all the time he, Jared, was well aware that it was Delyth's habit to leave parties in time to be home before midnight.

*

114

Jake turned to Delyth as, coming up beside him, she touched his arm. Out of the corner of his eye he had seen her approaching, and been glad – but then *not* glad. Because he would lose her that night: he knew it, but was finding it impossible to accept the only alternative he could see. To betray Sarsen was something he could not do. To betray him would be to destroy something of himself, for it would lay waste all he had become over the years; he was Sarsen's son by right of—

'Let's go over to the tree seat,' she said to him softly. 'I'm tired of party chat, I'd rather talk to you.'

Her voice and the touch of her hand reached deeply into him and, briefly, he forgot Sarsen. As they walked across the grass he took her hand in his.

But then when they sat down she said, 'Bad news from Gaza today. Tell me what it's really like, Jake, the situation in the Middle East. Here in England—'

'No, Delyth. Please, stop it; no politics.' In anger and despair he interrupted her sharply, but then softened his tone, going on quietly, 'It's your party night—'

'I've done the party stuff, I'd like a change. Why is it you never want to talk politics? With you living and working in the Middle East I'd have thought you'd be eager to talk about how things are there, to tell people.'

'I don't know enough,' he said bluntly.

'Then you ought to! How can you live there so close to it all without at least *trying* to? Head-in-the-sand as if you're an absolute moron—'

'Leave it, Delyth! *Please.*' He took her hand again, kissed it, held it, his eyes searching hers hungry for . . . what? Understanding? Impossible, surely, without any explanation being given. So perhaps *hope* of some kind, but then hope for what? There was no hope for him unless—

'All right, I've left it, Jake, It's gone, it never was!' The perceived angst in him had reached into her and eaten up her anger. Slipping her hand free of his she leaned back into the seat, gazing around her. Dusk had gathered in Jared's garden, masking its many imperfections with starshine mysteries. A breeze was whispering to the leaves of the chestnut tree.

'I'm sorry if I . . . disappoint you,' he said quietly.

'Disappoint me?' She laughed a little, looking up into the darkling sky. 'I *admire* you, Jake Messanger. The work you're doing, it's good. Do you think you'll get a satisfactory deal from those pharmaceutical companies you're seeing? They'll ratchet up their research programmes like you want?'

Don't let it get to you – don't let *her* get to you, he told himself desperately. You've got a job to do that will help advance Sarsen's cause across the world – *so do it!*

'Things are looking promising,' he said, 'but it's too early to tell yet. Their lead negotiator is playing his hand very close to his chest.'

'So are you, from what you've told me.'

It came at him cold across the twilight, but a quick glance sideways reassured him: Delyth was sitting back staring skywards, totally relaxed; she had been referring only to his cover agenda, at which he had been working hard.

'It's necessary to do that at all times, I've found,' he said carefully, hoping she would move away from the subject.

She did. 'Point taken,' she murmured, then sat up straight and smiled at him. 'The party is lovely, and I'm grateful, but do you know what I'm looking forward to most?'

Seeing her face full of happiness, Jake swiftly adopted a like mood. 'I haven't the faintest idea,' he said. 'Tell me.'

'One week today.'

'And why would that be?'

'Because by then the Watchman conference will have ended, and I'll have my father all to myself, for a fortnight anyway.'

'The Watchman conference?' He took it in his stride, but looked away, grateful for the night-dark stealing over the garden.

He need not have bothered: Delyth was on her feet, her head down as she smoothed her dress into place.

'You know, the one I told you about, air purity in underground rail systems,' she said. 'I'm not surprised you've forgotten, it's hardly a subject to set the pulses racing, is it?'

Delyth, *Delyth!* I can't stand this. But – I *have to!* Loyalty demands it: as Sarsen's son it is *not conceivable* that I should betray him.

Jake stood up. 'No, that's for sure. I'd clean forgotten about it,' he answered, seeing her hair swing forward hiding her face from him. 'I'm glad for you, that you'll be able to spend more time with your father.' Then he added – in order, he prayed, to preserve a sense of normality in the situation as it now existed between himself and Delyth, 'I hope it's not going to mean I'll see less of you, though?'

'Of course not.' She turned to him. 'I'd like you to meet my father, Jake. In many ways you're the same sort of man as he is. He'd like you, I think.'

'Is that really important to you?'

'That he'd like you? Oh, yes. Very.' A sudden stillness had come over her. The owl-light stole the colour from her eyes, but as he looked into them Jake Messanger saw there a tenderness – and he so longed for it to grow into a commitment that for a moment there was only Delyth and himself in the world; nothing else existed, *nothing.*

'I love you,' he said to her.

An instant longer she held his eyes, then – deliberately – she broke the spell. Touched his hand, said quietly, 'I know,' then turned away and began to walk towards the house.

The way she had responded seemed to him cold, dismissive even. He was not to know she had not meant it to be so, had only meant to make it clear to him that for her it was too early to commit. But at her perceived coldness towards him the world spun back into shape – for him a world dominated by Sarsen, by Operation Zephyr, and his obligations to both. He fell into step beside her, his mind now totally concentrated on those obligations, and working out the best way to phrase the question he had to ask her before they reached the house.

'I'm going home now; I'll just get my jacket,' she said into the silence between them. 'Would you see me to my car? I've parked in that little asphalted area private to Jared's property, like I always do. It's a bit scary there when it's dark, the trees and bushes shutting it in. Usually – at night – either he or Gemma comes with me. But I'd rather it was you.'

So there was no need for Jake Messanger to think out the phrasing of his question: she had just answered it,

'I'd be happy to,' he said, and took her hand as they walked on.

Chapter 13

London The same evening

Eleven-fifteen. Professor Stanton was working at his desk in the study at the front of the house when his doorbell rang. Irritated at being disturbed, as he had been engrossed in sifting through his notes in preparation for his final report to government on Watchman, he got to his feet and went to answer it, expecting his caller to be some friend or neighbour.

It was neither, and his absentmindedness in not verifying the identity of his caller before opening the door was to cost him dear. Edara's two heavies took him without any difficulty. Pushing him in front of them as the door was opened they charged straight in, then, as one of them pistol-whipped him across the face the other kicked the door shut then darted round him and – half supporting him as he staggered back under the shock and force of the assault, hands up to his bloodied face – grabbed both his arms, yanked them behind him and clamped his wrists together there, gripped cruel-tight.

'OK. Look at me now.'

That's the one in front of me speaking, the one with the gun, Stanton thought as, his head down, his eyes closed, he heard the words through a throbbing darkness of pain. He could taste blood in his mouth, feel it dribbling down his chin – wanted to wipe it away but couldn't, his hands prisoned behind his back. Tied there? No, held fast, fingers of steel.

'Come on! *Look at me*, I said!'

But while the professor was still dredging up the will to do so the tough behind him grabbed a handful of hair and jerked his head up. 'You're gonna have a hard time of it over the next few hours, Prof, if you don't obey orders quicker'n this,' he said, and Stanton smelled whisky on his breath.

He opened his eyes. The man facing him was wearing a balaclava but it wasn't pulled up over his mouth and the professor perceived that the man was an Arab, the very dark skin, the hooked nose, those deep-socketed brown eyes.

'You come to the car with us now,' the gunman said.

'Any resistance, mate – you try anything – and I'll break your fucking arms,' said the man behind him.

That one's British, Stanton thought, but found no comfort in the fact. 'Where . . . where are you taking me?' His voice unsteady, the words slurred.

'You'll see. Move!' Shoving hard against his spine the Brit propelled him towards the door.

'My gun is silenced,' the Arab said, opening the door with his left hand. 'You make one sound – one little sound, that's all – and you die,'

It took them three minutes, no more, to get him out to their car. The Brit drove; the Arab sat on the back seat of the black Volvo with Stanton beside him, his weapon pressed hard into his captive's side. In a matter of minutes the professor's head cleared. But even when, some thirty minutes later, the Volvo was pulled in and parked alongside the kerb in a quiet back street which he recognized and was very familiar with – knew Devon House was a mere four minutes' walk away – even then his brain still did not make the right connections.

The agent whom Edara had appointed to assist Messanger in the abduction of Delyth Stanton – a lean, fair-haired young man, lantern-jawed, wirily strong – was lying in wait for her in the cover of the five-yard wide windbreak alongside Jared's two-car parking area off to one side of his house. Relaxed but wide awake, he was leaning against the trunk of a maple tree, and the foliage of the shrubs crowding around it hid him from outside eyes. When he had peered at his watch a few minutes earlier it had shown nearly 11.30.

They should be coming along this way any time now, he thought and, straightening up, eased his handgun from its inside pocket in his custom-tailored jacket and squinted out through leaf-cover at the square of tarmac alongside him. There was only the one vehicle parked there, and he knew it belonged to his target: a white Fiesta with a roof-rack, it was standing three feet from him with the driver's door facing him. There was space for one more car on its far side but it was empty now. Behind the Fiesta a paved footpath led away towards the house. Since he had taken up position an hour earlier no one had come along it. My luck's in tonight, he thought – then suddenly tensed, hearing faint footsteps tapping across the quietness from the direction of the path across the tarmac. They were growing louder . . . and definitely coming towards him. It sounded like two people so, carefully parting leaves, he peered out at the path, searching it for any signs of life.

Can't see anyone – no, hang on! There's movement over there! Two figures are taking shape; blurry, though, can't see any detail yet . . . yeah, here they come. It's a man and a woman, walking side by side. Both're tall . . . and now as they come closer, the bloke's giving me the signal by turning once to look behind him – it's Messanger and the Stanton woman all right so be ready to take her the instant he holds her at gunpoint.

'. . . Jared say goodnight to you before he left?'

That's Messanger's voice, he's telling me it's OK to proceed as planned. They're crossing the tarmac to her car—

'Of course he did.'

'Did he say why he had to go?'

They're almost at her car now – driver's side – so I'll edge out on to the tarmac—

'Not really.'

They're rounding the bonnet. The woman's laughing – she's taking her car keys out of her bag—

'At least he remembered to wish me happy— *God! What—?*'

Messanger's stuck his gun in her side so *get on with it.*

'*Shut up.* Do as you're told, Delyth, and you won't get hurt.'

'Jake—'

'*Shut up*! Just do what the man says.'

'Give me the keys!' A stranger beside her. Fair-haired and cat-quiet he materializes out of the night with terrifying suddenness, one hand out towards her, palm up – and there's a gun in his other hand, pointed straight at her chest. 'Keys, pronto!' he orders. 'Car keys, *now!*'

There is no room inside Delyth's brain for constructive thought; there is only a chaos of disbelief and fear. She turns her head and looks up at the man she's just been talking to but discovers there only a man whose face is set against her, a man she doesn't recognize. 'Jake?' she whispers. But he gives her only a shake of the head. 'Hand him your keys,' he says, and there is nothing for her in his voice, nothing at all.

So she drops the car keys into the outstretched palm, and immediately the taut little tableau of two men with guns and a woman without one breaks up into its component parts. Then, within the space of a minute, re-forms inside the Fiesta. The fair-haired tough has put away his weapon and is at the wheel, the woman is in the passenger seat beside him while behind her, crouched on the edge of the rear seat, the other man keeps his gun on her, its muzzle only inches from the nape of her neck.

'She got her mobile with her?' the driver asks.

'It's in her bag.'

'The safe house in Hanger Lane, then. I'll get us there in twenty minutes.' His English comes easily off his tongue but is faintly accented.

'Don't break any speed limits. We're well within time.'

'OK. You're the boss.'

As the Fiesta is driven across Ealing the man holding the gun on the woman can smell her perfume and for some reason this fills him with a deep and sudden anger. With effort, he dismisses it. Her perfume is part of a dream that can never become reality, he tells himself, and sets his mind firmly on the tasks lying ahead of him.

Twelve midnight.

Closeted together in a minor safe house in Tottenham Court Road, Edara and Agent Nine had just completed a series of coded telephone checks with the three Zephyr agents assigned to release the toxic gas at the target sites, each one of them fully aware that, although possible, it is unlikely he himself will escape the death he has committed himself to inflicting on countless others this day.

'So, we remain on schedule.' Edara sat back from the table in the centre of the office-like room.

'But we've received no progress report yet from Messanger.'

'It is a little early for that.'

'All the same, I shall be happier when it comes in: the woman's co-operation is essential.'

'Should Messanger fail to secure it, our fall-back plan will kick in, and that precludes failure.'

Frowning, Nine strode across to the window and stood staring down at the street below. 'Not absolutely,' he argued. 'It leaves Stanton permanently blinded, yes, but when he's finally freed—'

'There has been a change to the original plan. Both he and his daughter are to be killed within hours of Zephyr's culmination.' Edara's tone was neutral but his eyes had sharpened, fiercely watchful of Nine's reaction to what he had said.

'On whose orders was the change made?' Nine swung round to face him. 'Has Sarsen sanctioned those deaths?' he asked blandly.

'Are you implying that I would take such decisions without his sanction?'

Agent Nine's answer did not come immediately. Through a count of ten he held Edara's eyes, striving to read in them exactly what lay behind his evasive reply to such a straightforward question as his own had been. But he did not succeed, and knowing Edara for the utterly ruthless predator he was, he ducked the challenge.

'I withdraw my question,' he said soberly. 'However, I would like to ask one other in its place.'

'You may ask; whether I answer or not is for me to decide.'

'It is this: does *Messanger* know that Stanton and his daughter are to be killed once Zephyr has been accomplished?'

Edara continued his close scrutiny of this lieutenant of his, confident of his own superiority over him. Agent Nine is indeed highly skilled in the art of being all things to all men, he thought, but over the years we have worked together I have come to understand the way he manoeuvres and manipulates people and situations. So, now I will manipulate him to the service of my own, covert purposes.

'No, he does not,' he answered, then rose to his feet and went round the table to Nine, stared him in the eye. 'The killing of the woman will fall to Messanger,' he said. 'I shall brief you later regarding the timing of the act. Meanwhile you will keep the decision to kill her hidden from him. Is that understood?'

'It is understood.' There was a narrow-lipped smile on Nine's face. 'Those two killings: it is a move I have advocated from day one of our planning—'

'Wisely, as is now apparent.' Edara turned away and resumed his seat at the table. 'For the rest of the day, do not leave your office without informing me of why you are doing so,' he ordered, then picked up the roster sheet before him and gave his full attention to it.

The dismissal plain, Agent Nine left at once.

By the time Delyth's Fiesta reached safe house Alpha off Hanger Lane in Ealing, Jake Messanger had taken one emotional and mental step along a road he could no longer resist taking. At the time he did not see it as a step along a road; he saw it as no more than one small statement of his own right to be considered a human being, whereas in fact it was a beginning, *the* beginning, of a fundamental change in himself.

Safe house Alpha was in a side street of terraced Victorian dwellings and, like several others nearby, had been turned into two flats, the entrance to the one on the ground floor being off the street while that to the upper one was at the rear of the house. Use of the ground-floor flat was confined to 'friends' of the owner: in this way he paid his dues to a certain hard-core terrorist organization and its associates.

As the Fiesta pulled up a few yards short of the safe house the man holding the gun on the woman spoke to her quietly. 'The three of us are going into this house now,' he said. 'As you can see, there's no one around. While we're going in I'll have my gun pressed into your side. If you make a sound I'll pull the trigger.'

'Jake.' Staring straight ahead of her Delyth Stanton whispered the name of this man she had so recently begun to open her heart to. 'What's happening? What's this all about?'

'I'll tell you when we're inside. Provided you don't cause trouble for us I can make sure you don't get hurt.'

'Your word on that?'

God! She still trusts *my word?* 'Yes. I swear it.'

For a second or two, Delyth hesitated, desperately scanning the road outside for help but seeing only a row of cars parked kerbside, glass and metalwork glinting beneath hoisted streetlamps. *There wasn't a living soul in sight out there.*

'Then I'll go with you and not try to get away,' she said, for – surely? – Jake could not actually be her enemy.

Yet his gun pressed hard into her ribs as they walked up to the house. Using his left hand, he took a key from the pocket of his jacket, unlocked the front door and slipped the key back. Inside, then, and she saw a carpeted corridor leading on through to the rear of the house; shaded overhead lighting revealing two doors off it and one along at the far end. Messanger opened the first one on his right, motioned Delyth inside. As she entered the room, the fair-haired man made a move to follow her but, quietly and authoritatively, Messanger barred his way.

'You return to base now,' he said to him. 'Rahman and I take things on from here. I'll call him in as soon as I've got this one ready to do whatever I tell her to do. That won't take long. I know her: pain'll break her fast; she's got no guts.'

'But Agent Nine said—'

'And now I'm ordering, so get on with it.' Messanger turned and followed Delyth in through the door, hearing the other man open the front door and go out. His strategy to secure Delyth's co-opera-tion was clear in his mind, but he was praying that he would be able to find the right words, that he'd be able to present his lie to her convincingly so that she would agree to do what he was going to ask her to do and, therefore, would not be hurt. For if he failed in that, he would have to go ahead with Edara's plan and she would be hurt. True, he would delegate the doing of it to Ahmed Rahman and make sure he didn't go over the top, but, nevertheless, Delyth would suffer.

'Jake, listen to me!' she demanded, as he went up to her. 'You have to tell me – please, *please* tell me what all this is about!' Standing straight and tense in the middle of the small sitting-room of the flat, she was in control of herself. There was no subservience in her, but, as he met her eyes, he saw she was desperately afraid.

He hardened himself against her fear: crammed down all feeling, blacked it out. 'Listen to me, Delyth.' He wanted to reach out and touch her, touch her arm or shoulder, but he held his hand lest it served only to unnerve her – or himself. 'We don't have much time so I'll give it to you straight. There's a plot to destroy the work of the Watchman conference, and I'm involved in it. In furtherance of this, the blueprints of some of London's underground rail systems will be photocopied tonight at Devon House—'

'I know about the blueprints, Dad's told me. Get on to how I figure— No! Wait! *Photocopied*, you say? So obviously your friends' – her lip curled and, suddenly, her eyes darted contempt and revulsion at him – 'by the look of things I suppose you count them your *friends*, they want my father's co-operation, need his handprint on the lock to open his cabinet.' She turned her back on him, put distance between them. 'He'll never co-operate, though,' she stated flatly. 'He won't do it, I know he won't.'

'If he refuses, they'll beat him up.'

'He'll take it.'

'Don't be a fool. No one but another professional could stand up to what these men will do to him. They're experts—'

'*And your friends!*' She rounded on him, accusing him again, her face white with anger but – he saw it clearly – the fear in her was even stronger than it had been before because now it was for her father.

Christ, what am I doing here? Jake Messanger thought, staring at her, a sense of total alienation harrowing him: a growing, remorseless alienation from his own past life and convictions – from Sarsen and everything he stood for. What *have* I become? he thought. I am only what Sarsen, who drew me to him as his chosen son having none of his own, has made me. I am his tool: nothing more than an instrument he uses to achieve his own ends. I can't escape from it, though. Not now. It's too late for that – no! Hang on a minute! Maybe it *isn't* too late? There's another approach might—

'But there's something *I* can do in this, isn't there?' Delyth said, standing tense, tight-lipped. Her mind had been racing: dismissing recrimination it had sought for, and found, firm ground on which she might stand and fight on her father's behalf. 'That's why you've kidnapped me, isn't it? *Isn't it?*' she repeated fiercely, infuriated by his self-enwrapped silence, her voice stabbing into it to make him listen to her.

'There's only one way to help him.' Quiet, Messanger's voice.

Holding his eyes, she stepped close to him again. 'And it's through me, isn't it?'

'Yes, it's through you. Because he loves you above all things, and you love him above all things.'

'And I was fool enough to let you see it. *You bastard!*'

He let that go past him, accepting it as no less than the truth. 'You have to persuade him to co-operate,' he said.

But her brain, ranging beyond the one immediate, personal threat, had perceived wider-reaching and terrifying possibilities inherent in the present situation. 'Let that stand for a moment,' she said urgently. 'There's something else here which I have to be clear about, for my father as well as for me. You said the object of all this is to destroy the work of Watchman. But that's too vague. Given today's climate of fear about security, and with the likelihood of terrorists striking where it's least expected, there is something here that I have to be absolutely sure about. So answer me this, straight yes or no. The plot you spoke of: is it in fact far, far wider than Watchman – is it part of some terrorist operation?'

'There should be no—'

'Answer me, *yes or no!*' Abruptly, anguish convulsed Delyth; panic fear and an appalled awareness of her own impotence in the face of possible disaster sucked all life from her face, her spirit was failing.

Casting wildly around for certainties, Messanger found none. To see her so broken destroyed his resolve – and he lied to her, seeing it as the only way forward.

'No!' he said strongly. 'No terrorist strike is involved in what's happening here, now.'

But his second of hesitation had betrayed him to her: the simple negative was not enough. 'You swear to me that no terrorist act – no bombing, no killing – will result from me getting my father to do what these people want him to do?' she persisted, watching him closely.

To lie to her a second time . . . to *Delyth*, and about such a thing? 'It's nothing like that,' he said, then quickly thrust at her the fact – the reality – which, he hoped and expected, would at once win her consent and thus avoid the physical assault on her that Edara had called for. 'However, there is one thing I haven't been entirely honest about—'

'Get honest now, then.'

'If your father continues to refuse them his co-operation after they beat him up, they will simply kill him. And you had better believe it,' he added softly. 'His life is in your hands.'

Delyth Stanton had no defence against that; the last vestiges of her resistance withered and died. 'Tell me what I have to do,' she said dully.

Shame and despair were in Jake Messanger. But he buried both and got on with the job Sarsen and Edara had planned for him. Nevertheless, deep in his mind he was again questioning the ethos Sarsen had instilled into him; he had taken one more step forward along the new road opening out before him, the road which had the potential to lead him into a world in which Sarsen had no place. Secretly as yet, and in spirit only, he had moved over to Delyth's side. Exactly where the new road might lead in concrete terms, he had no idea, but he had accepted the obvious now: the only way to find that out was to go along it.

'You have to speak to your father on your mobile,' he said to her. 'I'll explain exactly what you have to say to him. . . .'

'Right. OK, keep at it.' Rawlings cursed under his breath as he switched off the intercom.

'Sir!' Jared, seated in front of a computer on the far side of the room, seized the opportunity to claim Rawlings' attention; went on quickly as he turned to him, 'Should I get my sister on her mobile and check that Jake's still at the party?'

'Good idea. Do it.' Rawlings picked up one of the reports lying on his desk.

Gemma answered her brother's call and at once began telling him how the party was going.

'Is Jake still there?' Jared cut in.

'Jake? No, he went out with Delyth to see her to her car, you know how scary that little parking area is late at night. He hasn't come back since then.'

'You sure?'

'Of course I am, you idiot! This isn't a royal garden party, there's only ten of us here.'

'OK, Sis, leave it there – no, hold it! How long ago was it he and Delyth went off?'

'Shit, how should I know? I don't time people's comings and goings.'

'Roughly, then. It's important.'

'You are a bore. All I can say is, it must've been quite a bit ago, since, as you know, Del always likes to be home by midnight.'

'OK. Thanks. See you.'

'He's left your house?' Rawlings, having caught the drift of the conversation, was on his feet as Jared put away his mobile.

'*And* he went out with Delyth Stanton.'

'To drive her home?'

'No. She came in her own car, always does. But where she parks, it's just a tiny private area, only room for a couple of cars and not that well lit, usually one of us sees her off safely if it's late at night. . . . I'll go check up on this at once, shall I?'

'Do that. I don't want to lose sight of this half-brother of yours; we might get a lead of some sort from seeing who he contacts.'

'He came by car to my place, hire car—' Jared broke off, struck by a new idea. 'Sir, why don't I simply ring Delyth Stanton on her mobile? She always keeps it with her.'

'Right.' Rawlings nodded impatiently. 'Get on with it.'

Jared did so, but found Delyth's mobile was switched off. 'No dice, sir,' he reported. 'Maybe she's gone to bed.'

Rawlings frowned. 'If she had, wouldn't she have left the thing by the bed, switched on?'

'I'd think so. There's something wrong here, sir.'

'I agree. You'd better get over there fast.'

Five minutes later, Jared Messanger was behind the wheel of his dark-grey Mercedes, driving to his own home in Ealing. 'Check at your house first, then, if your half-brother's not there go straight on to the Stanton house,' Rawlings had said. 'Keep me in the picture every step of the way.'

'Recognize where we are?' Inside the black Volvo parked in a poorly lit side street, the Brit turned to the professor with the question, his right forearm across the steering wheel.

'Yes, I do now.' Conscious of the gun digging into his side, Stanton was peering out of the side window.

'Nelson Road; and Devon House is four minutes' walk away – that right?'

'Correct.' The only light within the car was that from the street-lamp six yards away: to the professor, the Brit's face was no more than a pale blur.

'And that's where you and me will be in a few minutes' time. Right, mate' – he nodded to the Arab beside Stanton – 'this is where you and me change places.' Sliding out from behind the wheel he got in beside Stanton, gun once more in his hand. The Arab took his place in the driving seat, his job now simply to watch and wait, make sure all was well until his mate and their prisoner returned.

'Listen to me, Stanton.' The Brit soft spoken – so far – and his throaty voice almost friendly. 'Here's what happens next. You and me walk round to Devon House together – I'll have my gun on you, you'd better remember that – and we go up to the conference room, where a friend of mine will be waiting. Then you use your handprint to open your filing cabinet for us and my friend photocopies three of your blueprints in there; that done, we close the cabinet up again.'

'And . . . after that?' Speaking was painful, his lower lip was split and there was blood in his mouth.

'We take you home, chum. Well, that's how it goes if you've done all we tell you to do, of course. Go with the flow, as they say – nice and easy, eh?'

'Why do you want the blueprints? What's this all about?'

'That's none of your business—'

'Of course it's my business!' Stanton straightened up suddenly, professional probity aroused, pain forgotten. 'Those blueprints are—'

Tiger-spring fast, the Brit drove his clenched fist hard into the professor's side and he broke off, hunching forward as the blow hit home then hugging the hurt, groaning, gasping for breath. 'You don't get explanations,' the Brit snapped, all softness gone from him. 'You do what you're told, and you keep your lip buttoned! OK? You ready to go?'

Leaning back, the professor held the flint-grey eyes. 'I'll not open my cabinet.'

'Then here's the choice open to you, the *only* choice: *either* you do every fucking thing we tell you to do, *or* your daughter gets killed – which'll happen fairly slowly, so you can hear how she feels while it's happening to her.'

A weird, lost sort of sound came out of Stanton's mouth, a hoarse, rasping moan retching up out of his guts – and for a couple of seconds it seemed as if life itself had gone out of him, his eyes vacant staring at nothing, his whole body slack. Then he snapped out of it: sat bolt upright, his eyes challenging the sandy-haired man beside him. 'I don't believe what you're saying,' he stated angrily. 'At this moment my daughter—'

'Is in a safe house somewhere in the care of pals of mine. They took her a while before we grabbed you. She'll have been roughed up a bit – to get her in the mood, like. You want to talk to her right now? Can do—'

Stanton went for him then, but, quick as light, the Brit's fist caught him on the underside of the jaw and he fell back against the fawn upholstery of the seat, dazed, already a prey to dreadful fears for Delyth, what they had done to her and would yet do.

'Enough chat,' the Brit said, taking out his mobile. 'I'll call my mate, and he'll put your little girl on the line to you. She'll wise you up on how things stand for her.'

Fumbling out his handkerchief, Stanton wiped blood from his mouth where the split lip had opened up again. His world was crumbling about him in catastrophe because, now, he believed every word the man had said. God give me strength, he thought. But it was no more than a wishful-thinking mantra from a long-gone youth: he had no faith.

'Spearhead,' the Brit said into his mobile. Listened for a moment and then went on, 'OK, put her on. I'll hand her over to the prof.'

Stanton took the mobile thrust towards him. His hand was shaking.

'Dad?' It was her voice: weak and trembly, but unmistakably hers.

'Delyth,' he said quite quietly, his heart lifting within him at the sound of her voice, but then across the line he heard her cry out as though in pain, and a newfound steadfastness surged through him because she needed his strength to lean on. 'Hang on in there, little lion,' he said, the secret to the two of them, fun love-name he'd given her during a childhood game but hadn't used for years suddenly coming into his mind. 'We'll work through this somehow, you and I—'

She screamed, thin and high. Then, 'No, Dad, it isn't *like that,*' she said, her voice breaking. 'Please just listen, *please,* or he'll cut me again; he's got a knife and he says if I don't get you to co-operate he'll cut me again and again so please just listen.'

'I'm listening, Delyth. Sorry, love, I'm so sorry. Say what you want to say, I'm listening.' She was the heart of his life, and horror at her suffering had eaten up his newfound strength, it was consumed, gone from him.

'I'm tied up, Dad. There's two men with me and they've both got guns, as well as the knife. They've told me what their people want you to do for them and . . . you've got to do it. You've got to—'

'I can't love. I'm responsible for the security of—'

'But nothing really bad will come of you helping them.'

'You can't know that.'

'Yes I can. They've promised me it won't.'

'Who has? And exactly what have they promised?'

'They've given their word that it's not a terrorist thing.'

'Who says it's not?'

'A man I trust.'

'But *who*? One of the two men there with you? Delyth, *who is it?*'

'I can't tell you that.' She screamed again – the cry stifled this time, but somehow that made it yet more devastatingly destructive of Stanton's will to resist. 'Dad, I have to get to the point,' she went on after a moment, and now her voice came to him quiet, agonized, but very clear. 'It's this: if you refuse to do what they want you to do, they'll kill me – and when they've done that, they'll kill you.'

The only light inside the black Volvo was from that streetlamp. The Brit could not see Professor Stanton's face, but he didn't need to; what he could see was enough, and he smiled: the old man was theirs for the taking, there was no resistance left in him.

'Believe me, Dad. You *must believe me.* It's the truth. I'm certain of that. They'll kill us both.'

'But Delyth. . . . Darling, are you equally certain that if I do co-operate with them, they *won't* do so?' He dredged the words up out of the coldness which had spread all through him, body, heart, soul, all freezing to death.

'Yes, Dad, I am. There's one person here who I trust. He says that once you've done what they want, you have only to give them your word that you'll say nothing to anyone of what's happened to us, that you'll keep absolutely quiet about it all for the next twenty-four hours, and they'll drive you back home as soon as you've done the job. You'll have a minder with you but you'll be home and safe. So do it, Dad! Do what they want, *please!*'

'But – you? Will they promise the same for you?'

'Yes. I've already given them that promise about keeping quiet. They'll drive me home, too, between two-thirty and three, they say.'

The Brit was right: for the professor, all hope of resistance was gone: all that remained was to salvage a couple of lives. But, 'Delyth, will they keep their promises to us? This one man, do you trust him? Trust him *enough?*'

'Enough, yes. He is not the man to lie to me about such a thing as this. I'm sure of it.'

'Tell him to come on the line. I want to hear him say these things himself.'

There was a brief pause, during which he heard his daughter put the request to someone fairly close to her. Then, 'No, Dad,' she said. 'He won't do that.'

'Why not? Delyth, *why not?*'

'I don't know – but Dad, you must do what they want! Tell the men with you you'll do it! Tell them *now*. Things're going bad here.'

In the Volvo, Professor Stanton handed the mobile back to the Brit. 'I'll open my filing cabinet for you,' he said. To him at that moment so-called freedom of choice was meaningless.

'Thought you would.' Grinning, the Brit punched out a number on his own mobile then spoke into it. 'Full agreement reached here,' he said. 'We're on our way. Be with you in a few minutes.'

Expertly handled, the Mercedes travelled fast across night-quiet London, dark-grey car slipping wraith-like through the city's streets, obedient to all the rules of the road but putting on speed wherever possible because Jared Messanger was harried by apprehension and a great anger.

The apprehension was for the safety of Delyth Stanton and was, so far, no more than a nagging anxiety. The anger was red-hot, and was against his half-brother because he was by now sure that some sinister and quite possibly criminally subversive intention lay behind Jake's disappearance from the party. Also, an appalling possibility lurked at the back of his mind: was Jake about to use Delyth – somehow, God alone knew how – in furtherance of whatever it was he was engaged in? And— ah, *shit!* Quit it, man. Just get yourself to the Stantons' place, he told himself. You could well be on a hiding to nothing here: when you get there all you'll find will be Professor Stanton incandescent at being interrupted in his work, and Delyth furious with you because her father is. So just drive, and get there. *Get there!*

No light was showing in the Stanton house. Parking just beyond it Jared pocketed the slim, powerful torch he'd chucked in on the passenger seat then got out, walked back to the gate in off the pavement, and took stock of the scene. Lit sometimes by moonlight but mostly only by starlight as drifting cloud obscured the moon, everything appeared to be the same as usual: prosperous-looking detached houses either side of the road, each with drive-in two-car garage and a fair-sized front garden; some of them, like the Stantons', comprehensively hedged into their personal privacy, others open-fronted to the world; cars parked kerbside here and there, not many, none close by. Delyth's wasn't one of them, but then it wouldn't be, would it, she'd have put it in the garage.

Opening the front gate he hurried along the path bisecting the garden, checking as he went that no light was showing in any of the windows, and pressed the bell beside the door. He heard it ring inside but then came only silence . . . and still, silence. Taking a step back he scanned the front of the house again . . . not a light anywhere, and not a window open. He looked around him but there was no movement anywhere, garden and road all quiet under the starred sky.

Hell! Jared thought, goddamnit to hell! OK, Delyth might have switched off her mobile, that could be. But what of her father? When he'd been talking to her at the party, he recalled, she'd mentioned that the professor was working at home that night as he often did, and would work on until she came in. So had she done so, and they'd both gone to bed? But no, there hadn't been time for that. Surely, something must be wrong here? Jake taking off from the party without a word to Gemma, and now this, apparently no one home at the Stantons'. He'd got to get inside, make sure everything was OK in there.

Decision made, Jared sought means of entry. No dice front windows or door, all solid shut. Round to the back, fast – same there re windows and door. Nothing else for it, it'd have to be forced entry. Better check first with Rawlings, though.

Darkly clad figure standing tense in the half-dark outside the back door of the Stanton house, mobile in hand. He spoke into it, his phrases short, urgent.

'Then break a bloody window!' his boss interrupted. 'Get in there quick and search the place. Call me back with a report soon as you can, I don't like the look of this. Then get back here.'

'You'll put a guard on after I've left, sir?'

'I'll send a plain-clothes officer straight away.'

Two minutes later, Jared's jacket-swathed elbow broke a kitchen window at the back of the house. Glass showered down inside but its tinkling fall on the floor was no more than a whisper across the blanketing quietness of the night.

Reaching in, he unlatched the window, pushed it open, spread his jacket across the glass-glinting window-ledge then hauled himself up over it and jumped down, landing crouched and easy-smooth, almost soundless. Straightening, he crossed the briefly moonlit kitchen to the door he saw facing him, switched on the light beside it, opened it, slipped through into the passage beyond and stopped dead, listening.

But no sound came to him. 'Stanton?' he shouted into the silent darkness around him. 'Professor Stanton! This is Jared Messanger—'

Suddenly, he broke off. There was no one in the house but himself; he felt it, knew it. Had to make sure, though. Didn't call out again. Simply went on through the house, using his torch – and the lights whenever he saw the switches.

Chapter 14

London The same night

His head sunk on his chest, his mind tortured by fears and despair, Professor Stanton walked unfettered at the Brit's side. Both of them were aware that the professor was a broken man and that from now on he would respond to one stimulus only: the safe-keeping of his daughter whose life, he knew, he was holding in the hollow of his hand that night. Leaving the Arab at the wheel of the Volvo, they made their way to Devon House. The streets were quiet; they were in one of those areas of London that dream away the night undisturbed by humankind because the nine-to-five 'suits' who worked there during the day have got back into their cars and made off to green field home, Chelsea flat, or whatever.

No word was spoken between those two as they walked the pavement side by side. They came from separate worlds, worlds which converse solely when they meet in conflict – and their particular conflict had just been resolved. Each of them, the winner and the loser, had accepted his status as such and, therefore, had at the moment nothing left to say to the other.

As they drew near to Devon House the Brit, touching Stanton's arm, guided him into a narrow alleyway opening on their left. A short way along this they turned left again, went on a few yards – the dark-windowed backs of tall buildings alongside them now – then halted at the rear door of one of these which had DEVON HOUSE printed black-on-white on the nameplate affixed to it. Taking a key from his pocket, cut from a template procured for Edara by Alain Oufkar, the Brit unlocked the door, shepherded Stanton into the corridor beyond, then relocked the door behind them, thinking, as he did so, thank Christ the job's been done OK, the alarm system's been put out of action. Some three minutes later, the corridor, a lift, and then another corridor quickly negotiated, he ushered his charge into the conference room and handed him over to Agent Nine who was awaiting him there. Two other men were also present but they were standing at one side of the room, on call for Agent Nine's orders.

When it suited him, Agent Nine was a man of few words; to him Stanton was no more than a passkey useful at the moment. 'You know what you have been brought here to do for us,' he said to him, then crossed the room to the row of filing cabinets standing along the opposite wall. 'Come over here and get it done.'

For the first time since he had got out of the Volvo, Stanton raised his head. He looked towards the man who had spoken, but then his eyes slid past him to his own cabinet and he stiffened where he stood, his mind racing as full realization of the magnitude – the shocking, appalling dreadfulness – of the possible consequences of what he was about to do struck home. What *purpose* lay behind what was happening? The answer given to him when he had put the question to them earlier, that his blueprints were to be used in a business deal of some sort, was not to be believed, surely? The two abductions, the Arabs, the hard men, the key to Devon House – such a seemingly well organized, synchronized operation surely must be in support of something more important than a business deal? Such a scenario seemed more suited to – *terrorism?* But then even as he thought that dread word, one other surged in over it, overwhelmed it and itself stood firm, primeval, paramount: *Delyth*. Delyth, my daughter: they will kill her if—

'Come, Stanton! The blueprints!'

The moment of truth. Robert Stanton strode across the conference room and confronted Agent Nine, looked him in the eye. 'Qualities and beliefs that we here hold dear and consider to be strengths are perceived by you and your kind as weaknesses – weaknesses you can use to your own advantage,' he said to him. 'So before I do what you want, I insist you make me one promise.'

'Name it.' Briefly, Agent Nine admitted to himself a certain admiration for this British professor.

'I understand from my conversation with my daughter that there is as such a bargain between those you represent and myself. It stands thus: a) I open the cabinet for you and b) I give you my word that for twenty-four hours thereafter I will say nothing to anyone of what has happened here tonight. In return, I am then driven home and, later, you free my daughter on the same terms as myself, she to join me at our home by or before three o'clock. I accept this – this trade-off, on one condition: that you swear on the Quran to honour, in full, your side of it.'

Bland-faced, Agent Nine smiled at him. 'I find in you a man after my own heart,' he said to him softly. 'I do so swear, on the Quran.'

But as he watched Stanton step forward and open his cabinet there was, now, nothing but contempt in Nine's face: contempt for a man so easily deceived.

'You handled that well.' But Jake Messanger did not go to her or use her name. Standing by the door where he had stood throughout her conversation with her father lest Rahman should come in, he watched her put the mobile down on the table beside the armchair she was sitting in and lean back, clasping her hands in her lap, eyes downcast. Then, after a moment, she looked up at him.

'Why, Jake?' Her voice steady, quiet. 'I'm finding I just can't believe this is happening. Why are you . . . part of this, whatever it is?'

Even a couple of weeks earlier he would have been able to answer her easily, succinctly, and confidently. But not now. Disturbingly aware of his own recent and increasingly intransigent uncertainties on that same question, he side-stepped the issue, taking up instead the tail-end of what she had said.

'What do you think it is?' he asked.

Looking away, she considered this. Got to her feet and stood fingering her mobile, staring down at it. 'I don't know,' she said finally, but then turned to him, a fierceness sudden in her. 'In fact

I've got a horrible feeling that I *do* know, and the knowledge scares me rigid! It's . . . it's *terrorism*, isn't it?' she accused. 'I think – now, I think – that you're a member of a terrorist organization, and have come over here to carry out some sort of mission on their behalf.' Then as he stood silent in the face of her onslaught, she thrust her question at him again. 'It's *terrorism*, all this, isn't it? *You lied to me just now!*'

There comes a time when you have to stop lying, Jake Messanger thought in cold honesty. For me, that time is now. Now, when I've betrayed two primordial trusts: that which is due to a man's family, and that which is surely a fundamental right of the woman he loves. 'I don't deny any of that,' he said – and saw a kind of death enter into her, vitality draining away out of her face, her body. 'But things will be different from today!' he went on urgently, hope rising in him that she cared enough for him to listen to the argument he'd been having with himself; that he would be able to make her understand the sea change which had taken place within him. '*I'm* different! I'm losing – have lost – belief in everything and everyone that brought me here—' He broke off sharply, swinging round as the door behind him was thrust open.

'I heard argument,' Ahmed Rahman said loudly in Arabic, standing in the doorway, angry, his eyes darting from one to the other of them in mounting suspicion. 'Why isn't the woman bound? Orders were that she should be kept tied after she'd used her mobile—'

'She was becoming worked up, started to make a fuss,' Messanger interrupted, but then quickly agreed the man's point. 'The ropes are in the kitchen, go fetch them. . . . Delyth,' he whispered to her, as soon as Rahman was out of hearing, 'for God's sake – for *our* sakes – don't resist when we tie you up. Bear with it else he'll insist on staying in here with us and I don't want that, you and I have got to talk.'

'There can't be a lot left to say between us, can there? Not after what you've just told me—'

But she broke off, hearing Rahman coming back along the corridor. Then he appeared in the doorway, a knife and lengths of thin rope in his hands.

'Shove her in that upright chair by the writing-table,' he said. 'Do it together, shall we? Muna's made fresh coffee for us, it's ready when we want it.'

They bound her firmly: ankles to chair legs, a couple of turns of rope cinching waist to chair back, then her arms pulled behind it and tied together there at the wrists. And as soon as it was done, both men went out.

Left alone then, Delyth Stanton. Lowering her head, she thought long and hard about Jake Messanger and the events and circumstances surrounding him and his arrival in London – those of which she was aware, that is – and his surprisingly swift integration into the social life of Gemma and, to a lesser extent, Jared. Then – strangely, perhaps, but incipient love, rooted as in Delyth's case it was in strong intuitive awareness and understanding of the other, may quite often defy reason – her feelings towards him crystalized into a new certainty. And when, some twenty minutes later, Jake came back into the room and went to her side, she looked up into his face and thought with startling clarity, I don't want this man to go out of my life. Therefore since it's plain to me that he's in the throes of some sort of crisis of belief, of trust, of personal identity even, which he must at once resolve – if I want him to stay in my life I've got to find out exactly what his crisis is, and then help him run clear of it: to run clear and away, be his own man. I have to think of a way. . . .

In the kitchen at safe house Alpha, Muna, a self-effacing Jordanian woman in her thirties clad in a long-sleeved blouse and an ankle-length black skirt, graceful in movement and her slender long-fingered hands deft in everything they did, served coffee to Jake Messanger and Ahmed Rahman as soon as they were settled at the cloth-covered table. Then she adjusted the black scarf covering her head and, withdrawing to a corner of the room, sat down and resumed stitching coloured silks into the embroidered cushion cover she had put down the moment they entered.

They had nothing to say to each other, the two men. But the soft beat of recorded Arab music from the CD player on a nearby shelf, its volume low, filled in the silence between them, washing over their mutual hostility but not eroding it. From one corner a blank television screen eyed them obliquely, two armchairs facing it, and along the opposite wall stood a refrigerator and an upholstered sofa.

Messanger had half finished his coffee when his mobile bleeped. He stood up to answer it, turning away from Rahman, assuming that since it was now getting on for two o'clock in the morning, his caller would be either Edara or Agent Nine.

It was Agent Nine. 'The photocopying has gone according to plan,' he reported, it having been agreed that he would keep both Edara and Messanger in close touch with the development of that part of the action. 'The agent carrying the pictures of the blueprints left Devon House ten minutes ago.'

'Which gives him an ETA at the command centre at the Red Pillars safe house of around two, allowing Edara ample time to plot the positioning of the suicide agents before briefing them.' Then, thinking it might be as well to confirm the timing for Delyth's release, Jake asked, 'So since we've got the photocopies OK, I take it the arrangements for the woman in my care here still stand? I drive her home' – he glanced at his watch – 'in an hour's time?'

For a moment Nine was silent. Then he said quietly, 'Didn't Edara tell you?'

'Tell me what?'

'A change of plan was made—'

'Hold it. I'm not alone.' Swiftly Messanger crossed the kitchen and went out into the corridor, shutting the door behind him. 'Continue now,' he said to Nine. 'What change has been made?'

'Stanton's daughter is to be killed.' Nine was enjoying himself, he had no love for the Brit. 'You hold her captive until eight o'clock, then kill her. That done, you depart from safe house Alpha immediately, leaving Rahman in charge there, and report to Edara at Red Pillars. Before leaving, you inform Rahman that a disposal vehicle will arrive there at nine o'clock.'

'*Why?*' The one word was all Messanger could get out, more would have choked him.

'Surely that is self-evident? In the interests of security, naturally.' Lightly, sarcastically, Agent Nine made a parody of the hackneyed, catch-all phrase, mocking Messanger. 'Both she and her father know too much, have seen too much to stay alive.'

'On whose orders . . . *who gave those orders?*' It had to be either Sarsen or Edara, and if it were Sarsen—'

'That, I deemed it wiser not to enquire about.'

'I do not believe you, and we speak of nothing else until you give me a straight answer.' Steel in his voice. '*Who gave those orders?*'

Game over, Nine decided. 'Edara told me it was Sarsen himself,' he said. 'It is only sense to silence them for ever,' he added, but even as he spoke, recalled that when he had asked Edara who had given the orders, Edara had evaded a direct reply, had refused to name names. 'You know as well as I do, Messanger, that it is the rule of our organization to safeguard its active service agents by the elimination of all potentially hostile witnesses.'

'But neither of the Stantons know enough to incriminate—'

'Do not call policy into question,' Agent Nine cut in sharply. 'Your job, like mine, is to carry out orders. Do that without disputation if you value your life.'

Rawlings looked at his watch: five minutes to two o'clock. Pushing his chair back from his desk he got to his feet and stood deep in thought, his mind still picking away at the brain-teasing situation which had been plaguing him since Jared Messanger had called to report the Stanton house empty, neither the professor nor his daughter at home.

Jake Messanger; Professor Stanton; Delyth Stanton, the professor's daughter: all three apparently vanished off the face of the earth, and their mobiles switched off. Yet try as he might Rawlings could think of no possible way those three could be connected, *together*, with any criminal, subversive, or terrorist activity. Messanger, yes, quite possibly: concerning him there appeared to be reason for suspicion. But Stanton? And his daughter, for Christ's sake? How the hell might *she* fit into any such scenario, a medical student home on vacation? The idea seemed utterly ludicrous.

But there the situation was, ludicrous or not: all three of them gone away into the night – and also, for some reason, incommunicado, a fact which intensified suspicion. Moving away from the desk,

Rawlings paced about his office, head down as he considered the three once more, one by one. Jake Messanger: Arab-Brit by parentage but domiciled – and working – in Syria for the last nine or ten years. But Intelligence hadn't discovered even the slightest tie-up between him and any Islamist terrorist grouping over there; and investigations into his business activities during his present trip to London had not uncovered anything open to question, he was doing the job he had come to do. Nevertheless, his half-brother suspected that he'd come over on a terrorist mission of some sort. And then there was the disappearance of Simon Croft: that stank to high heaven of foul play of some kind, and, with every day that passed, even suggested a killing? Besides, where was Jake Messanger now? His hotel, the party he'd been at, the Stanton house *and* his mobile – none of them had provided any information as to his present whereabouts, enquiries had drawn a blank at every one. And *why?* God alone knew.

And then what about Professor Stanton? Eminent in his field, currently London's delegate at the Watchman conference on security related improvement to ventilation systems in underground rail networks. A man with a blameless past, an open-book life, reportedly well known for his devotion to his only child, his daughter Delyth—

Hold it right there! Go back to Professor Stanton. To the Watchman conference's agenda, the ventilation of underground rail networks. . . . Think Japan – *Japan in 1995*.

As she sat alone and bound tightly to the chair beside the writing-table, Delyth found herself questioning her decision that it would be best to try to persuade Jake to turn his back on all his commitments and simply make a run for it, flee the country. Surely, she thought now, there must be a better way out of this? If the feeling between the two of us is to have any value, any real meaning or future, is to hold any promise at all of achieving a lasting result for either of us, then there has to be some more *positive* way to resolve the present situation. To just run away – that won't lead to anywhere worth going to; there's no merit in it bar the obvious one of *I'm* all right so to hell with everything else.

Dear God! Terrorism – this was *terrorism* she was caught up in! Suddenly, the true horror of what she'd just learned from Jake gripped her by the throat. No more than fifteen minutes ago he'd practically admitted it to her, but then the Arab had burst in before he'd had time to tell her the location and timing of whatever action he was involved in, so it was possible some sort of terrorist hit might explode here in Great Britain any place, any day or night! There'd be death and destruction— *Quiet now!* That way madness lies. *Think.* Yes, it is indeed possible that an attack is close at hand and could even be in London itself. So, the point is, what can I do to prevent it succeeding?

With a determination rooted in mortal fear, Delyth Stanton drove her mind forward in search of some constructive strategy to pursue, some course of action which had the seeds of hope in it, hope for herself, for Jake – and, quite possibly, for a great many others.

Alone in the corridor – Rahman in the kitchen behind him, Muna there also, embroidering five-petalled flowers on her cushion cover – Jake Messanger fumbled his mobile into its sheath, leaned against the wall at his back and closed his eyes. At that moment there lived in him two things only: an overpowering rage, and a bitterness that was running amok inside him clawing up all the love, respect, and trust he had ever felt for Sarsen and clamping the lot together into one obscene lump, so that within the compass of his mind and soul he could sick it up out of himself for ever – every last tainted scrap of it, *for ever* – in one tremendous jet of vomit. Be clean, then. Weaker, perhaps; cleaner, certainly.

He broke free of this catharsis. The realities of his situation – past, and now mercilessly present – were so stark and so appallingly plain to him that within a couple of minutes he broke free of mental agony and began to think rationally once more. But his priorities had changed: with his beliefs all drastically reorientated, his *élan vital* was driving him forward along new and uncharted paths.

The ley-line of betrayal stood all too clear to him, black on white: Sarsen had enticed the child with professed love, brainwashed him, then made the man his creature and used him, lying to him and deceiving him all along the line! That execution in Damascus: Sarsen had appointed him to carry it out with the express intention of then using Edara's photographs of the act to force him to accept the Zephyr mission. And he had sent him to London while keeping secret from him his true intentions towards certain people whom Jake would be required to use in the prosecution of Operation Zephyr and, in doing so, would betray to their deaths, placing them in Edara's sights as hostile witnesses who had to be eliminated. Unless. . . ?

Unless. There *was* one way out of this, wasn't there? One way to kill off Sarsen's creature and become his own man: *get out of Zephyr now, at once.* Delyth? Untie her, then the two of them could slip out into the night, she to make her own way home and he. . . ? He, to go on the run. Get cash from Gemma – yes, she could be counted on for that – then collect essentials, passport, wallet and so on, from his hotel and go into hiding. He'd have to warn Gemma and Delyth. Christ! he thought. So much to be done! I'll use Jared, get protection for them. First though, I must deal with Ahmed Rahman; allay any doubts he might be having about Delyth and me, and make sure he'll be out of action for a while.

He went back into the kitchen. As he entered, Rahman looked up at him. 'Trouble?' he asked.

'The reverse. That was Agent Nine. Everything is going according to plan. However, there has been an adjustment to the timing at the target stations.'

'Doesn't affect us.' Rahman's round, heavy-featured face registered discontent; he was bored. 'Just have to wait here, then, do we?'

'We do. You stay here with Muna. I'll watch the woman.' Messanger jerked a thumb at the two armchairs facing the television set in the far corner. 'Relax, make yourself comfortable. I'll call you when it's time.' He went out then and, glancing back in as he closed the door, caught a sideways look from Rahman to Muna, saw her meet it with a half smile . . . .

'Thank God you're back.' Delyth's voice was no more than a whisper because although by twisting her head round she could see Jake had come in alone, she could not see far enough to be sure the Arab was not just behind him, or waiting in the corridor. Jake closed the door behind him and came to her, so she went on quickly. 'Jake, I've been doing some thinking—'

'Quiet. Listen to me.' Laying a hand on her arm he spoke urgently. 'Like I told you just before Rahman came in, I've changed.'

'Yes, you said, and I believed you so—'

'Please, hear what I have to say. I've just been in touch with a senior agent in the organization. From him I learned certain things I'd never – things that made a nonsense of my life till now.' He paused a moment, a wry twist to his mouth. 'I'm not putting this very well,' he went on. 'What I mean is, I see that everything I've done in my life so far is rubbish. *I'm* rubbish – the way of life I chose, and lived, it disgusts me. Christ, I can't begin to express it, don't know—'

'Jake, leave all that for later, *all* of it. I understand what you mean, and that's enough for now. What was it you learned from this senior man?'

'I can't tell you that. I need you to believe in me without knowing. I'm going to drop out of the mission, cut myself loose from my past life – it's the only thing left for me to do. So I'll untie you and drive you—'

'But – you, Jake? What will *you* do?'

Already he was kneeling at her feet, fingers busy with the ropes around her ankles. 'I'll go to earth. Probably here in London; I know my way around. I'll make a new life—'

'Jake.' Simply his name, quietly spoken, but there was some subtly bewitching quality in her voice that made him look up at her sharply. Her eyes met his, held them: what he saw in them stopped him dead, words dying in his mouth, fingers dropping the rope because her eyes were telling him that she was with him. Not that she loved him – not yet? – but that she was close to him in a way he had never known before in his life; he knew it deep inside himself and the knowledge was wonderful to him.

'There's something I have to tell you,' she said.

'Wait until I've untied the ropes and you're free.' Should Rahman take it into his head to interrupt them he'd meet him with the gun, he decided as he set to work again.

'Thank you,' Delyth got to her feet, massaging her wrists, working her shoulders to relieve the stiffness, but going on at once, driven by a great fear and an even greater determination. She had to persuade him to deal with his situation in the way she had worked out during his absence – she *must!* 'This abduction of me and Dad, it's part of a terror plot of some kind here in Britain, isn't it?,' she said. Saw him swing away from her and grabbed his shoulder, forced him to face her. 'Don't you dare turn your back on me!' Her voice low but tight with anger, her face white, tense. 'And don't lie to me again, Jake, you and I have moved beyond that now. Agreed?'

Searching her eyes he said quietly, 'Agreed. You're on my side—'

'Not if you run away from all this.'

'Tell me a better way, and I'll take it.'

'I've thought of a better way – at least, one that seems better to me. But I'll only tell you what it is, and help you to take it, if you tell me the truth behind what's happened to Dad and me tonight. You lied to me about it earlier on – no, don't deny it, there's bigger things at stake I suspect, and no time to waste. Tell me the truth of it all, *now.*' Suddenly, she gave him a quick smile. 'We'll deal with it together then, you and I. *Trust me,* Jake.'

He did, seeing the fact that she was prepared to help him as a small glow of light – of human warmth – in the louring darkness surrounding and threatening to engulf him. Starkly, briefly, he outlined for her the plan for the Zephyr strike: gave her no names, simply informed her of the bald facts and timing of the operation.

Delyth heard him out. Faced him at first, but half turned away from him in horror when he spoke of the toxic gas Sarsen's suicide agents were scheduled to release that day. But after a moment she forced herself to face him again, to look him in the eye. The scale and nature of the terrorist action he was outlining shocked and appalled her almost beyond belief, but she heard him out without interruption because it was imperative that she retain his trust and confidence in her, for only if she had them would she have any hope of winning him over, getting him to accept the plan she had worked out. Hopefully, he would not need winning over if he was the man she'd come to think he now was, he would . . . would hold it in high honour to do what it would require of him.

'The release of the toxic gas is scheduled for twelve midday today,' he ended, and saw her grimly maintained composure disintegrate, her face for a moment bereft of all vitality, her eyes widening but – empty, frozen with shock. 'I'm sorry,' he said. He could think of nothing else to say: he had perceived in her an understanding of the rejection of human values implicit in what he was part of, and it was beyond him properly to express his feelings. I'd need a lifetime to do that, he thought.

'So that gives us ten hours or so.' Aware of the urgency, Delyth pulled herself together, brushing aside his grotesque attempt at apology. 'I only hope it'll be enough.'

'Tell me your plan.'

She laid it on the line. 'If you simply run away from it all,' she said to him, 'you'll be a hunted man for the rest of your life, I imagine – hunted by both sides, your organization *and* British Intelligence. Whereas my way, you'll—'

'Just tell me. I'll make my own decision.'

'Fair enough. Here it is. You've just told me you have full knowledge of the plans for this Operation Zephyr. Well, that's an ace in your hand: use it!'

'How?'

'You *barter* with it. Take it to MI5 and—'

'No way! For one thing there isn't time—'

'So you use that fact to get them moving!' Delyth's face was alight now with hope and belief. 'Don't you see? If you're ever going to have any kind of life from now on you need *allies*. So you take your information – *insider's* information – straight to MI5 and trade it to them. You give them all you know about Zephyr; they promise you protection and, in time, a new identity.'

Jake Messanger smiled wryly. 'Great idea. Only thing is, just how do I get to anyone high enough up in MI5 who'll both listen to me and, in the event of him actually believing me, possesses the necessary clout to take the sort of high-level, wide-ranging and urgent action required to smash Zephyr in the time we have left? MI5 would demand proof of all I claim, dismiss it as a hoax.'

'Not if you do it through Jared.'

'*Jared?*' Furiously, he swung away from her, reaching for his jacket. 'I'm off now. This is a waste of time and dangerous to both of us. Jared would never lift a finger to help me; he hates my guts, always has done—'

'So he's got all the more reason to be eager to bring you in! Besides, think of the kudos it'd bring him.'

'He's too junior anyway; no one would listen to him – no one who mattered.' But he was facing her now, intent on what she was saying.

'You're wrong there. He's been intelligence-gathering for MI5 for the last few months, and with him being ambitious to move into mainstream intelligence work it would be grist to his mill to—'

'Is that true? He's been upgraded?'

Delyth saw it in his eyes then: wariness there, yes, but hope also. And seeing it, she pressed home her attack. 'He told me so himself. Shouldn't have, of course, but did. It means he has contacts, doesn't it? MI5 people he can reach, and who'll listen to him? He can get you *listened to,* Jake!'

For a few seconds longer their eyes held, each seeking confirmation and commitment in the other. Jake found them first.

'All right, I'll do it your way,' he said. 'Let's you and I get out of here quick, make our plans once we're outside. Got your mobile?'

'Right here.' She slipped it into her bag.

'We'll use your Fiesta.' Taking out his gun he moved towards the door. 'Don't come into the corridor until I beckon you out, and be as quiet as you can.' Then, gun in hand he eased the door open and stepped into the corridor – only to spot Rahman at the far end of it. He was closing the kitchen door behind him, surely had to be intending to come and check up on the captive.

He ducked back into the room. 'Rahman's coming!' he whispered to Delyth, 'get back in the chair quick, sit as you were.' Then as she did so, he shut the door and waited for Rahman to one side of it, his shoulders pressed back against the wall, gun ready in his right hand.

Heard Rahman's footsteps approaching. Heard him pause for a

moment outside the door of the captive's room, then he opened it and came in – the shirt-jeans-trainers-clad figure padded forward towards the woman in the chair – *was clear of the door.*

In one smooth, surging movement Messenger stepped in behind Rahman, shot him once high in the right shoulder then, as with a strangled cry the Arab pitched forward to lie prone, arms outflung, one side of his face pillowed on the carpet, closed in on him fast and clouted him across the head with the butt of the gun. Swiftly then, he relieved him of his mobile, switched it off and slipped it into his pocket.

'He isn't dead?' Delyth was at his shoulder, her face white. 'He'll live. We'll gag him, tie his legs together and his arms behind his back, then leave him lie.'

They worked together, using the ropes which had bound Delyth. 'What about the woman Muna?' she whispered, as she knelt to tie Rahman's ankles.

'She'll assume he's stayed in here with us. Whatever, she'll never dare take decisive action on her own.'

No more words passed between them. When the job was done, they went out into the corridor and Messanger locked the door behind them, took out the key and handed it to Delyth.

'Put this in your bag,' he said, then turned to open the front door. 'Hopefully, now Rahman's out of the way we should have at least an hour's start on any pursuit. If it occurs to Muna to go and check on where he's got to, she'll find the door locked, conclude that he and I are both inside guarding you, and go back to her embroidery.'

'But suppose someone – someone on their side, I mean – calls him on his mobile?'

'Then they'll find it switched off. I can't see any way round that. Which is where luck comes in. We'll just have to hope that if Edara does ring him, he won't read too much into the fact he's not answering.'

Chapter 15

London Saturday 14 August 02.50 hours

In the study at the front of his house Professor Stanton was near to breaking point. Never before had he known such utter despair, such desolation. The Arab inside Devon House had sworn to him – sworn on the Quran – that Delyth would be brought home by three o'clock, but it was nearly that now and there was still no sign of her. So, where was she? Why wasn't she back with him yet? Why? The questions were tearing him to pieces because the only answers to them that his imagination could postulate were past enduring – and there was nothing he could do about it. Through the hours of waiting, that last thought was a kind of death to him. A living death.

Earlier, the two guards who had driven the professor home had escorted him straight through into the study then at once checked all of its lined, red velvet curtains, making sure that no light shone through to the outside world. Then one had left to return to base, turning out the hall lights as he went. The other, a lean, cadaverous-faced Brit, had sat down in an upright chair near the bureau to the left of the door, telling Stanton to make himself comfortable since they had some waiting ahead of them.

'Not very long, surely?' the professor had said then.

But the Brit had merely grinned. 'You never can tell, y'know, about time,' he had answered. 'Time's got a mind of its own, I reckon. It goes on doing its own thing all the while. Whereas the five minutes a patient spends in his dentist's waiting-room before treatment seems to him to go on for ever, to the bloke knocking back his pint in his local, hell, five minutes is gone in a flash.' And then as the seconds went by, crawled by, for the professor, it became apparent that the guard had a gift for relaxing as opportunity offered: he sat at ease, seemingly laid-back.

When the hands of his watch showed five to three, Stanton, who had seated himself at his desk near the front windows and was trying to occupy his mind by conning over a recently received historical memoir, looked up from it and challenged his guard.

'How much longer?' he demanded. 'Can't you contact someone higher up and ask him where my daughter is?'

'Sorry, mate, no can do. More than my life's worth to question the big wheels.'

'But the arrangement was—'

'Whatever it was, you sure won't get her back till they've got what they want.' A grin came on the bony face. 'And could be we aren't quite that far yet. You gave us the means to the end we want, sure, but that's only the start, see. I reckon our show isn't over yet, not by a long chalk.'

'But I gave you access! What else have I got to give you, for God's sake?'

'Time, Professor: time to be sure you don't wreck our spectacular by reporting what's happened to your police.'

'I gave you my word I wouldn't do that! I swore I'd wait—'

'Sure you did. Not good enough for my boss, though, that isn't. Him not being a bloke who trusts anyone easily, he decided it'd be wiser to slap up *two* checkpoints to stop you breaking your word, the second being to hold on to your girl until a few hours after our mission's climaxed.' The Brit's eyes were gleaming with malice now: he was entirely sure of himself and it was amusing him to taunt his prisoner, it helped to pass the time. 'See, he'd reason that while you would quite likely be willing to lay down your own life for what you doubtless consider "the greater good" of your country, you would emphatically *not* be able to find it in your heart to lay down that of your lovely and talented daughter to that same end.'

Cut to the heart, his last hope taken from him, the professor got unsteadily to his feet and stumbled away from his desk, his head down to hide the tears half blinding him. He simply could not be still any longer; he had to move about or he'd go utterly to pieces. And then as he passed by the curtained window he lifted both arms and, elbows out, pressed the heels of his hands against his forehead as if seeking to drive out the devils tormenting his brain.

'Get back from those bloody curtains!' Out of his seat in a flash, the guard grabbed Stanton's arm, jerked him away from the window, clouted him across the cheek then manhandled him to a nearby armchair and thrust him down into it. 'You bloody stir out of there and I'll hog-tie you so fucking tight you won't be able to lift a finger, you fucking bastard.'

Stanton barely heard him: to him, what was said was no more than a spate of words spoken at random; there was no meaning in them. Shutting his mind against them he accepted his own inability to influence the outcome of this nightmare that had somehow sucked him into itself, and steeled his mind to accept the situation and – wait. The hardest thing of all, to him that night.

In fact, however, the professor *had* influenced the outcome of his present nightmare. Unwittingly and unintentionally, that raised arm of his had caught against the edge of one of the heavy, window-masking curtains and flicked it clear of the one meeting it. Only an instant passed before it fell back into place. But during that instant a long streak of light flared out from the study of the Stanton house, a sure sign – were anyone to be watching from outside – that there were people within.

Once well away from safe house Alpha, Messanger turned the Fiesta into a side road, parked and switched off. Then for a few seconds Delyth and he sat quiet, each wrapped in their own thoughts – and yet together, since for each the other was so closely involved in what was soon to be done and what, surely momentous but as yet unknown and beyond conjecture, might come of it. Jake had made his decision. Nevertheless, now the moment was at hand for him to actually *act* on that decision, he found his mind suddenly clouded by memories. Pictures from past times raced across the eye of his brain.

Incidents showing the kindness and understanding with which Sarsen had assuaged his grief and unhappiness during the dark years following his father's second marriage, when his stepmother had, with malice aforethought, excluded him from the new Messanger family; of his mother La'ali, and happy days spent with her in Bahrain; of Sarsen as his mentor and role model while he went through medical school.

And Delyth: she at first racked with misery at the thought of the pressure her father had had to endure, and of what he and she together had just done, but then stiffening her newfound resolve with the fact that she and Jake were now on course to frustrate the terrorist strike of which he was – no, *had been*, no longer *was!* – such a vital part.

'Time to act,' she said quietly.

And at once Jake picked up his mobile from the dash, punched out Jared's number, and found it answered, his half-brother's voice loud and clear along the line as he identified himself.

'Jake here – no, don't interrupt, just listen. What I have to say is life or death and not for argument. You were right in your suspicions of me, but there's no time to go into that now. I'm told you've got access to blokes with clout in M15. Is that right?'

'Yep, it's kosher.'

'Then you must put me through directly to someone with the authority to act immediately and with extreme force. I have detailed information on an imminent terrorist strike here in London.'

'Targeted at?'

'Three Underground stations.'

'When?'

'Midday today.'

'*Christ*! How much do you know?'

'Everything.'

'Come off it, you've—'

'Named targets, positioning of sharp-end agents, logistics of the entire op, safe houses. Put me through to some high-up, Jared, and *do it now*.'

'Hold the line – no wait! Where are you speaking from?'

Jake told him. Jared must have moved fast then, Jake thought, for in less than a minute—

'Rawlings here,' said a voice in his ear. 'Superintendent, MI5.' However, Rawlings had been listening in on Jared's line and had realized that, via Jake Messanger, they were quite possibly on to something big. So after a few searching questions he put him straight through to his own immediate boss, Bob Allen, whom he had earlier provided with full information on the security situation re Jake Messanger.

'Allen here.' The new voice down the line came to Jake, clear, authoritative. 'Give me the sites of those target stations first, then I'll want the gen on the nature of the attacks, personnel and structure of the enemy command and, most importantly, the location of their operational base for the strike itself. Once I've got that last I'll organize a command HQ for our counter-attack within striking distance of theirs, and get a rapid reaction unit in position ready to take them out. Skin your info down to the basics – you know what I'll need, you're no rookie to the game. As soon as I've got all I want from you, I'll hand you back to Rawlings. He'll get you to clarify certain points for us while I decide where to locate our action HQ. When I've done that he'll give you directions on how to get there. I want you at that HQ, in person. By then I'll have reported to the chief and we'll be setting up the counter-op. You'll be debriefed there and, from then on, stay on hand to advise on relevant details as the situation develops.'

'First you'll want proof of my—'

'Later. You're not unknown to us. We've got enough on you already to go ahead now you've come over to us.'

Thus, sitting tense with concentration behind the wheel of the white Fiesta with Delyth Stanton at his side and the glow of the nearest street-lamp at his back, his face mercifully in shadow, Jake Messanger set in train the process of selling Sarsen – also and of far greater immediate importance, Operation Zephyr itself – down the river.

By 02.30 hours Edara, clad all in black, polo-neck, chinos and a light-weight drill jacket, had established himself in the war room on the ground floor of Red Pillars, the organisation's top-security safe house situated some three miles from the centre of Uxbidge. When upgraded to active service status, as now for the climax of Zephyr, it was staffed from a ten-strong élite cadre of hard-proven loyalty commanded by a seasoned intelligence officer. Red Pillars had a secret, built-in escape route for use, by operational commanders only, in an emergency. This functioned thus: the adjacent house on one side of it was also the property of the organization, and in the Red Pillars war room a bookcase against the party wall between the two concealed a six-foot door connecting them. To the casual eye this presented no great barrier, being merely a standard wooden interior door. However, behind it lay a second and by no means standard one constructed of solid steel. Without lock or handle, its existence known only to mission commanders and the captain of Red Pillar's security cadre, this was operated by two push-buttons, one of them lying flush to the underside of the table in the war room, the other in the front room of the support house, beside the steel door.

Within five minutes of sitting down at the central table, Edara had contacted the guard captain on his mobile to check that all was as it should be with the security arrangements at Red Pillars. He did not do this because he had any suspicions to the contrary; he did it solely because it was required procedure by an incoming mission commander engaged in ongoing direct action.

'. . . armed guards in position.' The captain, at his desk in the support house next door, was nearing the end of his check-list of security precautions for the final-action phase of Zephyr. 'Steel sliding door activated to operate on your given signal from war room. Getaway transport together with drivers in place in side street running alongside this building, ready for your use in the event of emergency pull-out.'

Edara pronounced himself satisfied, cut the call, settled his gun and shoulder holster to greater comfort and then prepared to study and go to work on the ground plans of the target underground stations, which he had set out on the table, beside the three photocopies of Stanton's blueprints delivered to him earlier from Agent Nine at Devon House. Before starting on that, however, he sat back and ran a quick mental check on the present state of Operation Zephyr.

Abduction of Stanton: completed, and the professor now under guard at his residence. Seizure of Delyth Stanton: completed, and she now in safe house Alpha, held there under duress by Messanger and one subsidiary and scheduled to die by Messanger's hand once her usefulness as enforcer of her father's continuing silence comes to an end. Agent Nine: now in safe house Four in North London, his duty to keep check on the observers operating at the three target sites, he to report to me at regular intervals on the general situation there and, later, on the arrival of the suicide agents.

So, all action was proceeding as planned. Hawk-face as carved in stone, Edara ran his mind over the respective responsibilities of his lieutenants Messanger and Nine, and decided it would be wise to contact the former and find out how Stanton's daughter was responding to her present situation.

However, he discovered Messanger's mobile was switched off. Waited a few minutes, then tried again: still no reply. His fierce face closed in on itself and, after a moment, he called the number of the subsidiary agent at safe house Alpha, Ahmed Rahman. But that also failed to elicit any response. Now, abruptly, Edara's whole demeanour changed. Pushing himself to his feet he stood stiff and straight, eyes narrowed to slits in concentrated, sharply focused thought, every nerve in his body alive with tension: something must be wrong at Alpha, where by rights the action should have presented no difficulty whatsoever. So what was Messanger doing? One fact was blindingly obvious – he was not following the set plan! Now, Edara's jealous hatred of the Brit Sarsen favoured as his successor added fuel to growing suspicion. Could it be that Messanger was working to some agenda of his own? Might it really be possible that he had turned against Sarsen? Were that to be so, the Brit had it in his power to destroy Zephyr. Stanton's daughter was under his hand, and the two of them together could alert British Intelligence.

No! Surely not? Such a possibility . . . it would be too monstrous a betrayal. And yet, how else to account for the silence at safe house Alpha? *How else?*

Doubt took root in Edara's mind, and he decided to act. Sitting down again, he called Agent Nine. 'Events have led me to conclude . . . to consider the possibility that Messanger has turned traitor,' he said to him, coldly matter-of-fact.

The statement rocked Nine, but he picked up on it fast. 'General alert, then?' he asked tautly. 'And we may have to abort Zephyr—'

'*Never!* Besides, it is not sure yet. I'll question him. If we act fast we may be able to take him at Alpha.'

'He's still there, then?'

'I see no reason why he should not be. He has switched off his mobile, but he could be operating from there using that of the Stanton woman. I want him here. I must talk to him face to face, I will know then. You will proceed at once to Alpha—'

'What of Rahman? He's—'

'His mobile also is switched off. You have the pass key to the house?'

'To all safe houses operational tonight.'

'Hand over to Ramadan where you are, until you return. Don't use your own car, take one from the pool. Contact me from Alpha, as soon as you've summed things up and *without fail.* Understood?'

'Of course.' But Nine was already on his way.

And in Red Pillars, Edara, satisfied that Agent Nine would soon report to him on the situation at safe house Alpha, set to work again on the ground plans of the target stations, using the photocopies of Stanton's blueprints, and employing the specialized know-how he'd acquired a month earlier for this explicit purpose from a French engineer flown in from Damascus, to pinpoint and mark on them the exact position at which each martyr must establish himself in order to ensure that as many enemy deaths as possible accompanied his own.

Just my fucking luck: pitched into a one-man surveillance stint outside an empty house, and for God knows how long! Resentfully, Detective Constable Jim Smith stared across the starlit lawn at the black-dark façade of Professor Stanton's house. There can't have been more than forty minutes since Jared Messanger left here to report back to Rawlings and me arriving, he thought, and it'd take one helluva slice of luck for anyone to have got into the house during that time, so what's the point of me being here? I've checked on that back window Jared busted to get in and do his search. No one home, he told the boss then. And for sure no one's gone in since I've been here. 'Keep in cover and keep your head down, Smith,' Rawlings said to me, 'and if anyone either goes into the place or seems to be loitering with intent outside it, you don't go in after him, you call in to me and report it.' So here I'm stuck, keeping in cover and keeping my distance as ordered, and shit-boring it fucking well is.

Nice enough night, though. Warmish, dry, bit of a moon sometimes, starlight. All rather lovely round here, really. Sort of area Amanda would like, lawn and flowerbeds round the houses.

Twenty-five years old, Detective Constable Smith: a burly, dark-haired young man, fit and agile, a keen sportsman, and no slouch at the job, either, in fact often too much the other way, some reports on him criticizing him as given to taking headstrong, risky action on his own initiative. His girlfriend was no help to him in that respect: quite a high-flier herself and ambitious for him to achieve, she was continually spurring him on with '*Have a go*, darling! Get yourself *noticed*. It'll pay off, you'll see!'

Wouldn't mind sitting down in that swing-seat over at the edge of the grass, take the weight off my feet for a bit. Evening off tomorrow, maybe take Amanda for a meal at that country pub she's so crazy about.

Hey, get focused! Light showed over at the house, there must be someone inside! Second window left of the front door: for a split second a slit of light showed, as if maybe a curtain was pushed aside but then shoved back into place quick.

Reckon I'll get in, see what's going on. There's that back window Jared bust, I can reach in and open it, no sweat. Hang on, though, that's just what Rawlings said *not* to do. I'm supposed to report back to him. But shit! If I do, and suggest I go in, then ten to one he'll tell me to wait for back-up. So – which? Be a good boy and call in? Or act now, explain later?

Within four minutes of glimpsing that flick of light between drawn curtains, Smith had reached in through the broken back window, unfastened the catch and pushed it open, hauled himself up and over the sill and dropped quietly to the floor. Hazed moonlight went with him across the kitchen he found himself in, but then, as he pulled its door closed behind him, darkness engulfed him. Shutting his eyes he stood dead still for half a minute . . . and on opening them discovered he was in what was obviously a dining-room, the polished surface of a central table gleaming dully in the half-light from a window, blurred shapes of chairs ranged either side of it.

Enough! The room where the light had showed was at the front, not here. Taking out his torch he switched it to pencil beam then advanced swiftly but warily onward through the house, using the torch only when necessary, alert for enemy personnel on guard against possible intruders. Light on his feet, strong hands smoothly persuasive of doors and their handles, DC Smith moved ghostlike through the night-quiet of the Stanton house.

Stopped dead: *voices!* Whispery through the darkness enclosing him, half heard but unmistakable for what it was, the murmurous susurration of men conversing. Two men only . . . one sounding virile and confident, the other tired, worn out. No words distinguishable, though, so moving one cautious step at a time Smith advanced towards the source of the sounds he was hearing. Opening another door, the voice getting louder as he did so, he stepped through into what was obviously a corridor and saw, to his right and facing him across it, a line of bright light showing beneath the bottom of the door faintly visible there.

Got you! he exulted, and padded closer, stood listening. But silence had fallen beyond the door. No movement audible, no talk. Slipping his hand inside his jacket, he felt for his gun, but even as he did so remembered he was unarmed, his orders to observe and report in. Hell, if Stanton is in there under guard his minder would be armed – mind*ers*, perhaps?

No way of knowing, bar going in. Could be it's simply Stanton in there with a friend, he thought, but there's no way of knowing that either, unless— and that's *verboten*, the boss said. So I'd best lie low, keep quiet, and listen to what they're saying. For a couple of minutes, anyway. There's at least two blokes in there and they were talking a while ago, no reason they shouldn't start up again, give me some pointers to report to Rawlings. Mustn't stop here too long, though, any moment one of 'em might take it into his head to come out.

Movement in there. Footsteps . . . getting closer – no, he's stopped . . . but he can't be too far from the door now, so see you're ready for him—

'Hey, Stanton, you ever met this bloke Jake Messanger?'

The words came clearly to the man in the corridor. *Christ!* he thought, the professor really is in there.

'C'mon! the voice went on. 'Don't just sit there staring at me like some fucking half-wit, Prof! I asked you. . . .'

But Smith did not stay to hear more. The words 'Stanton' and 'Prof' signalled mission accomplished, so he should get out of there and make his report to Rawlings.

But then as he reached the door into the kitchen he halted, struck by the possibilities inherent in his present situation. Shit, I'm really on to something here! he thought. This is big stuff. I'm pretty sure there's only the two blokes in that room, Stanton and his guard. Suppose I nick his guard – do it off my own bat – I'd get myself noticed all right then, wouldn't I? Besides, if I *don't* go in now we might lose out altogether. That guard might get orders to take the prof elsewhere, or God knows what, something worse, perhaps?

Nah. Best not? Do that, and whatever I say Rawlings'll probably slap that 'headstrong' label on me again – more likely 'insubordinate' this time, which'd really choke off the promotion I'm in line for. So do it by the book, Smith! Get out of here quick and quiet and call in to Rawlings for back-up. Tempting, though, the other. . . ?

Chapter 16

London, late Friday night

'Has he promised you immunity from prosecution? Whoever he is, did he give you that?'

Delyth's voice was taut with strain but as Jake turned to her, mobile still in hand, he saw in her eyes a pledge that whatever he had done she'd stay with him, would support his every action, and for a moment his world narrowed down to himself and her, alone together. Putting out one hand he ran his fingers lightly, briefly over the scar on her cheek. 'I love you,' he said. 'And no, I have not received any promise of immunity from prosecution.'

'You didn't ask, did you?'

'No.'

'Why not? You need—'

'What I need is to destroy Operation Zephyr,' he cut in sharply, turning away from her to the street outside but not seeing it, seeing only – inside his head and clear in every detail, in every cruel line of mouth and jaw, in hooded eyes – Edara's face. But then – and the nearest streetlamp behind the Fiesta, so his face in shadow – he smiled a little and, with cool deliberation, rubbed out that picture and put Delyth's in its place, sketching it in with swift, sure strokes, knowing its every detail by heart. And when he had it completed he asked softly, 'Do you understand? About Zephyr?'

After a moment, and very quietly, 'I believe I do. Now, I believe I do.' Then her voice hardened. 'MI5 – they've called you in?' she asked, staring out through the windscreen at the dead-of-night empty road. 'You'll go there at once?'

'For debriefing. Not to their main offices. A man called Allen's setting up a temporary HQ for the duration of their counter-attack at a police complex outside Uxbridge – only five miles or so from here, near Hillingdon Heath. I'll take you to Gemma now.'

'One thing first, Jake. I've held it back till now because . . . well, the terrorist strike's the priority here. But, what about my father?' Her voice was anguished but she did not look at him. 'Now he's done what was required of him, will he be safe? They won't . . . kill him?'

Oh Christ! he thought. What to say to that? When Edara discovers I've left safe house Alpha and taken Delyth with me, God alone knows what he'll do, or order done. He'll turn rabid wild, might lash out anywhere, any way. But I have to give her hope, she's got a right to that. 'He'll be home by now,' he said evenly, keeping his eyes on the street outside the Fiesta – no one out there, London was asleep. 'He's served his purpose, Edara will dismiss him from his mind. So the deal they made will stand, your father will be under guard but—'

'Thank you.' The words were quietly spoken, and then she sat silent.

'So I'll take you to Gemma,' he said, after a moment, 'then go on from there to Uxbridge.'

'Can't I . . . go home?'

'Better not, yet. I've got a feeling you'll be safer at Jared's place, with Gemma.'

'Safer from what?'

'I don't know. It's just a feeling.'

'All right. Sorry, I'm wasting time. Let's go, Jake. . . . Gemma and me together – yes, I'm happy with that.'

The roads being quiet, Agent Nine made good time to safe house Alpha. Parking the Renault a good fifty yards short he hurried along to it, turned in through the gate. Finding the front door locked he used his pass key to open it and went inside. Closing the door quietly behind him, he stood in the corridor for the moment, listening. But he heard nothing, there was no sound at all from the kitchen where Ahmed Rahman and the maidservant should be.

'Rahman! Come up here!' he shouted in Arabic, using a master-to-slave imperative. Got no response, so tried the door on his right, where Messanger should be holding the Stanton woman prisoner, but found it locked. Drawing his handgun then, he went on along the corridor to the kitchen. Didn't call out again and moved swiftly but warily now, his finger curled round the trigger of the small but lethal, silenced gun.

The kitchen door was shut. Light showed beneath it. Putting his ear against it he listened for any sound within. But hearing nothing, flung the door wide open, slammed it back against the wall and stepped inside, sweeping his gun from side to side across the kitchen.

No one to be seen. Agent Nine froze, feeling out the silence with his senses, searching it for lurking danger. Suddenly, briefly, a faint rustling whispered across the silence – ceased. But he'd identified its source and, weapon at the ready, stepped swiftly across to the refrigerator against the opposite wall.

Found her there. Muna, crouched on the floor trying to make herself as small as possible, her back against the wall and the black scarf pulled up over her head, one slim-fingered hand holding it to cover her face.

'Where is Rahman, woman?' Agent Nine demanded. Got no answer so leaned down, thrust aside her hand, grabbed the scarf and jerked it from her face. 'Rahman, tell me where he is,' he ordered, and now there was a quality in his voice that made it infinitely terrifying, a deadly threat implicit in it, and in him.

Her eyes screwed up tight, she pushed herself hard back against the wall and made no sound. Seeing her paralysed by fear, Agent Nine struck out at her – yanked her half-upright with his left hand, pistol-whipped her across the face then released her. 'Now, *answer me!*'

Slumped sack-like on the floor Muna turned her bloodied face up to him, tears streaming down her cheeks. 'Ahmed . . . he went . . . went into the room at the front of the house, sir. He must have. . . stayed in there, sir.'

'Did you go there, call through the door to him?'

'Yes, sir. Two times I went . . . two times, sir. But Ahmed . . . he didn't answer me. But I am not . . . I don't know about these things, sir. Ahmed does; he is an important man. Why should he answer me if he does not want to?'

'The other man, and the woman who came here with him. Are they still in the room?'

'I do not know, sir. The door is locked. I have no way to know.'

But the man whose gun was smeared with her blood had swung away and gone out of the kitchen. Sinking back into herself Muna pulled her scarf back over her head, thanking Allah for the given mercy of the man's departure. Then, huddled down into her corner, into the comfort of known kitchen wall and refrigerator, she dismissed from her mind all thought of outside people and their affairs; her own pain and fear were quite enough for her to deal with. After a few minutes, she made a quiet prayer to Allah not to allow the man with the gun to come back to her – *ever* – then struggled to her feet and shuffled across to the sink to rinse the taste of blood from the inside of her mouth and bathe her cheeks. When she felt truly clean once more, inside as well as out, she sat down and carried on with her embroidery, finding great solace and great beauty in the colours of the silks and the pretty patterns she was crafting on her cushion cover.

Agent Nine gave no more thought to her. Going swiftly to the front room he used his pass key – it slid unhindered into the lock, he noticed, there was no key on the inside – and went in. He saw Rahman immediately: he was lying face-down on the floor, gagged, trussed up like a goat, and there was blood all over his shoulder and across his head. Cursing, Nine cut him free with scissors from the writing-desk. Then, as he began manhandling him over on to his back, Rahman stirred and, groaning, using his elbows and feet, pushed himself up into a sitting position.

'Messanger and the woman – where are they?' Straightening up, holding back the fury coursing through him with an iron will, Agent Nine spat the question at the wounded man.

'Gone.' Rahman peered up at him through slitted, swollen eyelids.

'I need a doctor.'

'You'll get one later. Think now: did you hear them say anything to indicate their plans, where they would go?' Then, seeing the sweaty, tousled head jerk backwards as a spasm of agony shook his body, Nine leaned down and hit him across the face with the back of his hand. '*Speak!*'

Cramming the scream of pain back down his throat, Rahman fell back on one elbow then dropped his head, cowering before his boss, and told him the truth, praying that Agent Nine would accept it as such.

'I heard nothing of their plans,' he said, and shook his head to try to clear it. 'Messanger lay in wait for me beside the door, then shot me from behind the moment I was inside. I had no chance—'

'They drove here in the Fiesta, as laid down? The white Fiesta, the woman's car?'

'Yes, they parked—' But Rahman broke off, aware that Agent Nine had turned away and was heading for the door. 'Sir, I need a doctor!' he cried, fear surging inside him as he realized his boss was about to leave him alone, wasn't going to call in Zephyr's back-up medics. 'I'm still bleeding, I need something for the pain—'

But Nine was gone, leaving the door open behind him. From the moment he heard Rahman admit he had no knowledge of Messanger's immediate intentions, he was a man driven by one over-riding purpose: to pursue Messanger *to the death*. Because the half-Brit had indeed turned traitor: there was no other construction to be put on what had happened at safe house Alpha. Messanger must have ditched Zephyr, he thought. He's gone on the run, taking with him Stanton's daughter, the operation's prized lever for ensuring her father's silence concerning the blueprints, which silence *must* continue if both the success of the hit and the safety of its personnel are to be achieved. When it came to the crunch, Zephyr proved a strike too close to home for Messanger: his father's country, into which his blood-kin recently welcomed him so warmly, has claimed him for its own. . . . That was a state of affairs which chimed in with both Edara and Agent Nine's set-in-stone belief that, in life, it was *the father's* blood that counted. The seed of the father determined a man's ethos and, therefore, his allegiances. The mother, while vital to his material well-being, was simply the vessel there to give him birth and then safeguard and nourish the infant until he grew old enough to stand on his own two feet, a young man ready for *his father's* guidance and instruction.

Seated now at the wheel of the Renault, his mind cold and clear, Agent Nine analysed the situation. By his own actions proven an apostate, Messanger had to be killed, and it should be done as soon as possible. Was it a possibility that the Brit would go to MI5? No. For one thing it was inconceivable that he would betray Sarsen so utterly; for another, even if he considered doing so, he would not do it while Professor Stanton, Delyth's father, was in Edara's hands, his life immediately forfeit if British anti-terrorict forces moved against Zephyr. Speed being of the essence, Nine decided he would for the moment ignore Edara's order to report to him at once on the situation he had found at safe house Alpha. Instead, he would act on an idea which had just flashed into his mind: a gut-intuition that Messanger's next move would be to run to his half-sister for assistance. He'd need money, a temporary refuge from pursuit, help in buying airline tickets, or whatever. Reports from surveillance agents had shown the two to be fast friends, a relationship based on their childhood closeness to each other. So for the moment, Nine thought, I'll play my own game without reference to Edara: I'll drive to Jared Messanger's house where his sister is staying, get into cover and wait there: then if my guess is right and he does go to her, or if I find he's already in the house, I will kill him there and then. That way, Zephyr will triumph in spite of him.

However, by a twist of fate, as he drove along the night-quiet streets close to safe house Alpha, Agent Nine passed by a parked car he recognized as Delyth Stanton's. A white Fiesta with a roof rack, the very vehicle in which she had been abducted, it was standing kerbside midway between two streetlamps. As he passed it, he observed that there were two people sitting in the front seats, almost certainly a man and a woman. Being no believer in far-fetched coincidences, he drove one block further on then worked his way back and parked on the opposite side of the carriageway, some twenty yards behind the white car.

You are mine now, Messanger, he thought, mine for the taking! However, this is not a good place in which to make my strike, I see a café – lights, people – at the far end of the street. I'm sure you're not going to sit there all night. Doubtless the two of you are discussing your plans, so I will sit you out. When you move on, I will follow you.

Agent Nine did not have long to wait. In less than ten minutes the Fiesta slid smoothly out on to the carriageway and drove off. Side lights only switched on, the black Renault followed it. Always keeping its quarry in sight but never getting too close to it, the black car stalked the white, a shadow amongst the myriad shadows of the night.

As he drove to Jared's house, Jake Messanger was too engrossed in his own thoughts and plans to notice that although the black Renault on the road behind him vanished from his sight from time to time, it always reappeared among any vehicles behind him.

Inside Red Pillars, the war room opened off to the left of its small entrance hall in which one guard was stationed. Opposite it across the hall lay the prayer room, set aside for the use of the three suicide agents who were scheduled to release the toxic gas inside the target stations. Ascetically furnished, and with copies of the Quran on each of its three reading desks, this was a private place for their rest, prayer, or contemplation prior to their departure on their mission.

In the war room, Edara was sitting halfway down the long side of the table in the middle of the room. Facing him across it stood three chairs, empty as yet, awaiting the arrival of the suicide agents. In front of him were two small piles of papers. One comprised the three ground-plans of the underground stations to be targeted, on each of which he had marked the position from which the toxic gas should be released; the other, one for each martyr, a fulsome commendation of the man in question, naming him and signed by Sarsen, for his coming act of dedicated self-sacrifice. Getting to his feet and going round to the other side of the table, Edara placed in front of each chair the appropriate ground-plan and the personalized eulogy.

Then, resuming his seat, he immersed himself in the logistics in place for the post-climax dispersal of all agents working on Operation Zephyr: many complex and diverse exercises were involved in that sphere of the mission, and from time to time he contacted various key sleepers and commanders on the ground in order to clarify or check up on some vital point. This task was to him a labour of love: Zephyr was his cherished brain-child, a spectacularly destructive terror strike in the very heart of enemy territory, painstakingly nurtured to maturity over the last two years. Obsessed by it, Edara gave no thought to Jake Messanger, or to Agent Nine whom he had despatched to deal with him. Zephyr is on the last lap of its long march and nothing can stop it now, he thought, the glow of triumph on him. *Nothing.*

Chapter 17

Agent Nine was familiar with the area in which Jared Messanger lived. In the early days of the planning for Zephyr, he had run Edara's surveillance exercise on the Brit, so he had recced his house and its environs in person. And now as he saw the Fiesta ahead of him turn into a road he recognized, he smiled to himself: he had been right, Jake Messanger was intending to seek assistance from his half-sister. Aware that the house in question was the second one back from the corner the Fiesta had just turned, Nine parked before he reached it.

Got out and moved fast then. Went on along the pavement, rounded the corner – and stopped dead, pulling into the shelter of the conifer hedge alongside him on sight of the Fiesta no more than twenty-five yards ahead of him with Messanger getting out of it and his passenger already on the pavement. She was indeed Stanton's daughter, he saw now, but he had no interest in her. *Messanger* was his target, and must be killed before he had time to go to ground, to fade into a British background, possibly never to be caught.

Watching from his cover Nine saw the two of them go up the short path and into the house – Messanger had a key, he observed. What will the son of a dog do now? he wondered. Will he leave Delyth Stanton here with his half-sister and himself come out again? To fly out of the country immediately? Or to hide out with some contact?

No! He must not escape us! Like I thought, I must and will kill him here and now. Take him unawares while he is still confident that he is safe from us, that it is too soon for us to have discovered his treachery. So shall I break in, kill him in the house? No, that carries the risk that if he's decided to go on the run at once, even as I'm looking for him inside he might elude me and get away. I'll give him half an hour: if he's still inside by then I'll have to risk going in after him. Meanwhile I must be ready to take him if he comes out. I'll get into cover over by the front door: the bushes growing either side of it are tall enough and thick enough to screen me and to hide what's going on from the neighbours. This isn't the sort of area whose inhabitants go out as early as this, but one can't be too sure. Yes, it should be easy enough: my gun is silenced, and he will not be expecting trouble.

Slipping in through the front gate, Agent Nine darted along the path and concealed himself amongst the flower-studded foliage of the shrub growing to the left of the door, pressing himself close in against the house wall. And while he lay in wait he noticed that the flowers on the bush were pale yellow and had a sweet perfume, but although he remembered in passing that one of his surveillance agents had told him the name of the bush, he could not call to mind what it was.

In the hall of Jared's house Jake Messanger took off his jacket, tossed it over a chair and turned to Delyth. 'Best you wait here; I'll go upstairs and wake Gemma—'

'Why are you whispering?' A smile sudden on her face, surprising him. 'This is friendly territory, we're safe now.'

Her smile reached deep into him and he relaxed – a little. 'There's a great deal to be done before that last is true,' he said sombrely.

'So why not leave me to do the explaining here? You go straight off to Allen, MI5.'

'No. I owe it to her—'

'And just *why* do you owe me anything?' Gemma's question cut in sharp and clear and, turning towards the flight of stairs at the far end of the hall, they saw her standing on the landing above in a rose-red dressing-gown, blonde hair tousled, one hand on the banisters. 'Shit!

What on earth are you two doing here at this time of night?'

It was Delyth who answered. Jake stood silent, gazing up at her, seemingly rooted to the spot. 'Join us, and I'll tell you,' she said. 'A lot's been happening—'

'But – *MI5?*' Gemma was halfway down the stairs. 'And who's this bloke Allen? You said something about Jake going to see him right now. So what's happened, Jake? What's going on?'

He watched his half-sister as she came down the stairs towards him, her eyes never leaving his. And, as he was doing so, his conversion became complete: he understood – for the first time, and deep within himself, and irrevocably – that he did not belong with Sarsen and the ethos he lived by: he belonged with those who held to a very different ideal, the very one that Sarsen and his kind were seeking to destroy. He turned to Delyth.

'You're right,' he said to her. 'I should go at once to Allen. You'll tell her?'

She searched his face. What he was about to do was such a life-defining act that, for a moment, she was afraid of not being able to deal with it properly, with understanding – or even, on a more mundane level, with the right words. 'You . . . you trust me?' she asked.

'With my life.'

He saw his commitment get to her, go into her – her eyes suddenly brilliant, *for him.* Then present urgencies took over once more, and she reached out and touched his hand.

'Go at once,' she urged, then wished him Godspeed and, turning to Gemma with a quick 'Let's you and I go into the kitchen and brew up some coffee', led the way there, not looking back.

Jared, MI5, Rawlings, Allen: Jake Messanger's mind switched tracks and, turning on his heel, he went out through the front door, recalling as he closed it behind him Rawlings' instructions on how to get from where he now was to the new MI5—

'Stop where you are! I've got a gun on you; one move and I shoot you dead.' The voice was Agent Nine's, the language Arabic. Jake Messanger froze on the instant, his back to Nine, his arms held clear of his body.

Nine stepped out from shielding foliage. 'Face me. There is one thing I want you to know before I kill you,' he said. 'Sarsen has ordered the death of your half-sister after Zephyr has climaxed—'

'That won't be easy for you.' Turning as he spoke, Jake saw Agent Nine no more than six feet from him, the gun in his right hand silenced – like Edara's, like the one he himself was carrying – and perceived from what Nine had just said that he hadn't realized that Jake had already informed MI5 of the nature, timing, and sites of the Zephyr operation and that, consequently, the mission was doomed. So keep talking, he told himself, and get ready to jump him.

'Jared will look out for Gemma, he'll keep her safe,' he said.

'Not from me—'

'Ja-ake! You left your jacket behind!'

At the call, the set-piece situation exploded into action. Nine's eyes flicked sideways towards the opening door – and in that split second Jake sprang at him, driving his body in against the Arab's, his right hand grabbing for the gun. Getting a hold on the bony wrist he twisted it aside, felt sinews and muscles strain as he did so, and the trigger was pulled. But the bullet flew wide, buried itself in a treetrunk. Locked together in furious combat the two men fought for control of the gun because each knew that the man who lost that would die on the instant. Tooth and nail drew blood, fingers clawed for eyes, lifted knee jabbed for genitals but never quite struck home. Maintaining his hold on Nine's wrist, blood flowing from his hand where the Arab had bitten deep, Messanger inched his fingers towards the stock of the gun, forcing the barrel inwards towards Nine's chest – a couple of centimetres would do it, but Nine kept his finger on the trigger, resisted with all his strength – and again, the gun fired! Nine's entire body convulsed in shock, a rictus hideous on his face as agony raced through blood and tissue. Then he collapsed in Messanger's grasp, the gun falling from his hand, blood seeping from the entry wound in the side of his chest.

Messanger had fallen sideways under the deadweight of the Arab and now lay on the ground, sweating and panting, the lower half of his body pinned down by that of Agent Nine. Christ! he thought hazily. Oh Christ, *I'm still alive.* And no other thought came inside his head: for the moment that truth was wonder enough in itself, he could handle no other.

'Jake? Jake, *are you all right?*' Delyth was kneeling at his side, Gemma standing behind her. He looked up at them and the moment of wonder passed, reality won out and became a present and urgent force urging him to act.

'Thank God you came out when you did,' he said to his half-sister. 'Yes, I'm OK. Go back inside, both of you, I'll deal with what's happened here. Get out the First Aid box, and don't go near the windows.'

'But what—?'

'Come on, Gemma!' Delyth was on her feet. 'Don't you see? The fewer of us out here, the better; the last thing we want is to draw attention this way.'

As the door closed behind them, Jake quickly eased himself free of Agent Nine's body; then stood looking down at the man who had come so close to killing him. Cursed him briefly and silently, then bent down and checked for signs of life. Found none, and was glad.

Casting a careful glance around him, listening, he found road and houses all quiet as the grave and thought, lucky for me, Nine must've been working alone. Lucky, too, that there are all these tall hedges about, I doubt anyone can have seen what's happened here. And hauling Nine's body into the house he locked it away in the small lavatory near the front door.

Quickly then, went into the kitchen to fetch cleaning materials to wash away the trail of blood.

'We'll do that,' Gemma said, guessing his intention as he opened the cupboard beneath the sink. 'From what Del's just been telling me, surely you ought to get to this bloke Allen as soon as you can.'

'You're right. But are you sure you'll be OK?' Jake straightened up, eyed her steadily. 'Now this—'

'He is dead, isn't he?' Delyth's question from behind him and, swinging round, he saw her standing, straight and still, by the kitchen table.

'Yes, he's dead.'

'Is there anything we should do, then, Gemma and I, about him?

Ring the police—?'

'Nothing. It'll be dealt with by Allen. I'll report the killing to him at once; he'll send his own people. When I've gone you lock the front door, and when they turn up you make damn sure it really *is* them before you open it to them. One more thing: don't – I repeat, *do not*, either of you – call me on my mobile from now on, and don't you answer any incoming calls—'

'Hang on a moment, Jake,' Gemma said, and they both turned towards her. 'I've got Dettol and stuff here, I'll do your hands.'

'No time for that, I'll get it done where I'm going. Take care of yourselves, you two,' he said, and went swiftly out of Jared's house into the street.

But as soon as he was back in the Fiesta he used his mobile and, contacting Allen, reported the killing of Agent Nine and requested immediate removal of the body. '*Immediate* action,' he repeated. 'Is that possible?'

'Can do, will do. You get yourself over here *now*, I need you here. Rawlings gave you the location of my incident command HQ.'

But in spite of Allen's positive response, as Jake Messanger drove to Uxbridge, where by now Allen had established his temporary operational centre for the counter-attack against Zephyr, with its central thrust against Edara and the three suicide agents, he was plagued by unease regarding the continuing safety of Delyth and Gemma, for although it was *unlikely* that Edara or any of the Zephyr personnel were aware that Agent Nine had followed the Fiesta to Jared's house it was, nevertheless, *possible* they were. And it was also possible they'd called Nine's mobile number, found he wasn't answering so tried again and, eventually, had concluded that for some reason he was unable to answer and that, therefore, he might be in trouble of some sort and in need of back-up. . . .

Chapter 18

Hillingdon Police HQ. Four miles north-east of Uxbridge
Saturday 02.30 hours

Having been informed by Messanger that by 01.45 Edara would be
established at Red Pillars, on the outskirts of Uxbridge, Allen had
taken over a conference room at the police base in Hillingdon.
There Allen, Messanger, two MI6 officers, and the assault personnel
– two rapid reaction units, eight officers in all – were now in pre-
action session, with Allen using the information already given him by
Messanger. Jared was not present: he was working with Rawlings who,
on stand-by for action in expectation of a series of co-ordinated
attacks later in the day against Zephyr safe houses across London and
in the regions, was assembling his teams and had assigned Jared to
one of them.

'Right.' At the head of the conference table Allen turned to
Messanger who was seated between the two MI6 officers, halfway
down one of its long sides. 'I'll go into your info on subsidiary action
and provincial safe houses after we've dealt with our moves to arrest
our primary targets, Edara and the three suicide agents, at Red
Pillars. What we want from you is detailed gen on the layout of Red
Pillars, and a full account of its security. Security first, please.'

'Sir.' Leaning forward Messanger rested his forearms on the table
and, looking Allen in the eye, proceeded to lay on the line the facts
requested – as far as he was aware of them. 'With Zephyr set to climax
at twelve midday, from 01.00 hours there will be one guard on duty

177

in the entrance hall at Red Pillars, and one in that of the support house next door, plus the guard captain—'

'Seems pretty light?' Allen – ex-SAS, hard-faced – was frowning.

'It is, and intentionally so. As I pointed out to you earlier, sir, Edara deliberately went for a stripped-down-to-bare-essentials approach to the nucleus of his strike force for Zephyr.'

'And all his surveillance sources were reporting the mission secure. Yep. Right. Move on to the layout at Red Pillars and its adjoining support house.'

'Sir. Both are situated towards the end of a row of small terraced houses of the two-up, two-down variety. They face on to a main road, with the support house on the corner. Their ground floor plans are identical. I'll describe that of Red Pillars, where Edara and the three suicide agents will be at the time of our assault. Entering via the door facing the main road you find yourself in a small hall with one door opening either side of it. The one on the left leads into the war room, which shares a party wall with the front room in the support house. The one on the right opens into the prayer room—'

'Which is set aside for the use of the volunteers and has no guard assigned to it.' Allen interrupted again, following Messanger's description on the rough sketch of the two properties he had made while questioning him on the phone earlier. 'Go on.'

'The hall narrows into a corridor leading directly from front to back of the house—'

'So each house has only the one entrance/exit, which is on the main road? Neither of them has a back door?' This time the interruption came from the dark-haired woman facing Messanger across the table.

'Correct. They've been blocked up.'

'Thank you.'

'*But.*' Messanger turned back to Allen. 'But, Edara has an emergency escape route. From his war room he has access to the support house via a concealed door linking the two, and from it he can reach the slip road alongside it where the two escape vehicles will be in position, an Escort van and a Vauxhall saloon.'

'This side road: it's a public way, so I assume steps will have been taken re other parked cars?'

'Of course, sir. The Escort and the Vauxhall will have been in position since midday yesterday. Between them there'll be four parked rented vehicles, all unoccupied.'

'We'll take Edara before he has time to get to the cars.' The officer on Allen's left leaned forward, an impatience in him, an eagerness for the action to begin.

'That is what we hope for.' Allen spoke before Messanger got round to it, then put to him a vital question. 'This communicating door: exactly how secret is it, and how difficult to break through?'

'It's built into the party-wall between the two buildings, and on the war-room side is concealed behind a book case. The door itself is an ordinary wooden one—'

'Will it be locked?'

'I don't know. If Edara has time to go through it he may lock it behind him; but shoot off the lock, and you're through.'

'So if he makes it into the support house before we get to the war room, we should be able to follow quickly and – provided our assault teams have neutralized the two enemy in the support house – take him before he makes it to the escape vehicles? There'll be no further barriers for us to overcome?'

Messanger hesitated, running his mind over all Agent Nine had told him about the two houses and the security measures in place there.

'Well?' Impatiently, Allen prodded at his silence.

'I've only been to Red Pillars once, what I know is mostly what I've been told. All I can say is that *as far as I know* there won't be.' In the face of the M15 man's pressure – necessary pressure, no doubt of it given the time factor involved – Messanger pushed aside the sudden shadowy disquiet fretting his mind; at the time he could see no reason for it.

'Then I'll move on.' Allen cast a swift glance at the concentrated faces of the officers of his two assault teams: all were experienced in anti-terrorist work so in reaching the decision which must now be made, and on which the success of their counter-attack might depend, their opinion had to be taken into account – up to a point.

179

'Clearly, Zephyr is a complex op, comprised as it is of three separate hits each supported by ancillary measures,' he said to them. 'Equally clearly, we have only a short space of time available in which to frustrate all three hostile strikes *and* arrest all personnel engaged in those ancillary measures. Therefore, at Red Pillars we have two courses of action open to us. One: to attack just before the suicide agents set out from there and take into custody not only those agents but also Zephyr's commander Edara, thereby rendering the operation dead in the water.' Pausing, Allen stared Messanger in the eye, this man whose conversion he was taking on trust largely because, with the time so short, *he dared not do anything else*: a man who was half-Arab by blood, and whose change of allegiance had been abrupt and absolute. Mind-blowingly so? Yes. Suspiciously so? No, not that last. Messanger is levelling with me, Allen thought, perceiving in the man's eyes and body language an integrity, a steadiness of purpose and . . . what? Something else, something difficult to define . . . an intrinsic, self-contained certainty that invited trust. Besides, he reminded himself grimly, the bottom line is *we have to* take action, not to do so would be to risk the most dreadful carnage. 'That's a fair assumption to make, is it not?' he demanded.

'Without a doubt.' Messanger's answer shot back fast on the question, and at once Allen withdrew his searching stare and turned again to his assault teams.

'Our second option is to delay our counter-attack and strike mid-morning,' he went on, 'by which time the delivery agents can be arrested at or near their target sites and in possession of incriminating evidence. This second option has one further advantage in that at the target stations the support personnel will be in position and we can take them also.' Allen's eyes swept questioningly around the eight concentrated faces. 'Myself, I'm in favour of the first option. Unless any of you raise serious arguments against it, I shall implement it. Your opinions, please. Fast.'

'Happy with first option, sir.' Eve Martin leaned forward: a slim woman, severe of feature and her long dark hair caught up at the back of her head in a French pleat. 'The second's too close to zero hour; if anything goes wrong – well, considering what's at stake, the risk simply isn't acceptable.'

No one present favoured the waiting game implicit in the second option: within a few minutes the first option had been endorsed and Allen issued his orders.

'Eve, you and your team' – John Everett, veteran marksman, Tom Black and Des Jackson – 'you'll take on the arrest of Edara and the three suicide agents at Red Pillars, they'll be in either the war room or the prayer room. You will disregard any security staff – unless directly threatened by them, in which case you are authorized to use maximum force. Your job is to hunt down and arrest your specific targets. . . . Ted,' he went on, addressing Edward Turner, the stocky, hard-faced officer seated on his right. 'You and yours' – James Richards and brothers John and Charlie Swale – 'will deal with all security personnel at both Red Pillars and its support house, by which I mean immobilize and disarm them, employing whatever degree of force may be necessary to do so. You leave Edara and the suicide agents to Eve's people.'

Sitting back Allen rearranged the papers in front of him then looked up again at the assault teams. 'Straight after this briefing you will familiarize yourselves with the environs of the two houses and their ground-floor layout' – he slid the sketch-maps in front of him into the middle of the table – 'and draw up your plans of attack. I shall organize the arrest of enemy agents engaged in ancillary action, bearing in mind, of course, every possible thing that might throw your blitz on Red Pillars out of gear. We'll all work in this room. You have the IT equipment in here' – he waved a hand towards the mass of high-tech electronic appliances ranged on the work surfaces lining the wall on his left – 'to use as required. Also you have Superintendent Rawlings to refer to re logistical arrangements, and Messanger with his inside knowledge of the Zephyr mission—'

'Sir.' Jake interrupted, standing up as Allen, still talking, began to get to his feet.

'Yep?' The MI5 man faced him.

'I'd like to be in on the offensive against Red Pillars – with the people assigned to arrest Edara.'

Allen stiffened. 'Why?' he asked quietly. 'You'd be going up against . . . against those who were your own, men you were working with only hours ago.'

Messanger hesitated, momentarily uncertain of himself. The request had welled up from inside him, unreasoned, out of some deep subliminal pool of . . . of what? Aloneness? An aching sense of aloneness, perhaps? Or – again, perhaps – out of a desire to as it were *prove* himself to his new associates?

'Against men you were *working with*,' Allen repeated, still probing, needing to know.

Messanger perceived one facet of the complex truth of his situation then: it came home to him quite suddenly, complete. 'I suppose that's why,' he said grimly. 'I want to be in at the death.'

Allen frowned, searching uneasily for specific intention behind that last statement of Messanger's. But then with a decisive 'Permission granted. You will be subject to Eve Martin's orders for the duration of the exercise. Report now to Everett, he'll fill you in,' he went over to one of the computers, his attention reverting to the co-ordination of the widespread and disparate initiatives involved in MI5's counter-attack against the Zephyr operation.

Again, Edara looked at his watch: 04.15.

The first of the suicide agents will be reporting to me any time now, he thought, 04.30 is their deadline for doing so. Allah grant that no random occurrence such as a traffic accident befalls any one of them; for such men as they, it is not possible to have reserves on stand-by. But then close on that thought came another, and he used the intercom on one of the desks at the side of the war room.

'Sir?' The guard captain on duty in the support house answered immediately.

'The prayer room prepared for the martyrs – is all as it should be in there? They must lack for nothing.'

'Their sacrifice is great. I have checked in person, sir, and nothing has been forgotten. They will be close to God there.'

'Their names will be remembered for ever.' Edara cut the call. His mind had already moved on. Intoxicated by controlled exaltation as the climax of Zephyr drew near, it was roving over the diverse activities of the individual operatives engaged in its prosecution.

Agent Nine! Edara's thoughts stopped dead, then zeroed in on the one man. Why had Nine not yet called in with his report on the situation at safe house Alpha? Twice, recently, Nine – always self-willed, opinionated, and impatient of control – had taken action beyond the scope of his orders. On those two occasions I went no further than reprimanding him, he thought, but if now he has repeated that offence, then the moment Zephyr has been completed *I will see him destroyed.*

He controlled his anger. He would deal with Agent Nine later. His present imperative must be to ensure the success of the operation: he had to contact Nine, had to get information on the situation at safe house Alpha, and on Messanger.

But that course of action turned out to be more easily decided on than achieved. He called Nine's number, found his mobile switched off, so punched out that of Ahmed Rahman – only to find that still dead! Quelling a stab of apprehension, he used one of the telephones on the table, contacted Selim Ansari, one of the many agents on stand-by for the three days covering the Zephyr climax, and ordered him to proceed at once to safe house Alpha, to force entry were that necessary, and then report back immediately on the state of affairs he found there, with special reference to Agent Messanger.

As Edara replaced the receiver, the guard captain's voice came on the intercom. 'The first of the martyrs has arrived, sir.'

The words clear and confident in the room. *Zephyr is on course,* Edara thought as he heard them. And at once he concentrated his mind, his brain – his very soul – on the forthcoming briefing of the suicide agents which he would now carry out in his war room.

They were young, those three: not one of them over twenty.

Standing facing Edara across the table with their eyes fixed on him, all were wearing blue jeans and sneakers, but there the similarity in their clothing ended: one wore a dark blue shirt loose outside his jeans, the man next to him a grey polo, the third a denim jacket open over a white T-shirt. Physically, there was nothing about them to draw the eye: all were dark-haired; two were of average height, their build rangy, slim-hipped; the third was more solidly set – and had tied across his forehead a broad, red-and-white checkered headband.

Edara held that one's eyes. 'Remove the headband,' he said to him quietly. 'There must be nothing – *nothing* – to call attention to yourself.'

The young man looked down, then raised one hand and pulled off the headband, stood with it in his hand, at a loss what to do with it.

'Place it on the table,' Edara said. 'I will ensure that it is returned to your family.'

The young man did as suggested, then looked up at Edara again. 'Thank you, sir,' he said.

Edara saw in his eyes that he was afraid, was quite desperately afraid, and for a second then he saw inside his head the face of his own son, who would have been roughly the same age as this doomed young man had he not been killed in a road accident five years ago on his way home from school. But in the space of a single breath he expunged the memory. Said, holding the dark eyes with the fear restless inside them, 'You will live for ever in my thoughts.'

He took his seat at the table then, motioning the young men to sit down in the three chairs placed facing him across it. No alterations had been made to the individual plans of action, he told them. Before their departure from Red Pillars for the target stations, each would be armed with the holdall – presently concealed in the prayer room – loaded with the prepared heavy-duty plastic container of pressurized gas that was his weapon against the enemy.

'You have all been under intensive instruction to ensure you are fully conversant with the moves required of you at each and every stage of your mission,' he went on. 'Each of you has studied the ground-plan of his target station, and paid three familiarization visits to it. I would remind you that once you leave this house your behaviour and your body language must be that of a student. . . . Each of you will travel to his action site alone, following the directions you committed to memory during your training. On arrival there, you will place yourself' – Edara paused, indicating the ground-plans laid out in front of them on the table – 'at the exact position indicated on your station layout, which I have marked and will discuss in detail with each of you in a few minutes' time.'

Pausing again, he swept his eyes over the three faces intent on his own. 'If you are unsure regarding anything I have put forward so far, ask about it now,' he said.

But no question was asked: throughout the preceding month these young men had lived under the tutelage of their instructors, the waking hours of each day given over to mental, emotional and physical preparation for the endgame act each was pledged to carry out. Now, two of them gave a slight shake of the head; the third smiled serenely into Edara's eyes.

He had expected no less and went on at once. 'Watches will of course be synchronized before you leave here. At twelve midday you will lift your container from your holdall, place it on the ground, and release the toxic gas in the manner you have practised with your instructors.' Again he paused; as he went on this time his voice made it plain he was giving orders. 'You will then remain at your posts for at least three minutes, to ensure that all of the gas escapes. As the people around you observe your actions, some among them may read the situation correctly and attack you or attempt to close down your container. You will stand your ground, using your handgun to prevent that—'

'Sir, we understand our duty.' The words came quiet and clear, interrupting Edara. The speaker was the young man whose head-band would soon be returned to his parents. Edara looked at him and perceived that his eyes were now confident and at peace; he had killed the fear that had been in him.

'I am entirely sure of that,' Edara said; then for a moment allowed himself to imagine and exult in the havoc and devastation these young men would, in seven hours' time, cause to erupt inside the underground stations Green Park, Holborn, and Knightsbridge. He knew each of those places well, had made a point of doing so, and now visualized the wildfire panic of terror that surely would ensue as the lethal gas established itself in the air – not only on the target platforms but also, via the airducts and ventilation systems, throughout the whole of each of the stations under attack. People within its compass would have no choice but to take it into their lungs. . . .

Then he brought his mind back to the young men who very shortly now would bring it all to pass. 'After the three minutes have passed you will make your way to your designated safe house,' he said.

Each one of them knew as well as he did that, in reality, there was no real likelihood of any one of them being physically fit enough to make his way out into the street and effect his escape: their close proximity to the source of the outpouring of gas would be such that death would take them within the three minutes they were committed to remain at their posts. Nevertheless their faces remained impassive: each had made his choice.

To alter that choice at this stage requires an altogether different kind of courage, Edara thought cynically, watching their eyes; praise be to Allah that none of these three possesses it.

'It is now close to five o'clock,' he said to them. 'The first of you will leave here at 07.15, the other two will follow at half-hour intervals. . . . Now, with my help, you will familiarize yourselves in close detail with the positions from which you will release the gas; I have marked them on the ground-plan of each station. . . . The prayer room across the hall has been prepared for your use; it is arranged for your rest, prayer, and meditation. Avail yourselves of its amenities whenever you wish to do so.'

The minutes ticked by in the war room at Red Pillars. For Edara and one of the martyrs they raced by once the final briefing was done. But for the other two their pace was too slow: after half an hour had passed, one of them, finding it difficult to hold on to his certainty, touched his brother beside him on the shoulder – then when he turned, and his eyes showed him to be of like mind, both rose quietly to their feet and went into the prayer room.

Edara, however, was revelling in every minute of this time of waiting. His head down, and holding clear in his mind the complete picture of the complex network of actions and events comprising the climax of Operation Zephyr, he was living it with his brain, his heart, and his spirit.

When the two martyrs pushed back their chairs he looked up, watched them cross the room and go out of the door – then as it closed behind them his mobile bleeped. He answered it at once.

'Edara.'

'Ansari. Safe house Alpha.'

'Report.'

'Only two people present here. Agent Rahman, shot in the shoulder, semi-conscious, and the maidservant, Muna, unwounded but—'

'You got information on what happened from Rahman?'

'Very little. He is confused. The only facts I can get from him are that Messanger shot him and then left here with the woman prisoner, and that Agent Nine came here a short while back, refused to call a doctor for him and—'

'Facts, man, facts! *Where is Nine now?*'

'Not known. When he left here he did not speak of where he was going—'

'Or is it that Rahman does not remember?'

'I don't think so.'

'And Messanger? Nothing to indicate his intentions?'

Selim Ansari hesitated. Then, eager to offer his boss something, however small, said, 'Rahman told me that earlier on Messanger had mentioned his half-sister.'

'Saying what?'

'Rahman could not recall exactly; it was just something about seeing her.'

'Return to base at once, then.'

'But sir—' Ansari broke off, aware that he was speaking along a dead line. His boss had switched off, leaving him stuck with Rahman. He had been about to ask Edara for authorization to call in one of the Zephyr medics to attend to the poor sod groaning on the floor in front of him. Too late for that now.

But Selim Ansari was a compassionate man. He did his best. Going along to the kitchen, he ordered Muna to take warm water and towels, clean Rahman's wound and then make him as comfortable as possible.

'Sir,' Muna said, as he turned away to leave her, 'the housekeeper next door is a trained nurse; is it permitted that I ask her to come and help me? She has medicines—'

'No,' Ansari answered over his shoulder. 'You will *not* do that, it is *not* allowed.' But then, as he went out into the street, there came in him a complicated sort of anger. Anger against Edara, yes, but also against himself: a thin thread of self-disgust because although he had wanted to arrange help for a fellow agent who was in pain and badly in need of it, he had allowed his fear of the consequences of doing so, should Edara learn of it, to stop him from acting. *Coward*, he upbraided himself as he got back into his car. I should have forced the point upon Edara. Nevertheless he acknowledged inside himself that, were the same situation to occur again in his life, he would react to it in exactly the same way.

And as he drove away from safe house Alpha he was aware of a chilling sense of loneliness within him; a feeling of . . . *loss*.

Chapter 19

After Jake left, Gemma and Delyth, deciding it would be impossible to sleep and knowing that, anyway, they had to wait up for the MI5 men to remove Agent Nine's body, brewed coffee in the kitchen and drank it there, sitting at the table, talking over what had happened that night and wondering what might come of it.

'God! It's so hard, waiting like this, knowing damn all.' Her coffee long since finished, Gemma pushed herself to her feet. 'Let's go back into the sitting-room.'

'I'll come in a moment. You go ahead.' And watching Jake's half-sister walk to the door and go out, Delyth thought, both of us are so uptight, and so very frightened. We know that by now big decisions must have been made by the people at MI5 – life-and-death decisions with so little time left to prevent disaster, and we can't think about anything else. Gemma and I are talked out: we've nothing left to say to each other about it. Our minds won't leave it alone, though. . . .

As she went into the sitting-room she saw Gemma had sat down in an armchair with a book, so, going across to the window-seat she curled into one corner of it, put her mobile on the white-painted sill beside her, under the drawn curtains, and sat quiet, her head down, trying to make a coherent whole out of the – to her – wildly disparate events of that night.

Some ten minutes later, her mobile bleeped. Picking it up she spoke her name to her caller, listened.

'Delyth? Delyth, is that really you?' He was whispering, afraid to believe.

'*Father!*' Her voice was soft with wonder, the word was lovely in her mouth. 'Yes, it's me. I'm free.'

Hearing her say this, he believed: his daughter was alive and she was no longer a prisoner, and the revelation that it was so broke over his world like a shower of gold. '*Delyth,*' he said again, but then was lost for words.

'Are you all right? Where are you?' She was on her feet, her face, her whole body vibrant with the joy creaming through her. 'Oh God I can't believe this is happening – Yes, it's my father and he sounds OK!' she whispered in a swift, ecstatic aside to Gemma who had leaped to her feet and come to her, was standing at her shoulder.

'Delyth, little lion, you're not hurt? They didn't hurt you?'

'No, they didn't hurt me. I'm at Jared's house, with Gemma. We're safe here. But you—' Feeling behind her for the window-seat she sat down, gesturing to Gemma to do the same. 'Where are you, Dad?'

'I'm at home.'

'But they said—'

'The . . . they lost the initiative. At present I don't know how or why it all began to change, no doubt that'll all come out later. But apparently some time after they brought me back suspicions against them were mounting up and MI5 put surveillance on the house here—'

'Weren't you under guard, though?'

'There was only one of them by then, the other had left.'

'And how many did MI5 send?'

'One. Only one.' Professor Stanton paused for a moment; when he went on Delyth heard in his voice a quiet sort of. . . admiration? Humility? Both, she decided. 'But that one man was gifted with a quick eye, total commitment and great personal courage, and I thank God for it, I owe him my life. Good observation told him there were people inside the house, so he got in through a broken window. Then he listened outside the study – that's where the guard was holding me – realized I was being kept prisoner in there and. . . . He came in and freed me, Delyth.'

'Just like that?'

'No, my little lion, not *just like that.* . . . Sorry, I'm not telling this very well. You see, he was disobeying orders. He'd been told to wait for reinforcements, but seeing risk to me in doing so, he tackled the situation by himself, single-handed. He burst in and went for the guard – and he wasn't even armed. It didn't last long, their fight, but believe me it was vicious. He took a bullet in the side, Delyth. It didn't stop him.'

'My God.' Softly spoken, the words were a wondering, heart-felt salute to a man's courage. Then after a moment, 'May he live for ever,' she said. 'Is he OK? What's his name?'

'Smith. Jim Smith.' Stanton heard her quiet laugh come along the line and was content. And as soon as he had reassured himself that she was safe and well he ended his call, telling her he was in the middle of being debriefed by M15 officers on the night's events, and would call her again as soon as he was allowed another rest break.

Chapter 20

Having set in motion the various initiatives he wanted up and running against Zephyr's ancillary networks, Allen once more turned his attention to the one to be undertaken against Red Pillars itself, the enemy operation's command centre. To this end he called his assault teams back to the main table. As he watched them gather together and bring with them their photocopies of the layout of Red Pillars and its support house, he made a silent prayer that the flood of information which Messanger had given MI5 in the small hours of that morning was both correct in every detail, and flawed by no omission of fact which might prove fatal to the total success of their coming attack. Any slip-up in that could only too easily result in a committed terrorist armed with toxic gas – or, in worst-case scenario *three* such men – gaining access to their targets in London.

'Now, to the format of the assaults on the two houses,' he began, as soon as all his officers were seated at the table. 'Thanks to Messanger we know that at both, and right from their mission's conception, Zephyr commander Edara decided to deploy minimum-force security, reasoning that with neighbours being curious folk, especially Londoners after 9/11, anything bigger might arouse the very suspicions he had so far – according to reports he received from his secret agents – been successful in avoiding.' Briefly, a tight-lipped smile touched his lips; then he went on. 'Consequently, at Red Pillars he has only one guard, while in the support house he has the guard captain and one other. Because of that, we in our turn have been able to slim down our attack force. Back-up, in strength, will be on call, as you already know. . . . Questions?'

None was put forward, so he continued. 'Both assault groups will go in at 07.13. We have already covered their action plans. Group A, I would remind you that your prime target is mission commander Edara. The three suicide agents should present no problem, they're not experienced in combat and at the time we strike, their handguns will be in their holdalls. Edara's another matter; he'll likely react fast, given any chance at all, and he'll be carrying a gun – uses a shoulder holster. Hopefully you'll take him either in his war room or in the prayer room across the corridor from it. But maybe he'll make a run for it. If he does, and escapes through Red Pillars' street door, you will immediately call in back-up to cut him off and apprehend him. Should he escape via the connecting door into the support house you will continue to pursue him, remember he's *your* responsibility, not Group B's although they'll be in action in the support house—' He broke off, seeing Eve Martin raise a questioning hand. 'Yes?'

'Sir. This connecting door between the two houses. It still seems to me a bit odd it's not, well, more security-conscious?'

'I agree.' Allen turned to Messanger, challenging him. 'It really is simply an ordinary wooden door, as you said earlier?'

'*As far as I know* that's all it is, was the way I put it. I've only ever seen it there, closed. Like I told you, reliance was placed on it being concealed.'

'Fair enough.' Allen took in Martin's accepting nod, then glanced around at the other intent faces. 'Further questions?'

'The holdalls containing the gas cylinders, sir.' Jackson's eyes sharp beneath heavy eyebrows. 'It's sure there's only the three of 'em?' It was his job to secure them.

'Messanger?' Allen turned to him again.

'Only three. One for each suicide agent.'

'And the handguns they're armed with?' Everett put in: he was still finding it difficult to place absolute trust in this defector from the enemy terrorist organization. He had not wanted the outsider to go in with his assault squad but, since he did trust Allen, he had not spoken out against it, deciding instead that once the action started he'd watch Messanger like a hawk until events proved the bugger either on the level with MI5 – or otherwise.

'The guns will be in the holdalls. The orders to those men are that they must not on any account use their weapons until after they have activated the spray which emits the toxic gas – then, they may do so to prevent anyone getting at it to close it down.' Messanger had intuited Everett's incipient doubts regarding his good faith; realizing it was instinctive he respected the man for keeping it on hold until further proof was provided – and resolved to watch his own back during the assault on Red Pillars.

On receiving Jake Messanger's call reporting the death of Agent Nine, Allen had taken the necessary action, ranking the situation as an emergency calling for swift response. And soon after Professor Stanton had ended his call to his daughter a black, unmarked Transit van purred quietly to a halt outside Jared's house. Three men got out of it. All were casually dressed in jeans and dark sweatshirts, and there was nothing remarkable about any of them; they looked and acted like mates on a routine 'removals' job – as indeed they were, in a sense. One of them – the biggest, tall and heavy-shouldered, quick brown eyes summing up his surroundings the moment he was out of the cab – had a rolled-up tarpaulin under his arm, while his mate, walking beside him, carried in his right hand a slim black briefcase; the one following close behind them had his hands in his pockets and looked as if he had just been routed out of bed and was not at all happy about it. All three went up to the front door, and were let in by Gemma.

When the three came out some twenty minutes later, their tarpaulin appeared to be wrapped around something around six feet long by three across – a rolled-up carpet, perhaps, you might think if you spotted it, though you might consider it odd to see such a job being carried out in the small hours. Whatever it was, it required two men to carry it. They stowed it away in the back of their van, then got back into the cab and drove away – a classy engine that Transit had, it slipped quietly and smoothly away from the house with the yellow-flowering shrubs growing either side of its front door.

'Praises be that's done.' Gemma turned away from the window in the front room as the Transit merged into the shadowy half-light of the street and was lost to her sight. 'What now? . . . . Oh shit! I wish Jake would call us.'

'He will as soon as it's right for him to do so, and he's got time to.' Across the room from her, Delyth stood tense, her head down. 'I hope to God they'll play fair by him,' she went on. 'M15, I mean. He's . . . he's putting his life in their hands, isn't he? His *life*.'

Gemma had been moving towards her but stopped now, staring at her, her mind searching for the truth which had to be lying at the heart of all that had happened that night – the part of it she knew anything about so far. And when she had, she believed, found it, 'How much of Jake's decision to go to M15 was his, and how much was yours?' she asked, a certain harshness in her voice.

Delyth looked up, a nervy, almost defensive movement. 'I think you should ask him that. It's for him to say, not me.'

'Perhaps. But I'd still like to know how *you* think it was.'

'Why should that be of interest to you?' A stiffness in her, a sudden uncertainty.

'Oh come off it! Because he's in love with you – and I'm very fond of him, in spite of the way he's used us.' Gemma's face was flushed, her eyes alight. 'He and I grew up together!' she cried passionately. 'I loved him then and I still do! *I still do*, Del, so I want to know how much of what he's doing now is him, and how much of it is *you!*'

'But don't you see, *I* don't really know that! Only Jake himself does. . . . And Gemma,' she went on, quietly now, 'I don't imagine he's giving much thought to that side of things at the moment, so I suggest you and I don't either. There are far bigger things than anything about us three at stake – at stake *now*, right here in London.'

It got through to Gemma – hit her hard, and she went across to Delyth, laid a hand on her arm. 'I'm sorry, so sorry,' she said. 'To think small like that – it's horrible.'

'Not so. Wrong timing, that's all.'

'May I ask you one thing, though, before we leave it?'

'Of course.'

'Do you love Jake? Really *love* him?'

'Yes, I do. But as to what I'll do about it – *that*, I don't know. Yet.'

More questions sprang to Gemma's lips but she crammed them down because indeed this was was not the time to ask them. 'Let's go and have another coffee.' she said. 'I want to know more about how you and your father – well, I want to know everything you know about what's happened tonight, really. Piece things together, make some sort of sense of all that's been going on. . . .'

Chapter 21

07.00 hours. In the Zephyr war room at Red Pillars, Edara was sitting at the central table, oblivious to the presence of the third suicide agent who still sat opposite him, self-enwrapped, dark eyes dreaming ecstatic dreams of self-sacrifice in the service of the Almighty. An hour had passed since Selim Ansari's call to him, but he still had not succeeded in tracing either Messanger or Agent Nine. He had long since shrugged off his anger towards Nine for cutting himself off from communication and, secondly, for disobeying a direct order by failing to report on the situation he found at safe house Alpha. Inevitably, Agent Nine's career in Sarsen's organization was now at an end: by those two acts – both positive, not negative failures – Nine had committed professional suicide. Once Zephyr had been completed, Sarsen would destroy him; dereliction of duty in the course of a mission was a capital offence.

But – Messanger? True, the Brit had – temporarily? – disappeared from view, taking Stanton's daughter with him. However, the woman's only value to Edara was as the sword he was holding over her father's head to secure his continuing silence; and since there had been no action at any of the target sites by British anti-terrorist forces to indicate she had contacted her father and told him she had escaped her captors, it seemed likely that Messanger had no intention of utilizing her that way to kill Zephyr. So – just what was the rationale behind what Messanger had done?

Using one of the computers Edara refreshed his memory of events since he had learned of the Brit's departure from safe house Alpha, calling up and re-evaluating incoming reports from the two sleepers he had sent to the area following Ansari's call. But they contained nothing of value – hardly surprising considering the brief time they'd had. Impatiently he pushed the computer aside and sat quiet, making a mental resumé of how matters stood – at that moment, and to his knowledge – with Zephyr.

To his knowledge, there was no threat of any nature to the success of the operation. The three suicide agents had received their final briefing; the holdalls containing the toxic gas stood ready for them in the prayer room; Red Pillars was secure; himself and its guard at post; ditto guards in the support house. Both escape vehicles were in place in the side road, access to them available to him via the connecting door and its sliding steel barrier to pursuit. At the target sites, all personnel involved were in position including back-up, surveillance and observation people. All agents and sleepers engaged in the operation were on full alert and would remain so until stand-down orders were issued.

Nevertheless, to Edara's way of thinking, the behaviour of both Agent Nine and Messanger was a cause of concern. Did either of them now pose a serious threat to Zephyr? He debated the question in his mind. Nine's duties would continue to be carried out by his deputy who, since at this advanced stage of the operation those were largely logistical, would have no difficulty in handling them. Therefore, there was no need to detach men from present, vital duties to track Nine down; that could safely be put on hold until later. Which left – *Messanger.*

At thought of the Brit, all Edara's long-term malevolence towards him flared anew. Messanger has cut himself loose from our mission and from Sarsen, he thought: given the facts, there is no other interpretation to be put on the present situation. When it came to the point – Zephyr about to climax here in London, capital city of his homeland – *he failed us.* The Brit born in him took up arms against his Arab commitments – and won. . . .

Divided loyalties: yes, I have seen it before; have used it, in my time

– and seen far stronger men than he broken by it. And it is my experience that in some cases – no, now I come to consider it, in *most* cases – they *drift* when that happens; maybe only for a short while, but often for the rest of their lives. So, I believe Messanger will be thinking only of himself now: all his energies will be directed towards escaping us and positioning himself for a new life – with the woman, perhaps? Yes, it is possible; surveillance reported him definitely attracted. He has her now, and he is on the run. Therefore – as it is for Agent Nine although for totally different reasons – I can feel confident that he poses no immediate threat to Zephyr: both he and Nine will from now on be marked for a traitor's death, *but neither threatens Zephyr's success.* That being so, there is no call for me to use my time and my agents to track down either of them immediately. Indeed, to do so would be a dereliction of duty on my part: the success of Zephyr must be my priority *above all else.* I will set my men on Messanger and Agent Nine later today, after Zephyr's climax.

Decision made, Edara straightened in his chair and, as he did so, saw the third volunteer get to his feet and begin to walk towards the door.

'You are going to pray?' Edara asked.

'I would like to do that, sir, yes.' The young man had halted at once, his eyes direct to Edara's, burning with the exaltation in him. 'With your permission, I will join my brothers.'

'May all three of you go with God,' Edara said, his heart lifting as he recognized the inner glow of the martyr.

As the door closed behind the young man, Edara glanced at his watch. It showed 07.03 hours: in twelve minutes' time the first of the suicide agents, armed with his canister of toxic gas, would set out from Red Pillars for his target.

07.10. In the prayer room at Red Pillars, the suicide agent whose headband still lay on the table in the war room across the corridor, rose from his knees with the supple grace of youth. There was no fear in him, only an intense awareness of his own destiny.

Neither of the two young men sharing that destiny looked at him or spoke to him. They knew each other well by then, those three. All that they either wanted or needed to say to each other had already been said: during their period of programmed instruction each had learned a great deal about himself – and learned also that while much of that knowledge was to be kept to oneself alone, certain elements of it profited from discussion with the young men of like mind who, as training progressed, were becoming as it were one's brothers in the very deepest sense of the word.

07.10. In the Escort van parked in the road running alongside the support house, Harry Fox, its driver, a thirty-something Brit long trusted by the guard captain, slid his handgun out of sight just under the passenger seat then got out and stood on the pavement, easing his arms and shoulders. . . . Fucking boring this waiting job is, he thought, and there's another hour of it yet. Stick with it, though, Brer Fox, you stand to be upgraded if you do good here today. Then with a quick look up and down the street – no sign of life anywhere, hadn't been since that young bloke hared along the pavement ten minutes ago, half asleep he was by the look of him – Fox strolled up towards the intersection with the main road. No harm in stretching his legs a bit, he thought as he came up to it, only a few minutes since the guard captain did the seven o'clock check, so he won't bother us again for a bit— Jeez! Eyeball that, man! That blonde across the street over there, swinging along towards Red Pillars, sexy long legs and plenty of 'em on show, blonde hair thick and shining, she's on her way to work I guess—

Hey-up! What the hell was that caught my eye? A bit behind her – a shadowy man-shape there! Dead still he is now, pulled in tight against that house wall. Hard to see him but I know he's there and he sure is acting cloak-and-dagger-like, shit-certain *he's* not on the way to work. Watch yourself, though, Fox, he'll be keeping his eyes peeled same as you are now so act casual, don't give yourself away. Could be trouble for us? Could be he's making for Red Pillars? He's on the move again and— *Christ! There's a gun in his hand!*

Catching a split-second glint of light on metal as the man slipped closer to Red Pillars Fox darted into a doorway, used his mobile.

'Captain? Harry Fox, driver, the Escort. There's a bloke working

his way along the main road towards Red Pillars and keeping in cover
. . . he's around twenty yards short of it, I'd guess . . . yeah, he's
armed, handgun by the look of it . . . no, far's I can see there's only
him—'

The line went dead in his hand. '*Jesus!*' Harry Fox muttered, then
pelted back down the road and got in behind the wheel of the
Escort, reached down for his gun and put it on the seat beside him.

07.12. In his war room, Edara stood up and started towards the door,
it was time for him to go to the prayer room, the first of the suicide
agents would leave in three minutes' time. But no sooner was he on
his feet than the intercom on the table burst into life.

'*Red alert! Red alert!* Take emergency action *now!*' The guard
captain's Arabic hard and clear. 'Enemy attack imminent. You will
take emergency action *now,* repeat *now!* Out.'

For two seconds Edara stood motionless, at war with himself.
Pride, self-belief, his very soul were urging *Stand your ground, fight this
out* – but training and professional calculation were crossing swords
with that, stating one fact: *If you do so and are taken by the enemy it will
be a mortal blow to morale throughout Sarsen's network.*

Professionalism won. Grabbing the two top-secret files from
amongst those lying on the table he dashed across to the escape
door, opened it, stepped through into the front room of the support
house then turned and pressed the control button high up on the
wall to the right of the steel door. Saw the barrier slide smoothly out
and across the open doorway. Then, as it clicked into place on the
opposite side, drew his gun and ran towards the door into the hall.
Reaching it, he pressed himself against it, listening. . . . Heard an
exchange of fire in the hall – the fall of a body – a man's voice saying
in English '. . . straight on through to the back' and then the
padding of feet running on down the corridor . . . *past him.*

So *move. Get to the escape cars.* Quick but quiet, Edara slipped
through the door into the hall – seeing his guard captain sprawled
unmoving on the floor there, dead or wounded, he didn't stop to
find out – then shoved his gun back into its holster and, careful to
look unhurried, walked out through the front door, covered the

short path to the open gate in a couple of strides and went out into the main road. Heard windows being opened here and there but saw no one around, no traffic passing – so ran for it then, flat out: along the pavement, round the corner and into the side street.

In the Escort van parked there, Harry Fox had the engine running and the passenger door unlocked. 'Get in quick!' he shouted, leaning out of his side window.

'Leave her running and get out!' snapped Edara, stopping alongside him.

'But, sir—'

'Out! *Out now!*'

Seeing Edara's right hand reach in beneath his jacket, Fox leaped to conclusions and was out of the Escort in a flash. Pushing past him, Edara slid in behind the wheel, slammed the door shut then pulled away and drove off down the street.

Harry Fox stared after him for a moment; then, deciding against joining his mate in the other getaway vehicle, the Vauxhall parked further down the road, he turned and made off at speed, ran clear of the perceived danger zone. He was the first of the two front-line agents of Operation Zephyr who evaded arrest in that early morning raid by MI5; both of them let off the hook when the long-legged blonde swung along the pavement opposite Red Pillars and attracted Harry Fox's eye – thereby causing the red alert which enabled Edara to escape in the Escort with less than a minute to spare.

07.12 On the west side of Red Pillars and about ten yards from its front door, Jake Messenger stood tense in the cover of a recessed shop doorway, his eyes riveted on the entrance to Edara's command centre. Ahead of him there was no sign of Everett and Martin but he knew they were there, in cover like himself, just as surely as he knew that Black and Jackson were a couple of yards behind him. Their plan of attack ran through his mind again. Everett and Martin blast their way in and, using stun grenades, take out the guard in the hall. Self right behind them goes straight into war room to arrest Edara – but if he's been quick enough to escape through the connecting door I pursue him into the support house. Black and Jackson come in off the road right behind me into the prayer room, where Black arrests the suicide agents and Jackson seizes the holdalls containing the three handguns and the gas cylinders. Then, as soon as Red Pillars is under our control – sooner if something goes wrong and we have to call in back-up – Martin makes her report to Allen, who'll take over from then on, despatch transport and armed guards to convey detainees to designated interrogation centres.

Time to move. Ahead of him, Messanger saw Everett and Martin break cover and, crouched low with assault weapons at the ready, make a dash for Red Pillars and at once he snapped into action himself, went in hard on their heels.

'Armed police! Armed police! Drop your guns!' they shouted as they smashed the locks, rolled in the grenades, paused, then charged in, but to Messanger the frightful cacophony of their attack was no more than noises off-scene, everything in him was focused on his own target, Edara. Pelting straight through the entrance hall, aware of Everett standing over a guard who lay slumped on the floor at his feet, he reached the closed door into the war room, flung it open and darted inside, gun out in front of him, clasped in both hands and weaving from side to side in search of his erstwhile commander.

But the war room was empty *and the doorway into the support house was totally blocked by a featureless, solid sheet of steel!* For a split second then, shock and disbelief shook Jake Messanger's resolve because obviously this barrier to pursuit had been in place for a long time ready for use, yet Edara had kept him ignorant of its existence.

Messanger went after him. Reasoning that there hadn't been time for Edara to be far ahead and that he'd be making for the escape vehicles, he raced back through the hall, out into the main road then along it to the corner, turned into the side street – only to stop dead, sliding his handgun back into the pocket of his jacket because, although the Escort was gone, and presumably Edara with it, the Vauxhall saloon was still in place, parked alongside the kerb some twenty yards down the street *and he had to have wheels.* Assuming the body language of a man on his way to work he walked on towards the Vauxhall, observing as he drew closer that there was only the driver inside it and that the window beside him was open. As he drew level with it he whipped out his gun, leaned in through the car window and held the muzzle two inches from the side of the driver's head, just above his ear.

'One wrong move and you're dead,' he said to him quietly, seeing the handgun loosely held in the man's left hand where it rested on the passenger seat.

Matt Neeson sat frozen, eyes fixed on the empty road in front of him.

'Spread your fingers wide, lift your hand clear of the gun and place it on the wheel.' Messanger could smell the man's fear.

'I ain't—'

'*Do it.*' Gun rock-steady, Messanger watched the hand seen pale against the dark leather of the passenger seat. Saw the fingers splay wide . . . lift clear of gleaming metal . . . clamp hard on the rim of the steering wheel.

'You want to stay alive?' Quiet again, Messanger's voice.

'Yeah. Sure.'

'You're certain of that?' For he'd seen the man risk a furtive glance into his rear-view mirror and was praying that no one was approaching the Vauxhall.

'Certain. *Shit, get on with it.*'

'Then when I give the order you will leave the keys in the ignition, get out of the car and leg it right out of here.'

'You mean – you ain't nickin' me?'

'That's what I mean. Provided you at once run clear, beat it. Is it a deal?'

'Man, I'm on.'

Messanger straightened up, but his gun hand remained aimed and steady.

Neeson scrambled out – tall and thin he was, quick brown eyes in a bony face – then turned to the man who was holding him at gunpoint, looked him straight in the eye.

'Thanks, mate,' he said, with feeling.

Messanger smiled faintly as, just for a second, he saw the other man as – simply that, another guy living his life, only this one looking as if to his way of thinking a small miracle had just come his way.

'Can't spare the time, is all,' he said. 'Bigger fish to fry.' Then as the other turned and made off down the street, he got in behind the wheel of the Vauxhall, called Allen on his mobile and reported Edara's escape from Red Pillars and his own seizure of the second escape vehicle.

'Shit,' Allen said. 'The white Escort van – you know its number?'

Messanger reeled it off, then asked, 'The raids on the main safe houses I gave you, have they been successful?'

'All but one are in our hands now and I'm expecting that one to call in with positive results any minute.'

'There's a couple I didn't mention, though they'd be too far away to be used. But the situation's different now Edara's got transport.'

'So, give me their addresses and I'll get reception committees in place.'

Messanger obliged, then held the line while Allen detailed an officer to set up the appropriate counteraction. While he was waiting, Messanger watched the main road in the wing mirror: it was coming alive with police vehicles, two ambulances. Red Pillars' security cadre and the suicide agents are all under arrest now, he thought. Operation Zephyr's fangs have been drawn: those containers of toxic gas will end up in laboratories for forensic examination. . . . *But what I want is Edara.*

'Messanger?' Allen's voice from the mobile.

'Sir?'

'You've screwed up.' Allen's voice was taut, aggressive. 'Zephyr's broken, right, and we owe that to you. But you made one hell of a balls-up re that steel door, and so Edara's slipped the net. I want him, Messanger. You know the bastard, know how his mind works. So tell me this: what will be his next move?'

'Given the situation he's in, a top-level mission-commander's automatic response – his *duty* – would be to get out of the country immediately in order to save his organization from the humiliation of his capture, and attendant publicity. But. . . .'

'But what?'

'Edara . . . he's different from most of the big guns I know in the organization. He's good at the job, yes, but he's also a cunning and vindictive bastard and I suspect that, *now,* his overriding desire will be to hit back at us – at me in particular – in any way he can. So I think there's a possibility, a likelihood even, that he may have another ploy in mind.' But at that point Jake Messanger's nerve failed: he broke off and backed away from telling Allen the idea that had thrust itself to the forefront of his brain; it seemed too way-out. 'Ah hell, no!' he said. 'It's probably just my fertile imagination.' Yet, inside himself, he was convinced, it was more than that: the frightening possibility which had been haunting his thoughts from the moment he realized Edara had escaped from Red Pillars had suddenly hardened into such a terrifying *probability* that he knew he must act upon it.

'What sort of ploy?' Allen's voice still harsh, but he sounded interested.

'Listen, I'll tell you.' And then the words came pouring out as Messanger's certainty of their truth increased. 'I'm familiar with Edara's hang-ups and obsessions,' he said. 'I also know that when he's in dire straits – as he is now – he's wildly unpredictable, his motivation seems to change and he doesn't behave in the way others have come to expect him to behave.'

'You're saying?'

In the Vauxhall, Jake Messanger hesitated, but then heard inside his head the words Agent Nine had said to him so recently, *words he'd said he'd had straight from Edara*: 'Stanton's daughter is to be killed' . . . 'the elmination of all potentially hostile witnesses—'

'Messanger? Speak, will you!'

'I'm saying that Edara might not immediately try to get out of Britain, or take refuge in a safe house.'

'Convince me. And make it fast.'

'Zephyr's failed – which in Edara's book translates as *he* has failed, he himself, personally and disastrously. Therefore he faces the loss of everything he has worked for all his life; he's lost all hope of becoming Sarsen's heir-apparent in the terrorist organization he controls—'

'So?' Again, Allen cut in. 'I take your point, now let me hear your conclusion from it.'

'So the first thing he'll do won't be to get out of the country, it will be to take action which will go some way towards restoring his own prestige in *Sarsen's* eyes.'

'And what will that action be?'

But Messanger caught a change in Allen's tone: it showed him still sceptical, but less so.

'Sarsen has a certain obsession,' he said, 'and Edara is aware of its nature, has been for years. I believe Edara will now play to that obsession – no, don't interrupt, what I'm about to tell you is based on a long and very personal story that we don't have time to go into, so I'm asking you to take what I tell you on trust because I swear to you it's true.' Messanger stopped there, waiting for Allen's yea or nay but fear growing in him as no answer came, fear for—

'Right. Go on: leave the story, get to the action you want to take because of it.'

So far so good, he's still with me; now I have to keep him there. 'This obsession of Sarsen's calls for the killing of my half-brother Jared, my half-sister Gemma, and myself, all of which he and Edara have scheduled to take place soon after the completion of Zephyr.' Christ, put baldly like that it sounds the stuff of fantasy. Shit to that, keep going or Gemma could be dead within the hour, Delyth also if Edara finds them together. 'It's my opinion that Edara – now he's escaped us – is likely to try to achieve at least the second of those killings, which he assumes will be easy, before he looks to getting out of the country.'

'Vendetta. Fairly common in the Middle East, and other places. But – three murders. . . ? You must have a source for your info. Who is it?'

'Agent Nine. And I'm convinced what he told me is true.' Believe me. For God's sake, *believe me.*

Allen made his decision fast, on the grounds that provided he handled the situation in line with standing orders there was nothing to be lost by acting on Messanger's idea, while quite possibly much might be gained.

'I take it you're asking for my authority to go to your half-brother's house yourself, now, in the hope that Edara will arrive there – whereupon you will arrest him. Correct?'

Messanger closed his eyes for a second as relief swept through him. Said then, 'Sir, that is what I'm asking. And can you spare me back-up? Red Pillars is under control, a couple of men—'

'Out of the question. My officers have their hands full. It's your hunch, you do the job. Personally, I doubt you're right. But there's a chance you are, and in that case you'll have done us a service if you take him. So good luck to you. Allen out.'

Chapter 22

Uxbridge and Ealing 07.25

All over London the streets were coming alive as the working day began to get into its stride. The sun was up but there was no burn in it yet: sunlight had taken the city street by street and now reigned over it benevolently.

Edara was driving the Escort van fast through the early morning traffic, utterly oblivious to the people hurrying along pavements or standing in line at bus stops in various attitudes of boredom, impatience or – occasionally – life-satisfaction. He had relegated the mechanics of driving to habit and long experience. The feeling and being part of him was concentrated on the achievement of his immediate objective: revenge on Jake Messanger. *Messanger:* the half-Brit who, acting out his lies, deceiving and finally betraying, had destroyed Operation Zephyr, and, consequently, the ambitions of its commander whom, thereafter, Sarsen would perceive as abject failure. Unless Edara himself could somehow alter that perception, Sarson would shame and degrade him, cut him out of his inner circle within the organization – if not worse. And the best way to alter it would surely be for him to kill Messanger, Zephyr's saboteur. But as things stood at the moment, that was not possible; for one thing, he had no idea where the Brit was.

However I *do* know the present whereabouts of one of the Brits whom Sarsen has marked for death, Edara thought balefully, seething with hatred and bitterness as he drove through the sun-gold early morning with the need to kill a hunger in him. I accept it may not be possible for me to take *Jake* Messanger's blood for a while yet but, by Allah, I will take Messanger blood this day. The woman Gemma shall die by my hand: her death will be gall and wormwood in Messanger's mouth, and nectar in Sarsen's—

He hit the red Mini side on. Coming round a corner into a narrow side street too fast, saw the Mini pulling out of its parking space a few yards ahead of him, swerved in time to avoid direct impact, caught it a glancing, paint-damaging swipe, but then before he could straighten her, the Escort's front offside wheel struck the kerb and the tyre burst.

As he came to a stop a yard or two on, Edara sat back, closing his eyes, focusing his mind desperately on what he must do now in order to get on his way.

'You all right, mate?' The Mini's driver peered in at him through the Escort's open window, round boyish face worried, voice full of solicitude.

Dark eyes looked up into blue ones, broad finely chiseled mouth smiled at the tall, slim young man standing on the pavement. The Brit appeared truly concerned for his welfare, Edara observed and thought: I'm lucky here I believe, he'll be a soft touch provided I approach him the right way.

'Thank you, I have suffered no hurt,' he replied, getting slowly out of the Escort, taking stock of the Brit as he did so. 'And it is a great happiness to me to see that you also have taken no wound.' If I keep my language flowery and overdo the concern – he's young enough, impressionable I suspect, certainly not well off, and eager to help a visitor to his country – I think I'll be able to manipulate him.

So, continuing to phrase what he had to say with elaborate and formal 'foreignness', Edara apologized profusely – he had been driving too fast, yes, but he had a business conference to attend, he explained. Then he brought out his wallet. 'I see that in the collision my Escort has made ugly marks on your beautiful Mini,' he said, extracting four fifty-pound notes and proffering them hesitantly to the young man. 'So I would greatly appreciate it if you would allow me to recompense you for any money you may have to lay out for repairs to your car,'

'Ah, shit, no need for that,' the young man said, thinking the cash would come in very handy. What a word-spinner this bloke is, he thought, but from the look of him it's a fair bet he's got no idea how to change that fucking wheel on the Escort so reckon I'll help him out; give him something for his money, like. 'I'll give you a hand with the wheel change, if you want,' he offered, sliding the notes into the back pocket of his jeans.

Two hundred pounds well spent, thought Edara. And some fifteen minutes later got back behind the wheel of the Escort and drove on his way, the young man immediately forgotten.

Nice bloke, that, thought the young man as he watched him drive away. Then he forgot the Arab and planned what he would do with the little windfall which had just come his way.

Jake Messanger was making good time on the road. But he was harried by doubts. Had his intuition as to Edara's present intention been wrong, was he on a wild-goose chase? he wondered. For his own training advised that as soon as Edara had escaped from Red Pillars his professional duty would be to devote all his time and energy to getting out of the country. To pursue a personal vendetta when under such dire and immediate threat as he now was from the British counter-attack – surely no agent in his right mind would elect to do that? But then with Zephyr just gutted before his eyes – and given his lieutenant Messanger as its obvious betrayer! – what *was* Edara's present state of mind? Damn sure it wouldn't be normal. Mad-bull fury at Zephyr's destruction, and a ferocious desire to punish the man he perceived – quite correctly – as the traitor who had brought about that destruction: those gut reactions would be at war with the professional requirement to cut his losses and run. The point was, *which of those conflicting passions had won?* At that moment, was Edara speeding along some secret emergency escape route prepared for him by a sleeper loyal to him alone, or was he still in the white Escort van, out there not far ahead of him and heading for Jared's house? Was—?

Braking hard, Jake jerked the Vauxhall to a stop inches short of the broad white line indicating a junction with a main road. Sat forcing brain and body to relax while the right-of-way traffic streamed across in front of him. Saw red light change to green, and drove on more slowly. You'll find out the answers to your questions when you get to Jared's, he told himself – so bloody well stick to the rules of the road else you aren't going to get that far!

Eight minutes later and well into Jared's neighbourhood, which he was fairly familiar with by now, he began to search among the parked vehicles for the Escort, quartering the area, working ever closer to his half-brother's house. Early morning streets palely sunlit, quiet. Four minutes gone by . . . five – then he spotted a white Escort parked ahead, cruised closer . . . shit, wrong number. Drove on past it and, turning right, stole smoothly along a road running parallel to Jared's and halfway down it saw a second white Escort van, parked kerbside like the first. Coasted closer, read its number plate, saw there was no one in it.

Christ, he really is here – already! he thought, and as terror for Gemma and Delyth engulfed him, adrenalin surged. Parking the Vauxhall he switched off and was out of the car and running, trainer-shod feet flying pavement because Edara had a head-start on him, could be inside the house by now. No, shit, that's rubbish, he hasn't had time, wasn't that much in front me. With luck he hasn't got beyond doing a recce of house and garden to see if anyone's about, plan how to get in. Pray God he's too hell-bent wild to give thought to the possibility that I might read him, might understand his mind-set and come after him.

Turning into Jared's road, he slowed to a fast walk. Met a bloke going the other way – 'Morning', said the stranger but got no answer – and a few seconds later came in sight of the house with the yellow-flowered shrubs bracketing its front door. It was no more than twenty yards away from him, so hugging himself into the cover of a tall conifer hedge alongside the pavement he hurried on, then halted just short of the gate into Jared's property.

Still keeping in the cover of the hedge he scanned house and garden for signs of life, movement. Discovered none so slipped in through the gate, streaked across lawn to the left-hand corner of the house and stood pressed in against its side wall, his eyes raking the shrubbery flanking that side of the grounds – a mere fifteen yards of grass between him and it – for Edara. . . . Jake Messanger was *hunting* now: hunting, because the parked Escort proved Edara to be close to Jared's house and he must have come to kill Gemma; what other conceivable purpose could he have? And finding Delyth with her, he'd kill them both. Therefore like an animal gone rogue and out to kill, he had to be killed before he had time to strike.

With a startling *swoosh* of wings a blackbird burst out of the shrubbery and away – and at once Jake's eyes darted to the spot it had emerged from, searching amongst bushes and treetrunks but discovering no man standing or moving there— Christ! Get on with this! he told himself, and stole crabwise along the side of the house to the next corner, the one at the back overlooking the big lawn. Halted again, listening. . . . Traffic noises murmur and whisper across the quietness, but there are no voices making words or laughter

Where the hell is Edara? He has to be outside still – or am I too late? Has he been – and gone? *Are Gemma and Delyth lying dead inside the house?*

Hasn't been time for it, he told himself, suppressing an impulse to rush headlong into the house regardless. The only place he can be is over in the shrubbery, he *has to be* somewhere in there, spying out the land ready to—

Taking his life in his hands, Jake sprinted across the narrow strip of grass into the shrubbery, worked his way deeper into it then turned to his right and went on down its length, keeping parallel to the lawn and moving with great caution because Edara might be anywhere about and the lush untended greenery provided good cover for them both.

There! Suddenly *he's there!* Spotting Edara no more than ten yards ahead Jake shrank back into the green-dark mass of a rhododendron and froze. Then, careful not to make the slightest sound, he smoothed aside its leaves to create a small window for himself, peered through it and saw his quarry side-on to him: hunched close in against a treetrunk at the very edge of the lawn Edara was engrossed in studying the back of the house – and looking that way

213

himself Jake saw that the back door was standing wide open.

Christ! he thought, once he makes his move he can go straight in – but luckily at the moment he's engrossed in summing up the situation, trying to see if there's anyone about inside. Has he got his gun out? Can't see him clearly enough, difficult in this shadowy half light. So what's my next move? Better not challenge him in here with the light so poor, too chancy, and if it goes wrong there'll be damn all to stop him getting to Delyth and Gemma.

I'll hold off until I'm absolutely sure I can take him. He'll be seeing the same picture as I am from where he is: a stretch of lawn to cross to get to the house, kitchen door open, no sign of anyone about inside or out. So he has two choices: he can make his way back through the shrubbery till he's level with the house, then use its wall as cover to reach that open door, or he can run straight across the lawn from where he now is, go in and—

He's on the move! Seeing Edara step smoothly clear of his tree and begin to work his way back along the inner edge of the shrubbery, Jake drew his gun. Watched the shadowy figure come towards him slowly, stealthily. . . . No more than the width of the shrubbery separated them, but at no moment was Edara open to challenge, now seen, now hidden in greenness as he slipped from one bush or treetrunk to the next, his back always to the man hunting him, his attention riveted on the house across the lawn. . . . As Edara drew closer Jake caught a glimpse of his right hand . . . then his left – *and saw that neither held a gun.*

He's almost level with me now, Jake thought. A yard or two more then he'll go forward to the very edge of the shrubbery for a final look-see before he moves out into the open. As he does so, I'll take him from behind, arrest him at gun-point. So quickly but quietly Jake stepped out from the shelter of his rhododendron—

But at that moment Edara broke cover! His dark-clad figure suddenly in full view, half-crouched and running across the lawn towards the house, *towards the open door.*

All caution gone, Jake charged through greenery out on to the grass and set himself, feet astride, gun trained on the back of the running man—

'Halt or I fire!' he shouted. 'Hands in the air! Both hands in the air. *Now!*'

Edara stopped dead, arms stabbing up and out above his head in the age-old gesture of surrender and still he had no weapon in either hand.

But watch him every step of the way, Jake warned himself, and closed in, maintaining the pressure on him with a rolling string of orders. 'Keep those arms up high! Higher yet! Feet *still!* Eyes to the front – *your front. . . .*'

'Play this by the book, Messanger,' Edara interrupted coolly, not moving his head. 'I am not armed.'

'I don't believe that.'

'You haven't won, you know. Those two siblings of yours will both be killed soon. Nothing will change that; I have left instructions with people you have no knowledge of.'

He's trying to break your concentration. Don't fall for it. Don't answer and don't hurry; you're nearly up to him now. Just get in close, jab your gun in his back, march him into the house and phone Allen.

'Gemma will be the first and her death will not be an easy one; the men I have appointed to the task are experts in handling women—'

But on that last word and in one fast, flowing movement Edara dropped low, swung round and launched himself bodily at Jake, hands out clawing for his legs to jerk him off balance. Then, even as Jake began to squeeze the trigger iron-hard fingers locked vice-like round his ankles, iron-hard shoulder rammed into him – and his bullet rocketed skywards as the two men crashed to the ground fighting for possession of the gun which had bounced out of Jake's grip as his hand hit turf and now lay just within the reach of both men, promising victory to the one who could get hold of it first.

Their world narrowed down to the two of them alone they fought with wordless, primitive savagery, their grunts of pain, the sharp hiss of rasping indrawn breath as a fist struck home, the feral snarl of killer rage all coalescing into a brutish dissonance which seemed a denial of their common humanity.

Edara's knee jabbed for the groin, one stiff-fingered hand struck for his enemy's eyes as the other scrabbled earth, straining towards the loaded gun but Jake dodged the vicious hand and went for Edara's throat, a madness rising in him, a wild, blood-deep hatred boiling up out of the adrenalin-fuelled, elemental intoxication of mortal combat as inside his head he heard again the threat the Arab had just made: *Gemma will be the first.*

With his left hand closed savagely around Edara's throat he reached out for the barrel of the gun with his right, every muscle at full stretch – another three inches and he'd have it! Edara tried to knee him in the guts but didn't connect – Jake's questing hand gained another inch – his fingers touched metal and *he had it!* Gripping the gun barrel he forced his body into one final heave, swung the reversed weapon up over Edara's head, and with all his remaining strength smashed it down across the right side of Edara's face as, in the last split second, he turned his head away.

The Arab collapsed. Lay sprawled on his side, his legs pinning Jake's to the ground. Kicking himself free, Jake scrambled up and, teeth bared, chest heaving, stood glaring down at the man sprawled unconscious at his feet. Saw the visible side of the dark hawk-face a mass of blood and tissue, the eye there a pool of blood, cheekbone caved in. And at the sight, a brilliant and atavistic exultation swept through him then swiftly spawned a bloodier and equally primitive urge – *take the life of your fallen enemy!* He came here hell-bent on death for you and your kin, so make him pay; *his* death for theirs; *it is your right!* 'Gemma's death will not be an easy one' – 'the men I have appointed to the task are experts in handling women': with Edara's words yammering at the skin of his brain, Jake Messanger shifted his grip on the gun, felt it slimed with Edara's blood and closed his hand lovingly around the stock, curled forefinger into curve of trigger, leaned down and advanced the muzzle to within an inch of Edara's skull—

'*Jake don't shoot*! Don't *do* it, don't shoot!' A woman's voice – Gemma's! Gemma's; flinging down the gauntlet from a world other than the primordial one about to claim Jake Messanger for its own it struck lightning-fast and straight to the core of his being – and lodged there, branding her command into him. Hearing it, he stepped back from the brink and *reclaimed* himself. Slowly, Jake Messanger withdrew the gun, stared at it for a moment then laid it on the ground beside him. Straightening, peered down at his hands, frowning. Both were bloody; after a moment he hunkered down and wiped them clean on the grass. Lawn, he thought, seeing and feeling its living greenness, it's the lawn at the back of Jared's house; I was standing here when I first saw Delyth. . . .

Turning towards the house, he saw Gemma running towards him and thought, she must have called to me from the terrace. Then his eyes went back to Edara and he thought, thank God I didn't kill him.

Chapter 23

Ealing Eight days later

'Jake's late. Later than he said.' Stretched out on her side in the shade of the old apple tree in the far corner of Jared's garden, Gemma, clad in brief shorts and a sea-green bikini top, reached up and put her half-full glass of lemon tea back on the beechwood table beside her. It was 5.30 and she and Delyth, hot and sweaty from working in the garden since lunch, had brought out a tray of tea and were relaxing before going indoors to shower and change.

'He often has been these last few days.' In her brightly cushioned chair nearby, Delyth smiled, stretching her tanned legs out in front of her.

Looking at her sidelong, Gemma wondered what she was really thinking about. Del's too damn good at hiding her feelings, she thought wryly and, rolling over on to her back, gazed up at the shifting patterns the wind-ruffled leaves above her created against the clear blue sky, and changed the subject.

'Over a week gone by now,' she said thoughtfully. 'Weird, wasn't it, the way things worked out that morning? How it happened that with just the two of us in the house, it was me who got out on to the terrace first. Earlier on, when we were both in the kitchen, we'd decided to go upstairs to wash and get properly dressed for the day ahead. So when that shot was fired out in the garden, you'd just got out of the bath—'

'And by then you'd had yours and were already dressed.'

Frowning slightly Delyth flicked her hair free of the collar of her black cotton shirt, pushed its rolled-up sleeves above her elbows; for her, the memories of that morning were still sometimes hard to handle. 'I'm glad it was you who got out there first,' she added after a moment, and softly.

Sitting up and crossing her legs, Gemma studied her friend's face. 'Why's that?' she asked. Received no answer, so tried again. 'Come on, Del. Tell me why you're so glad about it.'

'It's because . . . only you could have got through to Jake *at once* like you did. He loves you, so you were able to reach right into him – right through what was happening inside him – and cut him free of it.'

'But *you* could have done the same! It's true he loves me, we were so close when we were kids, and when he came back here we bridged the years apart so easily. But he loves you—'

'That's where the difference is, though, don't you see?' Delyth looked up, her eyes brilliant. 'Jake and you, you've already lived one whole part of your lives together so you are . . . you are bound together because of it. Hundreds, thousands of things you've shared, the two of you: big things, little things – they've all built up into a whole *world* made up of you and Jake. And from that shared world the two of you created earlier you were able to reach out, into him. . . . You and him, you're the two halves of a tranche of lived life: you fit together to form a whole new entity.' She turned her head away. 'Even in that nightmare moment when he was way off in a world where violence is king – even then *you* could reach out and bring him back into the one you and he had made and lived in as children and, now, are again living in together,' she said quietly. 'I wouldn't have been able to do that. At that moment, when he was possessed by hatred, I would not have been able to get deep enough into him to stop him. Jake and me, we haven't been together long enough yet for that to have been possible.'

Gemma sat quiet, moved by what Delyth had said, thinking about it. Said after a silence, 'I see what you mean, but—'

'Hullo there.' Briefcase in hand, Jake rounded the corner of the house and started towards them.

'Hi, come on over and have some tea.'

'I'd rather have a beer; I'll go get one,' he said and, changing course, made for the back door.

'Don't be long, we're dying to hear how things went today.' Scrambling to her feet, Gemma seated herself on one of the benches either side of the table, slipped off her sandals and scrabbled bare feet down into the cool greenness of grass, smiling to herself, pleased that Jake was 'home'.

Two minutes later he joined them, put his can of lager on the table and sat down facing her, briefcase, jacket and tie left in the kitchen, shirt neck wide open. 'I asked Allen about Simon Croft again, like you wanted,' he said to her. 'He told me he thinks Edara may eventually come clean about it, but that at the moment other things have to take priority; we have to be patient.'

'So be it. I didn't really expect anything else.'

'You look as if it's been quite a day,' Delyth said.

'It has.' He ran his hands over tired eyes.

'New and important stuff?'

'Indeed it was. And is.' But then Jake focused his mind more sharply, warning himself to take care how much he told them. Many matters had been discussed and agreed between Allen and himself that day, and the greater part of it was top-secret and not under any circumstances to be passed on to any other person or recorded in any way.

'Elucidate, please.' Crisply, Gemma pressed him. 'Come on, tell us.'

'Allen asked me to undertake a particular job on his behalf, and I agreed to do it.'

'An intelligence job? A mission of some sort?'

'You could call it that.'

'Here, or abroad?'

'That will depend on how things unfold. . . . We'll leave it there, Gemma. No more questions.' And staring down at the table, Jake Messanger thought back over the two momentous developments in his life – *sea changes*, you might call them, so great would be their effects for him – which had come to pass between Allen and himself that day. First to what – willingly, even eagerly – he had agreed to do for MI5; and secondly, to the priceless gift Allen had presented him with shortly after that, a piece of good news, absolutely brilliant news – the truth of which he was still finding it hard to credit, and which Allen had told him he must keep secret for a while yet. Regarding the first: on the strength of the wealth of inside information regarding Sarsen and his Syria-based terrorist organization he had given to MI5 and MI6, Intelligence top brass had decided to initiate a mission aimed at infiltrating one agent, possibly two, into that organization, and had selected him, Jake Messanger, to run that agent. To do that job he would work with a retired MI5 officer, Ben Brodie by name, once Allen's oppo and still held in high esteem by him and MI5, who had vast experience in anti-terrorist programming and had amassed and collated considerable data re past Closed Circle operatives who were still active in the Middle East, in Syria especially.

As to the second: strictly off the record, Allen had given him prior knowledge of the wonderful, almost incredible piece of news that *no charges were to be preferred against him in Britain.*

'You look hugely pleased about something, Jake, any chance you might tell us what it is?' Delyth's voice sounded amused and, looking up, he saw her smiling at him, but then quickly turned away without answering, suddenly overwhelmed by what he saw as the magnitude of his own good fortune. God, but I've been lucky, he thought. Those very aspects of my life, those past actions which I'd expected would damn me for ever in the eyes of the decision-makers here in British Intelligence have, in the event, been the very ones to cause those decision-makers to co-opt me into the service.

'To us, Messanger,' Allen had said to him a few hours earlier, 'you are the chance of a lifetime because you're a man of two worlds – ours and that of the Middle East, which is arguably the most difficult area of all for our Western intelligence organizations to penetrate: age-old, poles-apart differences between the two – of religion, culture and ethnological diversity – make both the infiltration of agents and the establishment of moles, sleepers and the like extremely difficult for us. The few times we've thought we've achieved it, said moles or sleepers have turned out to be double agents and have dropped us in deep shit at well chosen moments. So, as I said, to us, now, you're a gamble but also a godsend. You're totally fluent in the language; you've got first-hand, long-term, *lived* experience of Syria in general and Damascus in particular, and you've got social, medical and political contacts out there. All in all you know the ropes, and you know the people: what better man could we hope to find first to finger potential agents for us and then to recruit, train and generally prepare those chosen?'

'Jake! You're not listening, you creep!' Gemma half laughing but slightly cross. 'You look as if you're a million miles away and that's insulting to your present company so – come *on!* Answer my question, if you please!'

Gemma. Gemma, her gamine grin taunting him, the blonde hair all over the place, a smear of earth across her forehead where she'd brushed away sweat. Gemma, by bloodline his half-sister but more truly his *sister.*

'Sorry,' he said, smiling at her. 'Didn't hear the question. Say again?'

'I asked you how you got on with Jared. You told me you'd be seeing him today.'

'So I did. I invited him for a pre-lunch pint at a pub round the corner from Allen's office. He seems pleased enough with the way things are going—'

'Oh it's a lot more than that!' she interrupted. 'He's thrilled to bits, actually. He's been working like a dog on the follow-up stuff involved in rolling up all Zephyr's ramifications – well, I don't have to tell you that, you must know it better than I do. Then just yesterday Rawlings told him he's put his name forward for that special MI5 posting he's been hoping for. Didn't he mention it?'

Jake shook his head. 'Not a word.'

'Then he's an idiot, and I shall tell him so.' Gemma slipped on her sandals and stood up. 'I'm going to shower, can't stand my sweaty self any longer,' she said, and set off for the back door. 'See you in a bit.'

'I'll be in soon,' Delyth called after her, watching her swing away across the lawn. Then she smiled at Jake and let a silence lie sweetly between them for a few moments before asking quietly, 'How is it, really, between you and Jared? You didn't actually answer Gemma's question, did you?'

'You're right, I didn't.'

'I hope you'll answer mine.'

Looking away, Jake frowned, then picked up his can of lager, drained it, set it down. 'He still doesn't trust me,' he said finally, staring absently towards the terrace. 'Not really, deep down.' But he stopped there, recalling and considering an exchange which had passed between Jared and himself earlier that day . . . and decided to use it, now, to discover the answer to a question he desperately wanted to put to Delyth. Until now I've funked asking her, he thought. Always backed away from it because I'm afraid I might get what for me would be the wrong answer, one that would blow apart the love which is growing between she and and I. But it's time now to face up to it: I need to know, I *have to* know.

Decision made, he turned to her again. 'I asked Jared a certain question,' he said to her. 'I asked him whether – if in the event I'd gone ahead and deliberately shot Edara dead as he lay unconscious, but then later claimed I had shot him in self-defence during the fight between us – he would have backed up my story.'

'But how could he? He wasn't there.'

'No. I put it to him as a hypothetical situation, to know how he'd react. . . . But forget that, Delyth. What I really want to know is whether, had it come to the point, *you* would have backed me up. You weren't on the terrace either, at the critical time. But, if I'd needed it in order to escape a charge of murder, would *you* have backed my claim to self-defence? Lied for me? Without having any visual proof of its veracity, would you have accepted my version, that version, of events?'

She prevaricated. 'What was Jared's answer?'

'Straight off he said no, he would not. But then he gave me a quirky grin and said, "It's still early days, Jake. I haven't really got my head round all you've done, and are, let alone what you have been. Ask me again in a year's time – if you're still interested, that is".' Jake got to his feet and went to her, stood by her chair but made no move to touch her. 'Never mind Jared,' he said. 'This is something for you and me, and I need an answer. Would *you* take what I said as true, without factual proof of it being so? *Would you?* That's what I'm asking.'

In one swift, lithe movement she was out of her chair and standing close to him, holding his eyes, unsmiling. 'I would believe you without the proof,' she said. 'Is that enough?'

'It's more than enough. I'll always—'

'Ja-ake! That shitty mixer tap on the shower's playing up again!' Gemma's voice light and clear and, turning, they saw her standing at the open door on to the terrace in her scarlet bathrobe. 'Oh, sorry, I didn't realize—'

'We're just coming!' Delyth called and, touching his hand as she passed by him, murmuring 'Welcome to the joys of being one of the family, Jake', set off towards the house. But after a few steps she turned back to him. 'We've all the time in the world, you and I,' she said. Then went on across the grass, smiling.

After a few moments he followed her. She *understands*, he thought. Way deep down inside her she knows me – and understands that, somehow, I have to pay back. Somehow, and in the best way I can – Allen's way. And she'll come with me.

East Dunbartonshire Council